Christmas in Connecticut

JASINDA WILDER

Christmas
in
Connecticut

Author's Note

Westport, CT is a real place, and I've done my best to accurately reflect its character and appearance, but at the end of the day, this is a work of fiction and my version of Westport is a creation of my own mind, as are the various inhabitants and most of the named businesses. If you're from there, hopefully I've made it feel at least a little bit like home; if you're not, maybe you'll visit and find it somewhat familiar.

1

"**M**iss Cole!" A young boy's voice calls my name. "Miss Cole! Miss Cole!"

"We were chased by a dog, Miss Cole!" A second voice joins the first, and now the two boys, Jake Tormey and Dane Woolsey, are running pell-mell down the hallway toward me, backpacks bouncing, voices overlapping as they both try to tell me the story at the same time.

I hold up my hands to quiet them. "Boys, hush." Their jaws clack closed. "That's better. Now, perhaps you were chased by a wild, rabid dog, or perhaps not. But, I need you to be on time, okay? Can we do better, do you think?"

They both nod.

Dane, towheaded, short for his age, and likely undiagnosed and -treated ADHD, glares up at me. "There *was* a dog, Miss Cole. He escaped-ed his yard and chased us. He was big as me and had big lion teeth and every time he barked he got this big drool everywhere. He almost got me, too. See?" He turns around and awkwardly lifts his left foot up behind himself while trying to see it at the same time. "Look!"

Sure enough, the cuff of his jeans is ripped and damp, very much as if a slobbery dog had gotten its teeth in the fabric.

I blink in surprise. "Well, I'll be—you're telling the truth, it seems."

He puts his foot down and nods vigorously. "Told you."

"Is there an adult that can walk with you?" I ask.

Jake shrugs. "Nah. Our dads work together and our moms do too, and they all have to be at work at the buttcrack of dawn. Before school even starts. So we gotta ride our bikes to school on our own." His eyes widen as if he's realizing he's saying something he probably shouldn't. "But, um, it's only like two blocks, and we been riding our bikes to school since forever."

Sounds like a tricky situation, indeed. I sigh. "Well, I don't like you being chased by mean dogs. Maybe there's a route you can take that won't make you go past that dog's house."

Dane considers. "Maybe? We'd have to go around the other way, and that's lots longer."

Jake shoves him. "Nuh-uh. We could go through the other school."

"The gates aren't always open."

"During school they are. That might be even faster than the way we usually go."

I put my hands on one each of their shoulders. "We'll look into it—I'll help you. For now, let's get settled for class so I can start the lesson."

They trudge in and find their desks—at the same table together, while I stand outside my door and wait for the rest of my first-grade class to arrive.

Like the kids, and my fellow teachers, I have a case of the first day jitters. I don't ever let the kids see it, of course, but I feel many of the same things they do—what's it going to be like this year? Will the class be fun, challenging, weird? I have thirty-two first-graders whose names I have to learn, whose learning styles I have to figure out, have to sort out the needy, clingy ones from the stubborn, independent ones, the ones who can already mostly read on their own from the ones who need a little more work yet.

But, overall, getting to know the kids is my favorite part. I mean, I think at least in part, I became a teacher because I like kids more than I do adults. They're honest, for one thing. Brutally so, sometimes, maybe, but you know where you stand with them. Their needs are upfront, and mostly easy to meet: be kind, provide structure, and make sure they have fun. There's a little more to it than that, of course, but that's the general idea, and if you can get those three things in place, the details tend to be the easy part.

My classroom is prepped, initial seats are assigned— things always shift around a little in the first few weeks…

such as Jake and Dane, for example; I foresee myself having separate them. I clutch my mug of coffee and stand outside my classroom as I hear the squeaks of sneakers and chatter of voices as the busses begin dropping off the children.

Saugatuck Elementary is bustling and noisy as the kids arrive. I wave and smile at faces I saw yesterday, and spend a moment chatting with a mom dropping her son off for the first day of kindergarten—she's nervous and emotional and he's clingy, and I reassure both her and the child; his teacher, my classroom next-door neighbor, Susan Delahay, is already busy comforting another nervous first-timer.

My kids start showing up, as most of them are on the second bus to arrive. I make a game of trying to remember their names as they arrive, greeting them with intentionally the wrong name—it makes them laugh and sets them at ease, and then they tell me their name and I win both ways. They find their desks and put their lunches in the lunch bin, and hang their backpacks in their lockers, and some find a book or a stack of blocks, and I'm filled with the eagerness to start a new year.

I have a few stragglers I'm waiting for, according to my seating chart, and since these are the same kids who were last to show up for orientation last week, I'm guessing they'll be the ones who always show up a few minutes late. I'm keeping an eye on the classroom from the doorway while the kids get started on our first assignment—a

Tell Me About Your Summer Break writing prompt to tell me where the kids are in handwriting and spelling, and to get to know each one a little better—when a scene down the hall catches my eye.

A little girl with her father, slowly trudging down the mostly empty hall, hand in hand, not speaking. She looks nervous and he looks no better. The girl is about seven, I'd say, making her a second-grader; my guess is confirmed when they stop together outside Kelly Fratelli's second-grade classroom, two doors down and across the hall. They look a lot alike. She's tall for a second-grader, with jet-black hair that has been inexpertly put into a ponytail—it's uneven, and there are flyaways already wisping into her wide dark eyes. She's pretty, with delicate, fine features. Jeans, sneakers, and a pink T-shirt with a unicorn on it, all brand new.

He's gargantuan.

And handsome, in a rugged, almost brutal way. I'm a tall woman at five-ten, but he's a good half a foot taller than me, making him at least six-four. His shoulders are broad and rounded with hard muscle—his shirt isn't tight or fitted, but still clings to his powerful physique. Jet-black hair, like his daughter's, curls up under the back of a faded, battered tan Carhartt ball cap; his beard is thick, curly, and a little unruly. Deep-set eyes, very dark, almost black. Like his daughter, he wears jeans and a T-shirt, but his are aged and faded, and he's wearing heavy work boots.

He drops to one knee and holds her shoulders in huge, weathered, scarred hands. Mutters to her. She nods, eyes downcast. He hugs her, and she hugs him back, and he rises to go.

Makes it approximately ten steps before she launches into a run. "Daddy, wait!"

He turns and catches her as she slams into him. "I gotta go, sweet pea. Can't be late for work."

"Daddy, I'm scared." Her voice is small, but it carries.

His is quiet, deep and rough, gravelly, almost hoarse. "I know, Riley. But it's going to be okay."

"I don't know anyone. What if no one likes me?"

"I don't know anybody here either, babe."

"But you're a adult. It's different."

"Just because I'm an adult doesn't mean I'm good at meeting new people. I got a new boss, new coworkers. Shi—uh, shoot, honey, it's a whole new job I've never done before. So guess what? I'm nervous too."

"You are?" Her eyes are wide and her voice awed.

"Sure. It's normal to be nervous starting something new."

She shifts side to side, clutching his hand. "You'll pick me up?"

"Sure thing. Right on time, guaranteed." He kneels again and kisses her forehead. "Now, I really gotta go. You're gonna do fine. Just...you know what I do? I think about just making friends with one new person. Not even make friends, just...talk to them. Get out of my shell, just a tiny bit. Can you do that?"

She nods, hesitantly. "I can try."

"That's all you can do, sweet girl, just try. So how

about this—if we both talk to one new person today, we'll get ice cream on the way home."

She brightens at this. "Well…if there's ice cream involved, it's a different story."

He laughs, rubs a big thumb against her cheek. "Yeah, I thought so. Now, you go on in, okay? I really have to go."

"Okay, Daddy."

"Love you, stinky pickle."

She wrinkles her nose. "You can't call me that in public, Daddy."

He snorts and backs away. "Fine. Farewell, Riley Kerr."

She rolls her eyes and shakes her head. "You're ridiculous."

"You know it." He winks and walks backward until it appears she's heading into her classroom.

The bell has long since rung. The man waves once more, and then pivots and fast-walks for the exit, long legs eating the space quickly.

The little girl, Riley Kerr, stands outside the classroom, watching him go. It's clear, now, she was putting on a brave face for him so he could leave, but she's still struggling. She brushes her hair out of her face, watching him round the corner and vanish, and then she lets out a little breath.

Glances at me, as if noticing me for the first time.

I wave. "Hi."

She gives me a shy wave back. "Hello."

I glance in at my class—they're all being quiet and

good, and my two tardy students still haven't shown up. I cross the hall and offer my hand to Riley. "I'm Miss Cole. I teach first grade."

"My name is Riley." She takes my hand and shakes it, firm and decisive. Definitely taught how to shake hands by a man.

"Nice to meet you, Riley." I crouch in front of her. "You know, Mrs. F, your teacher? She's really, really nice. Plus, I had most of the kids in your class last year, and they're all really cool kids. I bet you'll make some friends in no time."

"But I'm new."

"I was new here just a few years ago myself, so I know how you feel." I smile, glance behind her at Kelly. "But just be yourself and be brave, okay?"

She nods. "Okay."

"And if you ever need anything, you can come to me, too, even though I'm not your teacher."

Kelly nods at me, and ushers Riley into her room. Kelly hasn't ever quite warmed up to me, for reasons I'm not entirely sure about. She's super conservative, favoring tailored slacks and blazers, blond hair in a neat, pin-straight bob, and has a very traditional, straightforward teaching style. Whereas I'm...pretty much the opposite in every way; if I had to guess, I don't think she approves of me. But, she's a good teacher and so am I, so we keep it to a cordial, professional nod in the hallways and break room.

I finally decide my last two students, Mackenzie Dean

and Ellis Warren, are either absent or simply very, very late, and head into my classroom.

Throughout the day, though, I find myself thinking about the little girl, Riley. And her dad.

I'm not sure why, but whenever I have a moment to think, my mind wanders back to their interaction. His reassurance, his admission that he's nervous too—they're new to Westport, and while this little town is friendly and welcoming, it's also the kind of place where new people kind of stand out. Which can be hard.

Single dad in a new town. Yikes. That must be tough.

But…how do I know he's a single dad? I don't. But there are little clues that make me certain I'm right.

Her hair, for one thing. Her clothes, for another. It all smacks of "Dad" rather than "Mom."

None of it is out of place or concerning. But I'd be willing to bet he's a single dad.

And it makes me curious.

Which is, in itself, curious.

Because I haven't been curious about a man in…

Well, ever.

2

THE FIRST WEEK OF SCHOOL PROGRESSES INTO FAMILIAR routines. It becomes easier to get out of bed and onto my bike, requiring less of the mental gymnastics. I learn all my students' names. I learn who's always the first one to class—Blakely Alameda, a shy, sweet girl who reminds me a lot of myself at her age. She's always the first one through the door, quickly settling into her seat with a book from her backpack. Currently, she's reading through an early reader version of the Babysitter Club series.

That was me, always with a book, always early.

Jake and Dane are always late, always sweaty and out of breath, usually dirty—as if they'd stopped on the way to play in a dirt pile or throw mud at each other—and almost always with a new excuse that's even more implausible than the last. They're sweet boys, if energetic and easily distracted. Dane is almost certainly ADHD, and I'm always having to come up with new tricks to keep him on task. Jake is a quick study, and if he's interested in the topic he's an incredible student. If not, he'll be doodling. He's quite a budding talent with drawing, so I make a deal with him—finish your work, and I'll provide a sketch pad and colored pencils for him to draw to his heart's content…as long as his work is done.

It takes a little longer to learn the other students, the ones who don't stand out like Blakely, Jake, and Dane. Slowly, day by day, I get to know them all.

And every morning, Riley is walked into school by her dad. She gains confidence, and they're always sweet together. He's always got a little joke to make her laugh, and she always plays along.

But, despite her show of bravado for her dad, I notice she's usually alone at recess and lunch. And I notice, too, that her outfits don't change all that much. She has two, maybe three pairs of jeans, a handful of T-shirts, and the one pair of sneakers. Her ponytail is never quite straight, and there's always hair in her face.

But she's clean and she always has a lunch and he clearly adores the heck out of her.

She runs to get into his truck at the end of the day—sprints, really, to the point that several of us staff often have to remind her to not run in the hallways.

I want to help.

I want to braid her hair for her. Get a few dresses. Some cute leggings and tops that aren't plain screen-tinted T-shirts.

Put some style into her life.

But I know better.

I also want to help her make friends. Or, better yet, be her friend.

Why am I so concerned with Riley?

I can't quite figure it out.

I also can't quite get a handle on why I'm always posted outside my classroom every morning until she's escorted in with her dad, hand in hand.

He doesn't swagger, not exactly. His walk is strong and confident, but there's no arrogance in him. His eyes roam the hall as he walks her to her class. Sometimes, they pause on me.

Do they linger, once in a while?

Perhaps.

Does it make my heart palpitate, in those instances?

Also maybe.

The dismissal bell rings, Friday afternoon. I wish all the kids a good weekend and clean up, straighten desks, put away books, the usual pre-weekend routine.

Dane comes back into the classroom, big, floppy Guardians of the Galaxy backpack hanging from his shoulders. He looks downcast.

"Hi, Dane," I say, smiling at him. I gesture for him to come to me at my desk. "What's up, honey?"

He shuffles, shifts. "My mom bought a rabbit."

I nod. "Wow, that's cool! I used to have a bunny when I was little."

He hesitates. "He's really fluffy and cute."

"I bet." I'm waiting—I know there's a reason he's telling me this.

"Dad says we can't keep him. Says he's allergic. And ever since we got the rabbit, Dad has been sneezing and coughing and his eyes are all red and it looks like he's cryin', even though I know for a fact he don't cry. He didn't even cry when he accidentally cut off the end of his finger that one time. He just said a lot of bad words, and then told me not to ever say none of them." He blinks at me.

"Wow. Your dad must be pretty tough."

"Yeah." He hooks his thumbs in the straps of his backpack. "We gotta get rid of him, so I never gived him a name."

"Okay." I smile encouragingly. I don't show my impatience, even though my yoga class starts in thirty minutes and I still have to get home and change. "So, how can I help?"

"Can we keep him?"

I lean back in my chair. "By we, you mean…here? In the classroom?"

Dane nods. "Yeah. I already asked our neighbors, and my aunt, and Jake's dad said he'd turn it into stew and I believe him because Jake's dad is weird. So I thought maybe he could be our class pet."

I frown. "Well, um…I don't know."

"Please? I don't know where else he could go. If I let him go, he'll probably just get eated by a dog or something. He's big and fat and fluffy and probably can't even run good."

"How about I think about it over the weekend, okay?"

He brightens. "You'll think about it?"

I nod. "I'll let you know on Monday."

He stares hard at me. "Are you one of those adults that says you'll think about it but it really means no?"

I laugh. "No, Dane. When I say I'll think about it, I mean exactly that. I have to decide if the responsibility of a class pet is something I want to take on. It wouldn't affect just me, you know. You'd all be responsible for helping take care of him. So, I have to consider my decision carefully."

"I guess that makes sense. But Dad said it has to be gone by Wednesday, or he'll give it to Jake's dad for stew." He frowns. "Who even eats rabbits anyway?"

I shake my head. "I don't know, Dane. But I promise, I'll have an answer for you on Monday morning."

He nods. "'Kay. Thanks, Miss Cole!"

"You got it, buddy. Have a good weekend."

"I will! Me and Jake are gonna build a fort in his backyard. No girls allowed, so don't even think about trying to see inside it." He says this over his shoulder, a matter-of-fact order.

I laugh. "I'll stay clear, I promise."

I watch him run out, backpack bouncing. With my door open and the classroom across from mine also open, I can see Jake on the sidewalk out front of the school, on his bike, waiting. Dane whizzes by at top speed, and through the cracked-open windows I can hear Jake shouting for him to wait up.

Those two are going to make the year interesting, I think.

Eager to get to my yoga class, I quickly finish locking up and head for my car. I'm about to unlock my Wrangler—it's my baby, a 1987 CJ7 restored and updated by my dad and brother and then gifted to me when they decided they needed a new project; it's eggplant purple, has a four-inch suspension lift and 35" mud tires. I've got a hardtop for the winter and a soft-top for the summer, and my dad and brother taught me how to rig a lift in my garage so I can change them in and out easily myself.

It's not the kind of car most people would imagine a girl like me would drive, but I love my Jeep with sparkly hearts and unicorn sprinkles. I drove it here from Colorado, in the winter, through a crazy blizzard. It's cool. It's unique. The purple is pretty and kind of girly, but with the lift and the tires it's just…cool. It's unexpected, and I like to be unexpected.

As I'm unlocking my Jeep, I happen to glance off toward the pick-up and drop-off lane in front of the school, and I see a small form sitting alone in the grass. It's quite a distance, but even from here the person looks dejected, and it's a good twenty minutes since the last of the busses left, so the school is empty except staff and a handful of latchkey kids playing dodgeball in the gym.

With a sigh of regret for the yoga class I'm definitely going to miss, I head over.

It's Riley. She squints up at me. "Hi, Miss Cole."

"Hi, Riley. Why are you still here? Did your dad not pick you up?"

She shakes her head. "No, he didn't." Her voice quavers, and she pauses, gamely struggling to contain her emotions. "He's never been late picking me up before."

"Well, I'm sure there's a perfectly reasonable explanation," I say. "In the meantime, can I sit with you and keep you company?"

She nods, and I spread my skirt around me as I settle into the grass beside her. It's a beautiful early September day, not a cloud in the sky but not too hot, with the afternoon sun golden yellow and bathing everything in glorious warmth and light. I close my eyes and turn my face to the sky and inhale deeply, hold it, and let it out.

"I just love a little sunbath, don't you?" I say.

My eyes are closed, but I can hear the puzzled frown in her voice. "A what?"

"Sunbath." I brace my arms behind me, palms flat in the cool, prickly grass. "Close your eyes, look up toward the sun, and just…soak it in." I peek at her, and she's mirroring my pose. "Good, just like that. Now, take in a deep breath, and hold it, and just…let it all go. You're safe, you're not alone, it's a beautiful day, your dad will be here any minute, and everything is just fine."

For another beat or two, she's quiet, soaking up the sun and breathing.

"I do feel better!" she says, sounding surprised. "Cool!"

I smile down at her. My purse, which is so big as to nearly be classifiable as a duffel bag, is beside me. I always keep something to snack on in my purse, because I have a terrible snacking habit, and because of situations like this. Need to calm an upset child? Food. Works like a charm pretty much every time. Today, my purse snack selection includes packets of peanuts, beef sticks, some freeze-dried bananas and strawberries, and, obviously, emergency chocolate.

I pile it all in the grass between us, and tilt toward her with a grin. "Hungry?"

Her eyes light up. "I could eat."

I snicker at that—I hear her dad in those words, even though I've never even met the man. "Well, then, what would you like, Miss Riley?"

Her eyes scan the snacks, and land, not surprisingly, on the chocolate bar. Hesitate, and then flick up to me. "Chocolate?"

I cackle. "A girl after my own heart." I open the wrapping and break the bar in half.

She accepts her half from me and nibbles on a corner. The smile on her face as she eats the treat makes missing yoga worth it. "I haven't had chocolate in a long time."

I tilt my head. "No?"

She shakes her head. "No. Daddy says sweets should be a special treat only for once in a while, because a treat's not a treat if you have it all the time."

I laugh. "That sounds like something you've heard your dad say a million times."

Another eye roll. "More like a bazillion times every single day." A huff. "He'd tell me I'm being melon-dramatic. But he does say it a lot."

I laugh at that: *melon-dramtatic*. "Well, a bazillion times every day might be a *tad* melodramatic." I over-enunciate as a form of gentle correction. "So, what counts as a treat, for you and your dad?"

She finishes the chocolate and fastidiously wipes at the corners of her mouth, her lips, and checks all her fingers. "Strawberries and blueberries. He goes to the market on the way home from work on Fridays and then on Saturday mornings we make French toast and bacon." A tip of her head. "Actually, the French toast is a treat too."

I open the freeze-dried fruit, dump some into my palm, and extend the bag so she can take some. "French toast with blueberries and strawberries—now *that* sounds like an amazing treat."

Riley nods. "It's my favorite. We watch Looney Toons while we cook and eat. I like to help him. I'm really good at flipping."

"That's the hard part, if you ask me."

She nods, expression reflecting assured wisdom. "It is. He's teaching me how to make the mix you dunk it in, but every time I try to do that on my own, Daddy says I make a cats-a-trophic mess."

"Catastrophic," I correct, automatically. "And you know, the last time I tried to make French toast, I made a horrible mess, too. It took me like half an hour to make everything, and an hour to clean up when I was done. There was egg and cinnamon literally everywhere."

There's a distant rumble of a large truck engine, and a big red pickup rolls to a stop in front of us. It's an older model, maybe ten years old or so. Nothing fancy, but well-maintained. There's a big silver toolbox in the bed, just behind the cab, and there's what looks to my untrained eye like an engine in the bed, or at least part of one. It's heavy, clearly, since the truck is sagging low over the rear tires.

Riley's dad jumps out the moment the truck is stopped, engine on, door still open, and jogs over to his daughter. "Riley, baby, I'm sorry. I'm so sorry. I didn't forget you, I swear." He drops to a knee and wraps her up in a hug.

She hugs him back and then steps back, resting her hands on his shoulders. "Sure you didn't forget? I've been waiting for forever."

I stand up and smooth my skirt down, brush my hands over my backside to make sure there's no grass stuck to me. Stay a step or two away while father and daughter talk.

"I got held up at work," he says, wincing. "There was a guy with an engine problem and he was willing to pay double our labor rate if we fixed it today so he could get back out tomorrow. I tried to tell my boss I had to go, but he said if I left before it was fixed, I could look for a new job."

"Well, I guess that's a perfectly reasonable explanation," she says, glancing at me. "That's what Miss Cole said. That there was probably a perfectly reasonable explanation for why you're late."

He seems to see me for the first time. "Miss Cole, I presume?" He stands up to his full, towering height, extends his hand to me, and I shake it.

His grip is firm but not crushing; his hands are huge, hard as stone and rough as cinderblocks, tanned the brown of old walnuts from the sun.

"Emma Cole," I say, meeting his gaze.

His eyes are a brown so dark they're nearly black, set deep in his rugged face. His beard is thick and curly, jet black. He's wearing a small, ratty old beanie, pushed back on his head so hair protrudes from underneath it, curly tendrils dark against his forehead.

My heart palpitates, and I have to force myself to simply meet his gaze and then look away, rather than staring at him like an awkward goofball.

"Rory Kerr," he says, in his deep, rough voice. "Thank you for staying with her. I really appreciate it."

I smile at him, and I'm just sure my smile is too bright, too silly, too eager. Too happy to finally be meeting him. "Hey, it's absolutely my pleasure. She's a delightful conversationalist."

He glances at her. "What'd you guys talk about?" He gives her a wink and a smirk. "Boys?"

Riley rolls her eyes and huffs in disgust. "God, Dad, *no*. I'm seven. Boys are stupid." She gives him a flouncy grin. "Don't worry, you still have a few years before you have to start worrying."

He cackles at this. "Good to know. So, not boys. What'd you and Miss Cole talk about?"

"French toast." She smiles at me.

He laughs. "French toast, huh?" He shakes his head, as if the ways of women are simply mystifying to him.

I kneel down and look at Riley. "I'm glad we got to

talk, Riley. You can come see me in my classroom anytime, okay?"

She nods, hesitates, and then leans in to hug me. "Thanks for staying with me."

"Of course, sweetie. Anytime."

I rise and back away, waving. "See you Monday."

Rory's eyes linger on me. "See you."

I walk away, and I feel his eyes on me, watching me walk, I don't exactly mind. I wouldn't admit to adding a little *zhuzh* to my walk, but I also can't say it didn't happen.

A glance at the clock in my Jeep tells me I did indeed miss my yoga class. But hey, it's a beautiful Friday afternoon, so I might as well make the most of it—I head home, change, put back the soft-top, and strap my paddleboard to the roll bars.

I spend the afternoon at Compo Beach, enjoying the sun and the warmth and the movement.

I only spend most of the time thinking about Rory Kerr, and his deep, warm, kind eyes, strong shoulders, and massive hands.

Only some. Not all.

I have some dignity, after all.

3

SECOND AND THIRD WEEKS OF SCHOOL PROGRESS APACE. Things settle in. Jake and Dane continue to be… not trouble, exactly, but…challenging. They're sweet, funny boys, and are never mean to their classmates, but they're always challenging me, as a teacher.

I appreciate that challenge, and make it a mission to meet the challenge and make a difference in their lives. I get a sense that they need some adult affection and encouragement, and I do my best to provide it, within the parameters of my position.

My favorite part of the day—but don't tell anyone else—is the end of the day, after the other kids have left. I'm not sure how it happened, and it's not even a verbal arrangement between Rory and me, but Riley comes over to my classroom after the bell rings and she helps me pick up and we talk—by which I mean, I listen to her talk, mostly—and then I walk out with her, by which time her dad is usually there to pick her up. It's not much, only fifteen minutes or so, but it seems to make it easier for Rory, and I genuinely enjoy the time I get to spend with Riley. She's sweet and funny and insightful, and always surprises me with the things she says and observes.

I haven't had any other exchanges with Rory yet, other than a friendly wave and a smile as Riley climbs into his truck.

Which is fine.

Absolutely fine.

It's not like his eyes haunt my dreams or anything.

Oh no.

I've for sure *never* daydreamed about running into him at a cafe on Sunday morning, and having coffee together. Nope, nope, nope.

Nor have my dreams ever been concerned with what he looks like under those T-shirts he wears.

I'd never act on any of those thoughts or daydreams or anything. I'm not that forward. I'm not shy, but I'm not a make-the-first-move girl, either. And also, I don't even know if he thinks about me that way. It's not like there's some professional taboo preventing us from having a relationship, since Riley isn't even my student, so it's not that. I'm just not the girl who's going to ask him out first.

And he doesn't seem inclined to talk to me any more than he has to either, so I guess that's that.

My friendship with Riley Kerr has nothing to do with my middling crush on her dad.

Just so that's clear.

Monday. A rainy, dreary, cold, gray day. Inside recess, which means some kids go to the gym and do activities there, and some play educational games on the classroom iPads, and others read or draw.

I'm going over my notes for the next lesson after recess—a multimedia art and science project on the water cycle—when my door slams open abruptly and a sobbing, hysterical Riley burst in, beelining for me.

Kelly is right behind her, frazzled and irritated. "I'm sorry, Emma, she's incoherent and—and she's demanding she can only talk to you."

I accept Riley's body against my legs as she slams into me. She's sobbing, wracked and breathless. "Hey, hey, hey, Riley, I'm here. I'm here." I kneel down, and she clings to me. "Do you want to go talk to me in the hallway?"

She nods against my shoulder.

I meet Kelly's eyes. "Can you just monitor them for a minute?" I glance specifically at Dane and Jake, who are huddled together at a table, drawing something; the whispers and giggles tell me whatever they're working on is probably gross at best, if not inappropriate.

"Sure." She huffs. "I'm sorry again. She got away from me."

I bite down on a comment about how she's not a

runaway dog, she's an upset girl. Instead, I lead Riley by the hand out into the hall. The music room, two doors down toward the main office, is empty, so I take her in there, turn on the lights, and close the door. We sit on chairs beside each other.

For a minute or two, I just hold her and let her cry.

Eventually, she calms a bit.

"What happened, Riley? Who hurt you?"

She sniffles. "They…they said mean stuff about my mom."

"Your mom?" I've been assuming she's not in the picture one way or another, and this is the first mention I've heard from Riley about her mother.

She won't look at me. "We had to draw pictures of our family. I drew me and Daddy and our sailboat, *Dreamrider*. And…and Max asked where my mom is. When I said I don't know, he—" she swallows. "He just said…" She shakes her head. "I don't want to say it."

I wrap an arm around her shoulders. "It's okay, you don't have to."

A shudder, as she works through another quaking sob. "It's not my fault Mom left."

Ohhhh shit. Danger, danger.

"Of course not, Riley."

"Daddy said so. He tells me all the time. It's not my fault. I didn't do anything wrong. I…she…sometimes things between adults just don't work out." She looks to me, as if for confirmation.

"Riley, I don't really know anything about what happened between your mom and your dad, but if I can say anything with any kind of certainty, it's that what happens between adults is never, *ever* the fault of the child involved. It's *not* your fault." I sigh. "And sometimes, unfortunately, kids are just mean."

She nods, and leans away from me. I watch her as she visibly works to shake off the grip of the emotions. "Thanks, Miss Cole."

"If it's just you and me, sweetie, you can call me Emma. Around other kids or adults, I should still be Miss Cole. But if it's just us two, I'm Emma."

Her eyes brighten. "You're the best." She emphasizes this by leaning back into me, arms wrapping around my middle.

She pulls away, and we stand up. I notice, as she wipes at her eyes, that her hair, in its usual loose ponytail, has come nearly totally undone.

"Riley, would you mind if I helped you with your hair?"

She brushes it away from her face. "Could you? I've been trying to learn how to braid my own hair 'cause Daddy can't, but it's hard 'cause I can't see the back and it always just falls apart."

I move the chairs so they're facing each other and have her sit on one with the chair-back to her belly. It's more difficult without a brush or comb, but I use my fingers as best I can to pull it all back neatly and evenly, and then set about braiding it. I always do a fishtail braid in my own hair as a matter of habit, so that's what I find myself doing with her hair. She has long, thick black hair, dense and glossy and tangle-free.

"Your daddy must make sure you brush your hair, doesn't he?" I ask.

She nods, then remembers I'm braiding. "Uh-huh. Every night before bed, he reads me a chapter from a book while I brush my hair, and then he brushes it in the morning before school."

"He's a good daddy, huh?"

"Yeah. I wish he could braid, though."

I laugh. "Well, he can't do everything, can he?"

She snorts. "I guess not."

I make quick work of the braid, tying it off with the elastic band. I have my phone in my cardigan pocket, on silent, and I take a photograph of her hair so she can see. I show it to her, and her mouth drops open, eyes wide.

"Oh my gosh, it's so pretty! Thank you *so* much! Can you show me how to do this?" She gingerly touches her braid with her fingertips, feeling it, tracing the pattern.

Such a simple thing.

"Well, I have to get back to my class, and so do you, but I think maybe we could work something out so I can help you learn to braid your own hair. Once you get the hang of it, it's pretty easy."

"When did you learn how to braid your own hair?" She asks.

"Oh, about your age. My mom worked a full-time job and had to leave for work before I got on the bus, so there wasn't always time for her to do my hair, and my dad sure as heck wasn't about to learn to even help me with a basic ponytail, so I just sort of had to learn on my own." I smile. "And I had help. My second-grade teacher,

Mrs. Pritchard. I'd stay in from recess and she'd help me with my hair, until I could do it myself."

She takes a deep breath, holds it, lets it out. "Okay, I feel better now."

"Don't let mean boys bring you down, Riley. And don't let anyone tell you that boy is mean to you because he likes you. That's dumb and not true. If a boy is mean, he's just mean. If a boy likes you, he should be nice." I'm treading in uneasy territory, here, especially in this day and age. But I feel compelled, and just have to hope this doesn't come back to bite me in the ass, someday.

Riley just nods, firmly. "Dad told me that, too." She uses her deepest, gruffest voice in an earnest and funny impression of her dad. "'Mean boys don't deserve a second thought, Ry. If he's mean, he don't like you—he's just a butthead. And what do we do with buttheads?'"

She pauses, where I imagine him pausing for her to answer.

"I don't know," I put in, with a bit of apprehension as to the answer. "What do we do with buttheads?"

"'Ignore 'em!'"

Phew. I was worried for a second her answer would be to punch them or something.

"Good advice," I say.

She nods. "He's pretty smart."

"Sounds like it." I take her hand and we return to the hallway, pausing between my classroom and hers. "I hope the rest of your day is better."

She smiles. "It will be. Thanks again…" She looks around, with melodramatic exaggeration, "Emma."

I can't help a laugh as I wave and head back to my class.

Kelly is helping Keller Benton work through a reading assignment. I watch and listen for a moment as she patiently corrects him here and there with some of the harder words. She sees me enter, and waits and listens as Keller finishes a sentence, then gives him a smile and a murmured encouragement.

She joins me near the door. "She's okay?"

I nod. "Yeah, she just needed a minute."

"I still can't believe what Zeke said to her. I'm going to have to send a note to his parents. You know, I don't report home every little squabble between kids. I'd never do anything but communicate with angry parents if I did that. But some, you just can't ignore."

"Oh, I know," I say. "Kids fight and argue, and most of it you can settle in class yourself. But some stuff?" I shrug. "She didn't even want to repeat what he said."

She lowers her voice a whisper. "He said Riley's mom was probably a dirty slut."

I cover my mouth and gasp. "He didn't."

She nods. "He sure did. Loud enough for the whole class to hear—and then laughed about it." A roll of her eyes and a disgusted smile. "I'm probably being judgmental here, but I'm sort of anticipating a no response from his parents, which is where I'm sure he's learned to use such awful language. And it's not the first time he's said things like that."

"You know what's worse than no response?" I ask. "The whole 'boys will be boys' BS."

She narrows her eyes and growls. "Don't get me started on *that.*"

"Same." I glance across the hall and see a yellow block fly across the classroom. "Uh, I think you're needed in your room."

She follows my gaze, and her eyes widen. "Oh shoot. Dana said she could only stay a minute or two to make sure everyone was settled." She heads out the door. "Thanks for helping with Riley."

"She's a sweet girl. I have kind of a soft spot for her."

She gives me a wave and heads back to her class.

The rest of the day is simple enough.

Dane stays after class, and I have my answer prepared.

"So, didja think about it?" he asks, eyes wide and hopeful.

"I have."

He grins. "And?"

"And I'll accept responsibility of the bunny. *But—*" I hold his eyes. "*You* have to take the lead on caring for him this year."

"And what about next year?"

I smile. "Well, I can deal with that then. But for now, make arrangements with your parents to bring him by. I have some work I have to do this afternoon before I can go home, so if you can have him here by, say, five, we can get him settled into his new home in the classroom."

He considers. "Mom and Dad don't get home till

after that." His eyes brighten. "But I got a wagon. Jake and I could bring him here in the wagon."

"I suppose that would work, as long as you're careful." I eye him seriously. "Would your parents allow it?"

He waves dismissively. "If it gets the god-dang rabbit out of the house, they'll be glad of it."

I frown. "I'm not certain how much I trust that answer."

"I'm allowed to ride bikes with Jake after school, long as we don't cross any of the busy roads. And I don't, to get here."

"Very well, then." I lift an index finger. "But, Dane, I have to leave at five, okay? So don't dawdle."

"The heck does that word even mean? I think adults all use it 'cause other adults use it, and nobody actually knows what it really means. Is it even a word?"

I laugh. "Yes, Dane, it's a real word." I pluck a dictionary from the shelf behind me and hand it to him. "This is a teachable moment. Find it in there."

He rolls his eyes. "You ever *not* a teacher, Miss Cole?"

I snort. "Nope."

He shakes his head as he flips through pages, muttering under his breath as he reads the entries until he finds the one he's looking for. "Dawdle—verb, waste time, be slow."

I smile at him. "See? A real word, in the dictionary and everything. Not just made up to make your life more difficult."

"I don't dawdle," he protests. "Everybody's always telling me to slow down, Dane, slow down. Calm down,

Dane. Use your inside voice, Dane. Bring it down a level, Dane."

I bite back my smile. "Well, you just have a lot of energy and you're very…passionate, and excitable."

"Mom says I'm her greatest trial. And if she can get me to adulthood intact, it'll be her greatest achievement."

I snort. "Well, I think you're wonderful."

He frowns. "You do?"

"Of course! You're fun, you're almost always kind. You always have something interesting to say. Sometimes it's hard to get you to focus, but good grief, you're a six old boy. In my experience as a professional dealer-with of six-year-old boys? You're, like, one of the best."

He's glowing, vibrating. For once, he doesn't know what to say, blushing and shuffling. He quickly recovers. "I'm gonna go get Mr. Tulip."

I splutter, my hand clapping over my mouth. "That's his name? Mr. Tulip?"

He nods. "Yeah. We ran out of the stuff he's supposed to eat, so I tried giving him different stuff, like carrots and grass and stuff, and I accidentally gave him one of Mom's tulips from the front yard, and he loved it so much he ate like six, and Mom was *so* mad at me. And so now he's Mr. Tulip."

"Mr. Tulip." I can't help a laugh. "All right. Well. I'm excited to meet Mr. Tulip."

He turns out to be an absolutely enormous white Angora. Enormous, as in growing up I had a terrier smaller than Mr. Tulip. Granted, most of his size is fur, but still. He's huge.

I did do my due diligence before agreeing to this, asking parents via our classroom app if anyone is allergic, and the answer came back negative for everyone. The jury is still out whether I'll keep him past this year, but for now, Miss Cole's first-grade classroom has a pet bunny. Named Mr. Tulip.

I'm cackling about the name all the way home, once Dane, Jake, and I get his cage settled in the corner by the bookshelves and blocks, feed him, and fill his water.

We raised rabbits on the farm I grew up on, so I'm well versed in the care and feeding of rabbits. They're not my favorite animal to raise as a pet, which is why I've never considered getting one of my own. But I just couldn't stand the idea of something untoward happening to the poor thing, and a class pet is always fun. And rabbits are pretty easy.

I just hope Mr. Tulip isn't one of the messy ones. Some rabbits are just...uck. They kick their bedding everywhere and just make a general mess. But, even that can be a teachable thing.

I'm at school a little early, the next morning, to set up for a project.

Rory and Riley are already waiting in the hallway. It's the end of September by now, so she's wearing a sweatshirt. Rory seems like the type who wouldn't notice the cold if it was blizzarding, so he's still in a T-shirt.

I unlock my door and smile at them both. "Hi, you guys. You're here early."

Rory hesitates, and Riley squeezes his hand, looks up at him expectantly. He harrumphs. "Uh. Miss Cole."

"Mr. Kerr." I do my best to exude welcoming, professional calm.

Inside, I'm freaking out a little. His hair is longer, shaggy under the back of his black beanie, and his beard is thicker than ever, curly, glossy.

He's the absolute definition of rugged. You could break boulders on his jawline. Diamonds would shatter on his cheekbones. His shoulders could double for anvils.

Pull it together, Emma, I scold myself.

He frowns, thick black eyebrows lowering. His beard shifts side to side, subtly, as if he's grinding his molars.

"Dad," Riley hisses. "She's *nice*. She won't eat you."

I barely suppress a snicker. "No cannibalism here, I assure you."

He sighs, a sound more like a growl than anything. He stares down at his daughter, and her loosely tied hair, already getting in her eyes. "What you did with her hair, yesterday. I watched videos online, and I tried." He holds up his hand—the palm is the size of a decent-sized dessert plate, and each finger is thick and blunt-tipped. "Her hair is just slippery, and I couldn't get the hang of it. These big ol' sausage fingers ain't so good at finicky things like that."

I reach into my room and flick on the lights—and sigh; Mr. Tulip has, indeed, kicked out a bunch of alfalfa and bedding from his cage. "Silly rabbit."

Riley immediately squeals, drops her backpack, and sprints over to the cage. "Ohmygosh, he's *so* adorable! Look, Daddy, look! He's so fluffy!"

Rory's face hardens further, which I wouldn't have thought possible. "Yeah. Fluffy."

She rolls her eyes at him. "You're such a grump, Daddy. Stop being nervous. Miss Cole is the nicest."

"Not nervous. Just don't like rabbits." It's hard to tell under the beard, but he could be blushing. Or it could be my imagination. "Friend had one when I was a kid. Said I could hold it. Tore the shit out of my arms." He winces. "Don't use that word, Ry. My bad."

"You owe me a treat after school," she says, without turning away from the cage.

He huffs. "Come back here, girly." He holds out his hand, and Riley immediately obeys, walking over to take his hand. "Will you show me?" He looks away from me, then back; this is requiring enormous humility from a big, strong, macho man. I have to say, I'm impressed. "How to braid? Or…just how to get her hair out of her face, at least."

I smile, and reach into my purse—after school last night, I bought packets of hair ties of varying sizes, a little baggie to hold them in, and a good comb. "Sure can." I bring a chair over to my desk, and lower my desk chair a bit. Riley sits facing away from me; I pull her hair free of the loose pony and comb it back.

"So, one simple thing you could do is simply pull this front section back by itself, first." I comb the section around her temple and forehead into a little ponytail. Show him the small, thin elastic band. "Use one of these. Doesn't have to be super tight or perfect, just enough to keep it back. Then, put the rest into a ponytail. Which, you've just been not making it tight enough. Twist it once more than usual and then pull it through."

I finish, and show him the final product. He nods, and I pull it all out so her hair is loose once more. "You try."

He takes my seat, and combs her hair back. I stand behind him, my hand resting on the seat back, inches from his shoulder. His touch is gentle, slow. Carefully, he pulls the hair around her face into a nice little section and ties it off. It's messy and off-center, but it's an improvement. Then, he does a regular ponytail, and this time makes it a little tighter, and now her hair looks much neater, and isn't in her eyes.

"See?" I smile at him. "One little change makes all the difference."

"What about the braid?" he asks.

I don't quite laugh. "I think maybe it would be better if I taught her how to braid her own hair. Save you pulling out your own."

He blinks at me. "You'd do that?" A puzzled frown. "She ain't even in your class."

I look at Riley with affection. "She's my friend. We talk after class, most afternoons."

He nods. "I been meaning to thank you for that. Being able to get here a few minutes later makes it a lot easier. So, thanks."

"It really is my pleasure. You're raising a remarkable young lady."

"Well, I think she's remarkable, too." He glances at my clock. "I should get going. You all right, Ry?"

She nods, and twists in the chair, leans into him. "I'll be able to do my own hair, soon."

He sighs. "Can I still read to you at night while you brush it?"

My heart melts a little, at that.

She laughs. "You *have* to. It's traditional."

"Good." He kisses the top of her head. "See ya this afternoon, stink-bug."

She rolls her eyes at him. *"Dad."*

His grin is like a bright bolt of sunshine breaking through heavy cloud cover. "I'll be calling you stink-bug even when you're grown, so best get used to it." His eyes cut to me when he pauses in the doorway. "Thanks again, Miss Cole."

"My name is Emma." I can't quite help the smile on my face.

"Emma." He says it like he's just…tasting my name, testing it out. Savoring its flavor and texture on his tongue.

"Rory."

Something crackles in the air between us, real and palpable.

He slaps the doorpost and nods at me, abruptly brusque. "Well. See ya."

"Rory?"

"Ayuh?" It's a distinctly Mainer inflection, the way he said that.

"If you ever need…um, anything else. With Riley, or…or not. Just let me know, okay?" Good grief, I botched that all up. Awkward much, Em?

He just nods, scrapes his hat off his head, rubs his fingertips over his scalp, and replaces the hat. "Thanks."

When he's gone, I notice Riley is almost too focused on Mr. Tulip, watching him do what rabbits do best: absolutely nothing at all.

"Riley?" I say, knowing I should leave well enough alone.

She looks at me with wide dark eyes. "Yuh-huh?" Innocent, guileless.

I just sigh, biting down on a grin. "You want to work on braiding?"

She laughs. "He was so nervous to come meet you."

"I think it was more that he probably doesn't like asking for help. Most men I've ever known are that way."

She shrugs. "Maybe. But he's weird around you."

"If you say so." I have to leave it there. I put my hair up in a bun this morning, anticipating this lesson; I let it down, shake it out, run my fingers through it, and sit in the little seat facing away from my desk chair. "So. I think the first thing to do is get comfortable learning to braid someone else's hair. Like mine."

She's quiet a moment. "You have a *lot* of hair, Miss Cole."

I laugh. "I sure do. I've actually never cut it, other than trimming the ends now and then."

"Never?"

"Nope, not ever."

"Do you think you ever will?"

I shrug. "I don't know. Maybe?" I use the comb to separate my hair into three equal sections, and then, moving slowly, I weave the three strands into a basic braid. "Like that. See?" I pause, holding the sections in my fingers. "You take over."

"What if I mess it up?"

I shrug. "Take it out and try again. No big deal."

I feel her fingers take over, and then I feel the gentle tugging of my hair being braided. It's a weird feeling, honestly; no one but me has braided my hair since I was a little girl. Just judging by feel, she's doing okay, so far.

A few minutes later, she binds the end in a hair tie. I hand her my phone with the camera open, and she takes a photograph.

I look at it, and turn in the chair to smile at her. "Great job, Riley! I can tell you really have been practicing."

She nods. "Daddy got me one of those Elsa dolls that's a real life-size head and hair, and I braid hers all the time. But when I try to do it on my hair, I just…always mess it up."

"You know what Mrs. Pritchard made me do to learn?" I ask. "She made me practice braiding with my eyes closed. So you have to do it by feel, like you do on your own hair."

We spend a few more minutes practicing, braiding my hair and undoing it and starting over. By the time I hear the first few squeaks of shoes of the earliest arrivals, she's gotten a lot better. I tell her to practice with her eyes closed at home, and then tomorrow we will try some braiding of her hair.

She's excited, bright-eyed. I twist the braid she did to my hair up into a bun, tie it off, and give her a quick hug. "Okay, you better get to class. I have a project I'm supposed to be getting ready for."

She skips to the doorway and her backpack. Pauses. "I think Daddy likes you. That's why he's nervous around you."

"Well then, I hope he's nice." I say this with a wink.

"He's always nice. Except when his boss is a butt stink, and then sometimes Daddy comes home cranky. But he's still nice to me, he just doesn't think anything is funny for at least until after dinner."

"His boss is a butt stink, huh?"

She nods sagely. "Daddy's the new guy, so he gets all the poop jobs. Except Daddy uses a different word I'm not allowed to say." She sighs, as if such seemingly arbitrary rules are beneath her, but yet she suffers them, for his sake. "He wants to go back to fishing, but there's no work here doing that and he can't afford his own boat yet."

"He's a fisherman, huh?"

She nods. "Not the kind of fisherman in the little boats with the fishing poles, though. He says that's not a fisherman, that's an angler. He's the kind of fisherman in the big huge boats with the nets, out in the ocean."

"You ever go fishing with him?"

She nods. "Yeah huh. It's one of my favorite-est things to do. Except he only lets me go with him when it's sunny outside. He says it's not safe for little nuggets when it's stormy." Her face takes on a concerned look. "Daddy says sometimes I overshare and that not everyone needs to know all the details of our lives."

I mime zipping my lips closed. "I won't say anything

to anybody." Students begin to stream into my room, and I give her a look. "Get to class now, Riley. See you after school."

Last few minutes of the day before the last bell rings. I'm going over their writing assignments from earlier in the morning, and they're all reading quietly. My classroom phone rings.

Donna Bellanger, the school secretary is on the line. "Emma? You have a call from a Mr. Rory Kerr? His daughter, Riley, is in Kelly's class, but he says he needs to talk to you."

"Yes, put him through, Donna, thank you."

A quiet click, a silent pause, and then his gravelly, cavernous is saying my name. "Emma, this is Rory."

Are my toes supposed to curl just from the way he says my name?

"Good afternoon, Rory. How can I help you?"

He clears his throat, a gruff huff. "I have a problem."

Getting words from him seems to be rather a trick, I'm finding. "Okay?"

"I repair boat engines. My boss's best friend's trawler broke down a couple miles offshore and he's sending me to go do an on-site repair." He pauses again, perhaps hoping I'll fill in the rest for him and thus spare him the need to actually say the rest; I don't, and he audibly sighs. "I have no idea how long it will take. Could be a quick fix, I could be out there for hours. And…ah…I got no one to hang out with Riley. You're literally the only person

I could think of to call. Could she—would you watch her for me?"

I have a thousand questions, but I choke them all back. "Certainly, Rory. It would be a delight to spend the evening with Riley."

His sigh, this time, is one of relief. "Thank god." Louder, then. "Looks like some weather is brewing out there, or I'd bring her along."

"Nonsense, Rory. She and I will have fun together."

"Can't begin to thank you enough. I just…I can't afford to turn down work, you know?"

"No need to explain. Riley and I are great friends." I hear noises in the background—the bass rumble of a diesel engine, a caw of seagulls. "Is there anything I should know? Allergies? Dietary restrictions? I already know you don't allow sugar."

"Nope. No allergies. She'll eat just about anything." A voice in the background, yelling his name. "I gotta go. You sure about this? I know I'm askin' a lot, when she ain't even your student."

"I am a hundred percent certain—I'm looking forward to spending time with Riley. Go. Fix the boat and call me again when you're back, and I'll give you my address." A thought occurs to me. "You should probably have my cell number, huh?"

"Yeah, probably," he agrees. I give it to him, and he mutters the numbers back under his breath as he writes it down. "Got it. I'll call you. Thanks again, Emma. Talk later." He clicks off, and I hang up.

This is getting…interesting.

4

FROZEN 2 PLAYS ON MY TV, A BOX OF PIZZA SITS ON THE coffee table, half the slices gone, and Riley has my left foot in her lap, a bottle of bright pink nail polish in one hand, tongue sticking out as she carefully applies the pink paint to my toes.

Apparently, it's not a quick repair. We've already been to the town library to get Riley her own card and picked out a few books. We went for a walk downtown and got a snack. Now, we're almost done with the movie, we've painted her fingers and toes and she's almost done with mine. After this, it's time for dessert.

Riley has talked nonstop since I told her what was happening today—a literally endless flow of chatter, with barely a breath between thoughts. It makes me smile—Dad always said I was a chatterbox as a kid; I'd do chores around the farm with him, and he'd just let me talk. He rarely said anything back, but he never shushed me and never seemed frustrated or impatient.

"Last time this happened we still lived up in Maine, and I had to stay with our next-door neighbor Mrs. McKay, and she was, like, old. She couldn't even walk, hardly. She didn't even have Netflix! Just the weird TV with all the commercials."

"She didn't even have Netflix? Wow. What did you *do*?" I wonder if she'll catch the sarcasm?

She huffs. "I was so bored! How did people in the olden days even watch TV? There was like a million commercials. And all there was to watch was some dumb show about a weird school bus that shrinks. I dunno. She didn't have any good food neither. I ate old graham crackers and apple juice. You're so much cooler than Mrs. McKay. I haven't had pizza in a long time. Daddy almost always cooks all our food. Getting something from somewhere else is a special treat."

"*The Magic School Bus!*" I said, laughing. "I used to watch that show after school every single day."

"But why did it shrink?"

"Magic! Duh!"

She shrugs. "It was kind of weird." She dips the brush into the bottle, scrapes it off on the rim, and goes back to my second to last toe. "I like YouTube better."

"YouTube, huh? What do you watch on YouTube?"

"Just stuff. Daddy says it's dumb and a waste of time, but it's harmless so he can't tell me not to watch it, but he sure wishes I'd watch regular cartoons or something."

"That's very open-minded of him."

"He makes me wear headphones with my iPad though, because he says it gives him a splitting headache."

"Reasonable request, I suppose." It's so tempting to fish for information. It'd be so easy to get her to talk about Rory, but that feels like cheating, so I don't.

Instead, I just let her chatter.

She proceeds to explain who her favorite YouTuber is and what it's about and what the last…episode, or whatever…was about—toy unboxing, believe it or not. By this time, my fingers and toes are all done and we just sit together on my couch.

Once our nails are dry, I break out Quest cookies and Rebel ice cream and I let her show me Rainbow High House videos on my laptop. She chatters through this, too, talking about which toy she would want and what she likes about it and the colors and everything.

It's going on nine o'clock, and she's starting to yawn.

Conundrum, now: let her stay up this late on a school night, or have her try to get some sleep, knowing she'll be woken up by her dad?

My problem is solved halfway through our sixth video, when she looks at me, then turns off the video, closes out the window, shuts the lid, and hands the computer to me. Yawns, slumps sideways and curls up into a ball, half on my lap.

"I'm tired." She closes her eyes, and immediately, her breathing starts to slow. "You're the best, Emma," she mumbles.

"No, you are."

She smiles, but she's already mostly asleep.

So…now what?

I've got a sleeping child on my lap. No clue when Rory will be done.

My AirPods case is just barely within reach, so I open my laptop, put in my earbuds, and turn on an episode of *Blown Away*.

I make it roughly eleven minutes into the episode before I start drifting off.

I'm jarred awake by my phone ringing via my AirPods, still in my ears. I jolt upright, blink, try to figure out what the noise is and where it's coming from and what it means—and then I have to find my phone.

Answer it. "H'lo?"

"Shit, I woke you up." Rory's voice in my ears.

I rub my eyes, struggle to find some mental coherence. "Yeah."

"Sorry."

"Did you fix the boat?" I ask. I glance at the time on my phone—11:36 p.m.

"Just got it running.'"

"Must have been really broken, huh?"

He chuckles. "It was damn near seized. Still mostly shot, but I got it running enough that he can limp back to shore. Gonna have to get it replaced, though."

"Couldn't it have just been, like, towed, at that point?"

A sigh. "That's what I said. Billy insisted on getting it going. I think I'm gonna have a top-end rebuild in my future. Yay me." He yawns. "I'm sorry, Emma."

"Hey, don't be sorry. We had fun. She's asleep."

"I'll be there as soon as I can. I just—you really went above and beyond. And I'm grateful."

"Not a problem, Rory."

Quiet.

This feels…intimate, somehow, this conversation. I can feel his exhaustion through the line.

"You know what?" I hesitate, even as the words bubble out. "She can just stay here tonight. I'll bring her to school with me. If you're comfortable with that. Or, you, um. You could crash here. My couch is a pull-out, so you and Riley could share it. It's just super late and you've had a long hard day and she's sound asleep."

"Shit." The curse word is an exhausted sigh, drawn out into several syllables: *sssshhh-yyy-iiiiiit.* "Let me get there and figure it out then, okay? I'm stuck riding back with Billy and we can only make like five or six knots at best. So I'm gonna be a while longer before I'm even ashore. I just…I just wanted to get ahold of you and let you know I haven't, like, vanished."

"I appreciate that, Rory. No worries." I rattle off my address for him, and he repeats it slowly, haltingly, indicating he's writing it down.

"Got it."

"I'll leave my side door open, so just park behind me and let yourself in through the kitchen, okay?"

"You're awful trusting, Emma. You don't even know me."

"I have impeccable radar. I can spot a creep from a mile away." I pause. "You're not one." It's the truth—I feel it in my bones and my gut. He's a good and decent person.

"Well, I'm glad to hear you think so." There's a noise on his end. "Awww fuck, man. Come on! You gotta be kidding me!"

"Did it just crap out on you again?"

He sighs heavily. "It's just struggling. He's got a major hitch in the pistons. One whole side is misfiring, and one of them is knocking like there's a gnome with a sledge-hammer in there."

"Well I'll let you go. Just...get the job done and don't worry about Riley. She's safe, she's sleeping, and every-thing is fine. Don't rush and don't worry."

I can tell he's moved. "You're a real-deal angel, Emma Cole. Thanks."

"It's all Riley. She's such a great kid that she makes it easy. You're doing an amazing job with her. Truly."

He clears his throat. "She tell you things?" A cough, and a rattle of metal on metal, and then the grumble of the engine—I hear the knocking and the misfiring. "About us? My ex, I mean?"

"Not as much as I think you're thinking. And I'm not prying, either. I respect your privacy." I can't help my-self. "Sounds like the spark plugs are bad, for one thing."

He laughs. "Bad? Try half a century old and jer-ry-rigged so much they're...they're just shot to hell." A pause, and if you can identify types of silences, this one would be incredulous. "You know engines?"

I huff a laugh. "Grew up on a farm in Colorado. If something broke and we couldn't fix it ourselves, we did without it. So I learned how to keep our forty-year-old tractor going without having to call for Dad. Plus, my dad and brother are gearheads and as the baby of the family, my favorite thing in the world was to hang out in the barn and watch them wrench. So I guess you learn a few things along the way."

"I hope you don't take this the wrong way, but you just don't seem the type, I guess."

"Well, you're not going to find me under a car on the weekends getting my hands greasy, but I can do my own tune-ups and fix most problems myself, in a pinch." I laugh. "I suppose you can be forgiven for thinking I'm not the change my own oil type of gal, though."

"You're just so pretty, and…I dunno. Girly." A pause. "That probably came out wrong."

"Well, I *am* a girl. I like pretty dresses and flowers and I read romance novels. So I am girly. But that's just not *all* I am. I can change my own oil and brakes, I can fix knocking and squeaking in my engine, I can change my own flats and plunge my own toilets and stop my faucet from dripping. I don't mind getting my hands dirty, and I'm not going to run screaming at the sight of a mouse or a snake."

He's unresponsive for a moment. "I'm sorry, but that's hot."

"If it's hot, why are you sorry?"

A laugh. "I guess I'm not sorry."

"Growing up, I resented my dad for making me do all that stuff. I just wanted to stay inside and read my magazines and watch TV. But he made me learn how to do things, especially when I got closer to graduating high school and going out on my own. He made me take kickboxing lessons three times a week for eight years." I laugh. "I'd rather have taken ballet lessons, but now I can walk down a dark street alone and know I can handle myself."

"Shouldn't have to have eight years of kickboxing in order to feel safe walking down a street," he grumbles.

"I agree, but that's just the sad reality of life as a woman."

"Makin' me think I need to get Riley started on self-defense classes."

"Yeah, it's not a bad idea. Golden Glove Self-Defense in town is really good. I go there once a week, just to keep my skills sharp. I know they have a beginner class for kids Riley's age and even younger."

"Thanks for that, I'll check it out." A pause. "Looks like this old bitch is gonna hold for now, so hopefully I'll be back in half an hour or so, if our speed holds."

"Crossing my fingers, then. See you soon."

"Yup, bye."

I rest my head against the couch and ask myself why it feels so easy and familiar to talk to him. Why just talking to him on the phone makes my skin tingle and feel too tight.

I mean, I know the answer—attraction.

Physical, at the very least.

I need to know more about him to know if it's attraction on any other level. It's tempting to assume that because I enjoy his appearance, and it's easy to talk to him, that it could be something between us. Unfortunately, experience has taught me that it's not always so simple.

Physical attraction does not equate to emotional compatibility.

And vice versa.

If anything, experience has taught me it's more likely that the two are going to be mutually exclusive. If there's one, the other cannot exist with it at the same time.

But for now?

I'm trying to keep my cynicism at bay, and allow myself to simply take things one step at a time.

Right now, I'm at step one: admit my attraction to him.

Step two is to determine if he shares that attraction.

Seems that way, but it doesn't do me any good to assume.

I doze off thinking about him.

"Emma?" The voice is deep, rough and hoarse and gravelly.

I blink my eyes open.

Rory.

He's in my home. Dressed in faded blue coveralls, the top pulled off and tied around his waist, a gray tank top baring thick, brawny arms the size of most people's thighs. Curls of black hair show at the neckline. His shoulders are like boulders, his chest broad and dense enough to stretch the fabric of the tank top.

I notice he's wearing three different friendship

bracelets on his right wrist—judging by the workman-ship, those bracelets were made by Riley. Practicing her braiding, it seems. On his left wrist, a thick, profession-al-quality dive watch.

His head is, for the first time since I met him, hatless. His black hair is a shaggy, curly, tangled thicket, hanging around his jaw and nape, sticking to his beard, which is normally clean and brushed and glossy, but now shows signs of having been tugged on out of frustration.

He's filthy. His coveralls and tank top are liberally stained with grease, his hands are nearly black with grease, and he's got smears of it on his forehead, nose, and cheekbones.

He's gorgeous.

I can smell him.

Ocean, and engine.

What a heady mixture of scents.

I tap the screen of my phone: 1:59 a.m.

"Guess it didn't hold," I murmur.

He closes his eyes briefly, rubs the bridge of his nose and blinks hard. "No," he growls. "It didn't."

He's swaying on his feet, and he can barely keep his eyes open.

Now that he's in my home, my offer to let him crash here seems far riskier than it had over the phone.

Not for my personal safety, though.

For…other reasons.

But I can't let him drive home in this state. There's not even a question of that.

I gingerly move out from underneath Riley, and she

stretches out in her sleep to take up the whole couch, snoring delicately. I cover her with a blanket, and then wave for Rory to follow me away from her where we can talk without waking her up.

I lead him into the kitchen and bring a beer out of my fridge, offer it to him. "Beer?"

To my surprise, he declines. "Nah. Thanks though. Water would be good."

I don't ask the obvious question, instead fixing him a mason jar of ice water.

He takes a few long drinks, and then eyes me. "I should get her home."

I shake my head. "You're dead on your feet. You're not driving anywhere."

He holds the mason jar by the rim, revealing black streaks on the glass from his hands. "I'm making your house dirty just being inside it."

"I do have this nifty new invention known as indoor plumbing." I smirk at him. "You could take a shower."

He narrows his eyes. "Your shower would be black by the time I'm done."

I shrug. "I know how to clean grease out of things, Rory. In fact, I have some heavy-duty hand cleaner, like you'd find in a mechanic's shop. As I mentioned earlier, I do most of the upkeep on my Jeep myself, so I keep it on hand to get the grease off my hands."

He eyes me, assessing. "I do have a change of clothes in the truck." A frown. "Sure you'd be comfortable with that?"

"Yes, I'm sure. I wouldn't offer otherwise."

He rubs his face, further smearing the filth on his face. "I *am* pretty beat."

"Go get your clothes."

He takes another long swig, his eyes not leaving mine. "Emma…"

I hold up my hand. "Another time, Rory. For now, just accept this as hospitality. Mainly because I'm so fond of Riley. Okay?"

He nods. Seems relieved. "I'll be right back."

I breathe out a long sigh when he's gone. It's hard to breathe around him. Hard to keep from staring. From wanting to put my hands on his arms, his shoulders.

I would never. Not unless he initiated it. But I can want.

While he's out, I pop into my bathroom and check it over—no stray undergarments on the doorknob or floor; I pull my hamper with my dirty clothes and stick in my closet, for now. No tampons or wrappers in the garbage. Some makeup on the counter, some face cream, my brush, my hairdryer. Nothing embarrassing. He's a grown man with a daughter, so none of that should be embarrassing, but still. He's a relative stranger.

I put out a clean towel and washcloth and set my container of heavy-duty hand cleaner with it so he can't miss it. I find him outside my bedroom, a stack of clothing in his hands. He shuffles awkwardly.

I indicate the bathroom. "Through there. Take your time. And please, don't bother trying to clean the shower afterward, okay? It's fine. I promise."

He just nods and moves past me toward my

bathroom. His gaze, naturally enough, does a brief scan of my bedroom. My eyes follow his, and take in my room from the eyes of a stranger: my bed is neatly made, a white, floral-print comforter, a chunky-knit throw blanket rumpled just so across the foot end, with probably half a dozen too many pillows; my hope chest at the foot of the bed, a four generation-old seaman's chest; a pair of slouchy, knee-high leather boots sitting flopped over by the chest, where I sit to put on and remove them; my blinds are drawn, with decorative, gauzy lavender curtains; a nightstand with a drawer and a pair of shelves featuring my perennial favorite books, a range of biography, romance, thriller, and diet-and-nutrition; my phone charger cord lays in a comma shape on the nightstand top, curled around the ceramic owl lamp; also on the nightstand, forgotten until this moment…my cordless Hitachi wand.

Which I do *not* use for massaging my shoulder and back…*ahem*.

Shit.

If I rush over there to put it away while he's watching, it'll just draw attention to it. Maybe he hasn't seen it. Maybe he thinks I just have tight shoulders.

His gaze lingers on the wand, momentarily, and then flick to me.

He knows.

I feel myself blushing, but refuse to be embarrassed. I'm an adult woman with needs and desires, and this is my bedroom, in my home. I hold his gaze without flinching, ducking, or trying to make excuses.

He doesn't quite grin, and certainly doesn't smirk. Says nothing. Just continues on into the bathroom. I hear the door latch and the lock click, and then a moment later the water turn on.

I let out the breath I hadn't realized I was holding, and fast-walk over to my nightstand to put away my vibrator.

We handled that like adults, I think. No awkward jokes or stammered excuses about how it's not what it looks like. It certainly is exactly what it looks like: I'm a woman who enjoys pleasuring herself in the privacy of her bedroom.

I head back to the kitchen and put my electric kettle to heating. I'm not sure if he's a tea guy or not, but a cup of herbal tea to relax is always nice, especially since he declined a beer.

I wonder what that was about. Is he sober? Does not he like beer? Is he worried I'd judge him for accepting? No way to know without asking, and I'm not ready to start asking personal questions just yet. If I ask personal questions, I have to be ready to answer them.

The kettle clicks off after a few minutes and the sound of the rolling boil subsides.

I hear my door open, and Rory appears in my kitchen. His hair is damp, jet-black spirals flat against his scalp and sticking to his neck. He needs a haircut. I'm tempted to get out my kit, but again, we're not quite there yet. Cutting a man's hair is pretty intimate.

Good lord, though, the man has an incredible body. I got a decent idea what his body looks like just from the T-shirts and jeans he habitually wears, but his emergency clothes are a pair of rather small running shorts that barely clear mid-thigh, and a baggy old Led Zeppelin T-shirt with the sleeves cut off, leaving a gaping hole big enough that I can see the side of his ribcage in the opening.

He's just brawny. An archaic word, perhaps, but it's just the best word for his physique. He's not a pro body-builder, nor is he IG model-shredded. He's heavy with muscle. Shoulders like mountains, thick arms, broad hard defined chest. I can't take my eyes off of him. His thighs are powerful, too—this isn't a man who skips leg day.

"Thanks for the shower," he murmurs, voice quiet. "I feel like a new man."

"No problem," I say. "You care for some tea?"

He frowns thoughtfully. "Don't drink too much tea. Not on my own at least." A pause. "Ex used to make tea all the time. But after she, uh—well, it just doesn't occur to me to make it."

"I find it helps me relax," I tell him. "The warmth, the herbal flavors, just the process of the whole thing."

He nods, seems like he's going to say something else. "I guess I'll try some tea."

I pour two mugs of my favorite herbal nighttime tea. "We could go sit on my back porch, if you want."

He nods. "Sure."

My porch is screened in, and the overhead light fixture features a low-wattage Edison bulb, shedding a soft orange light. Crickets sing. The waning moon shines bright over the trees lining the back of my yard. My only seating out here is a small wicker couch, just barely big enough for two people. My nerves sing as we take seats—he's close. So close I can smell him—clean male—and I can feel the heat radiating off of him.

He rests the mug on the arm of the couch and dunks the tea bag a few times, takes a tentative sip—hisses. "Still too hot."

"Just off the boil, still."

Awkward silence. He clears his throat. "Thanks again, Emma."

"Hey, no problem. I really do enjoy spending time with Riley."

He nods. Despite having just said it was still too hot, he takes another slurping sip. "She talks about you all the time." A wince, as he considers how much and what to say. "I think she...shoot, I know she needs a positive female role model and presence in her life. I don't want you to think I'm putting that on your shoulders or nothing, I'm just saying, she really looks up to you and can't get enough of hanging out with you. So I...I appreciate it. What you do for Riley."

"Well, like I said before...you're doing an amazing job with her. I'm an elementary school teacher because I like kids more than most adults, so I'm sure that's part of it, but I just genuinely like her company, as a person. She helps me clean up my classroom after school, and she just does it on her own. I've never asked her to. She just...helps. She's smart, she's fun to talk to, and she always has interesting observations about her class- and schoolmates."

He smiles. "I talk to her more than I do just about anyone else. Most of my work happens in the engine rooms of ships in the marina, so it's not like I'm in a shop to talk to other guys. So, Riley is it, for me, most of the time. And I guess I've just always spoken to her like I would anyone else. Guess that's rubbed off, some."

"Oh, it for sure has. In a good way, though."

He bobs his head side to side. "I'm a loner, and I'm always worried she's not learning enough social skills from me. Like, she only ever talks to her old man, and she's alone with me during the summer and I just don't know how to set up, like, a play date or some shit. I just worry she's not able to just be…a kid. I dunno if that makes sense."

I sip my tea, and then smile at him. "Well, I'm not her teacher, obviously, but I do have the opportunity to observe her in the lunchroom and during recess, and I think you don't have any reason to worry. She socializes normally with her peers. She plays like a normal little girl. She engages in games of pretend. She's never been ostracized for being weird or anything like that, that I've seen. She just is more capable of conversing with adults than most kids her age."

He nods. "Good. I appreciate you saying that. Takes a bit of the edge off my worry."

Another silence, both of us sipping tea.

He glances at me. "You're really not gonna ask?"

I shrug. "It's your business, Rory. I would never pry. Not with you, and not with her. Pumping little kids for information simply because they don't necessarily understand that that's what's happening is manipulative, in my opinion. If she volunteers information as a child would, that's fine, and I'll keep it confidential. But I'm not going to try to get her to tell me about you or your ex or anything, simply to satisfy my own curiosity."

He holds my eyes. "But you are curious."

"Of course I am."

He sips tea, gazes into the mug. "It's not that crazy or unusual of a story. I'm a Mainer, born and raised. Dad was a fisherman, Mom was a clerk for the township. I grew up on the boats with Dad. Never finished school. Mindy was from away. Boston, from old money. Maybe you know the type. Her family had a cabin Downeast, and one year she took her own little road trip from their cabin all the way up north, where we lived, and when I say way up, I mean Eastport, on Moose Island. About as far from everything as you can get, for a girl like her. She was the prettiest girl I'd ever seen, and a flatlander. I guess she thought I was interesting, because she ended up staying the summer. Came back every summer after that, and turned into a thing with us." He sighs. "I asked her to stay, and she did. Couple months later, asked her to marry me, and she did. Was good for us, for a while. When it was just us two. I was working on the boats with Dad and she'd complain once in a while about how living in the middle of nowhere sucks and isn't what she thought it would be. But she'd take trips down to see her family pretty regularly. She'd be gone most of the weekend, and sometimes for a week at a time. I didn't mind too much, then. Not gonna begrudge a flatlander time Downeast with her family where she's used to living."

A silence.

"But then she got pregnant, and that was hard for her. Then she had Riley and it made the trips down home even harder for her, if not impossible. And then when Riley was three, Mindy packed up and took a trip down to Boston, and she just never came back. Coupl'a months later, I got papers in the mail. Gave me custody and full rights, in return for not having to pay support. I didn't argue it. I had Mom and Dad to help, and I was making a decent living at fishing. Wasn't gonna get rich, but I could put food on the table."

"Generous of you."

"I'd just as soon not deal with the back and forth and the courts and all. I was pissed and confused and hurt. She didn't say nothing, didn't leave a note, just made like she was leaving for a weekend trip to see her mom and dad and never came back. Left most of her stuff. I shipped it all to her, once I'd signed the thing."

"I'm not a mother, granted, but I just don't understand a mother leaving her child like that." I shake my head. Sigh. "I really don't. Especially one as sweet as Riley."

A shrug. "I don't either. I guess in a sense I'm just grateful she left, instead'a taking Riley with her. Maybe that's selfish. Maybe she'd have been better off with Mindy and her family, down in Boston, with all the money and the best schools and all. But I'm just glad I've got my girl. Can't picture life without her."

He's on my left, his mug in his left hand and mine in my right—I cover his right hand with my left, a brief touch. "Just my opinion, but if Riley's mother was capable of walking away without a backward glance, then I think Riley is better off with you. It's not my place to judge, but that's just something I can't excuse. It's child abandonment."

He nods. "I agree. Been angry about it for a long time. Or, more confused than anything, honestly, but the confusion usually feels like anger."

"That's understandable." I slide my hand between my thighs in an attempt to quell the leftover tingling from merely touching his hand. "And I do truly understand how confusion can feel like or turn into anger."

He sips tea and glances at me. "Oh?" Not a direct ask, more an invitation to share.

"Mine is a little more complicated." I sigh.

He nods, shrugs. "Well, like you said first—I'm not gonna pry. You want to share, I'll listen. You don't want to share, well, I understand that, too."

To my own great surprise, I find myself sharing. Highly unusual—I typically avoid any mention of my own painful romantic history at all costs.

"Trace was my high school sweetheart. He lived on the farm adjacent to ours, and we grew up playing together. Climbing the round bales and chasing calves in the back forty. Swimming in the creek, up until it got weird to swim together. He was a year above me, so we never had a class together. We'd sit together during lunch, sit together on the bus, or sometimes we'd just walk home and make out in his family's fields. Then he got his license and his dad's old truck and he'd drive me to school and home." I do smile at the memories. "Hanging out and making out turned into real love by the time we graduated. We both went to Colorado State University together."

I shake my head, remembering. "I, um, actually took summer classes and tested ahead so I could graduate with him. Which I did." Another pause. "We got married right out of high school. Neither of our families approved, but when you've got two eighteen-year-olds convinced they're in love and this is the future and it's everything, there's no listening, right? So we eloped. Lived in married housing together. He was going to major in sport science. He wanted to be a physical therapist. I was working toward education."

I swallow. Sigh. Take a drink of tea, which has cooled enough by now to be drinkable instead of requiring careful, slurping sips.

"Senior year. Like, less than two months before graduation. I was in student teaching. He got certified as a personal trainer. Life was good. We had plans. He was going to find work as a physical therapist in Denver. He had applications out and was interviewing, and I was applying at schools. He was on the way back from an interview in Denver. Driving late. It was winter. He crossed the centerline. Smashed head-on into another car."

Rory winced. "Shit."

"He survived. Barely. He was in a coma for three and a half months." I swallow hard. "He suffered pretty severe brain damage. He had all his memories, he knew me, knew his family, knew our life. At first he was just focused on recovering. Getting out of the hospital. Fine motor skills, walking, talking, all that. He didn't have to totally relearn, but…he had a lot of work to do to recover. And he was just…different."

"Brains are crazy," Rory murmurs. "You never know how things will affect you, if you get brain damaged."

I nod, clutching my mug in both hands. "Exactly. That's what the doctors all said. Especially when he kept acting…weird…toward me." I blink hard. It's old and scarred-over pain, now, but it still hurts. "Distant. Cold. Like…he knew me, and he knew I was his wife…but…" I shrug. "It was like he'd kept all his memories except loving me. At first it was just…weird. Acting like he was nervous around me, not wanting my help, asking me to leave him alone when he needed something from the nurses. Then he got out of the hospital and had to go to PT and he'd want me to drop him off instead of staying with him. It was hard. I was confused. And he didn't want to talk about it—I tried, several times. A year after the accident, he was mostly back to normal. He'd gotten a job at the physical therapy facility he'd been going to for his own recovery. I'd gotten us an apartment while he was in the coma, and I'd gotten a job as a kindergarten teacher near the hospital. But he…finally, I confronted him. Asked him why it felt like he didn't love me anymore."

I steady my voice. "He said he couldn't explain it. He just…didn't. He said he'd been trying. And I can recognize now, more so now than I could then, but even then I could sort of see how he'd been trying. Making an effort to get back to normal with me. But…it was just… never there, for him. He never…um…we were never together, after his accident. He just…couldn't. I wanted to, once he was cleared, medically. But he just…didn't feel that way for me. Emotionally, physically. It was just gone, and he couldn't explain it and neither could the doctors. And he told me that he didn't feel like it would be fair to me to keep me trapped in a marriage where he didn't love me anymore, through no fault of mine or his. Something about the accident just…damaged that part of him, somehow. I don't know. I've never gotten an explanation that made any sense other than what you said—that human brains are a mystery."

"Damn," Rory whispers. "That's fuckin' rough, Emma."

"Yeah. It was." I sigh. Shake it all off. "So we divorced, and he moved out into his own apartment. I finished out the year, and then I left Colorado. I took some time off. Drove out to California and lived in my Jeep and learned how to surf. Got into yoga—got certified to teach it, actually. But I couldn't just be a bum forever. Marrying Trace had strained my relationship with my family, so I didn't really feel comfortable going back home to the farm. I put out applications to schools all over the country. San Diego, Austin, Boise, here, Chicago, Seattle. I got interview offers from quite a few, and chose this place based on my visit here. It was just so…charming. And so very different from the little farming community where I'd grown up and then college in Fort Collins."

He nods. "So, you can surf. You can teach yoga. You can work on cars." A grin, turning the conversation into lighter-hearted territory. "What else about you would surprise me?"

"Well, I grew up on a farm. So, I can take a chicken from walking around to meat in the pan. I can ride horses like nobody's business—I was a barrel racer in high school. I can shoot better than most men. I told you I took kickboxing—I'm a black belt." I smile at him. "That enough surprises?"

He nods. "That's a lot of different skills."

"What would surprise me about you, Rory?"

He shrugs. "I'm not a very surprising person. I don't have a high school diploma—I got my GED just a few years ago, after Mindy left. I dropped out sophomore year to work with Dad on the boat full-time. By the time I was eighteen, I was first mate of a trawler, on my own, earned through my own merits and not just because my dad was well-known in the fishing community. I learned early I had a knack for engines, and Dad would lend me to friends who could teach me. So I'd spend summers on boats all over the Maine Coast, fishing and working on engines. It's all I've ever known. Doesn't leave a lot of room for surprises."

"You're doing yourself a disservice, I think."

"Something surprising?" He shrugs. "I gave up drinking, and not because I had a problem, but because I didn't. When Mindy took off, I had Riley depending on me. Her mom had already abandoned her, and I felt like for me to start drinking to deal with the pain would be abandonment just the same, only in a different form. So I gave up alcohol and got into powerlifting. Whenever I was ashore, I'd be in the garage, lifting. Became my outlet and my solace. Still is."

His physique makes even more sense, now.

"And you've stuck to that, ever since, the not drinking?" I ask.

He nods. "I'm better off. I'm a better person. I was never a heavy drinker in the first place. And I've met enough people whose lives are defined by their relationship to alcohol, you know? I don't want that to be me. Being a single father is hard enough, right? Adding a struggle with booze on top of it would just make it that much harder, I guess. And everyone struggles with it, to some degree. That's my personal feeling."

"I think that's amazing."

He shrugs. "Eh. Don't make a mountain out of it. Just the best path to survival that I can find. I want to remember my life with Riley, I want to enjoy it. Not just survive it. And I want her to remember me as being sober and present, not…" A waving gesture with his now-empty mug. "A drunk."

"Your parents influence that decision at all?"

"Smart girl." A smirk. "Yeah. Dad drank a lot. I didn't like it, how it made him. And, in the end, I think it was a major contributor to him dying of a heart attack, about a year after Mindy left."

His life is divided into two: Before Mindy Left, and

After Mindy Left. It's something I understand on a personal, visceral level. My own life is similarly divided: before the accident, and after.

"Your mom?"

A shrug. "Eh. She was never healthy. She had medical issues my whole life, and passed away, not unexpectedly, when I was eleven. After that, it was me and Dad. He sold the house and we just lived on the boat year-round. I didn't have a permanent home again until Mindy and I got our first apartment together."

"Wow," I say. "So, we've both been technically homeless."

He nods. "Yeah, guess so." A look at me. "How long did you live in your Jeep?"

"About a year. I had savings, and I worked odd jobs to supplement it. That's not the same as you living in a boat for however many years it was."

"Almost ten. Mindy moved up to Eastport with me when I was twenty-one. So yeah, ten years."

"Did it have actual living quarters, the boat you lived in with your dad?"

He rolls a shoulder, chuckles. "Sort of. Not the kind meant for year-round living, but we made it work, and Dad was always working on it, jerry-rigging improvements and such. His boat was his life."

"Riley said you guys have a sailboat named *Dreamrider*?"

He nods, laughs. "Yeah. It's a tiny little sailboat. Barely big enough for two people, but she loves sailing more than just about anything in the whole world. I've been taking her out to sea since she was a baby. Mindy'd leave, and if I couldn't find anyone to watch her, I'd bring her with me. Usually there was someone on board who could keep an eye on her downside while I worked. Wasn't the best environment for a little tyke, but what could I do? Mom was years in her grave, Dad was gone, Mindy was gone. So, she grew up around fishermen. Boozing and cursing and telling stories and smoking, but they cared for her like she was one of their own."

"Kids are resilient. She was loved and cared for. In my experience, that's what really matters." I play with my teabag. "So what brought you down here?"

A sigh. "A few factors all combined. There was a bad storm and the boat I'd been working on nearly went under. We barely made it to shore. Thank god my neighbor was watching Riley that time. It was a wicked bad storm, the dregs of a hurricane. Swamped us. We were pumping like nobody's business. How we even made it back, I'll never know, but we did. After that, I had trouble finding a boat to work on. Everyone had a full crew, and everyone knew I had Riley and they didn't want that additional responsibility. I dunno. Plus, I'd been born and raised in Eastport. Mom died there, Dad died there, and Mindy had left me there—I was alone. Alone, with way too many memories. I couldn't find work, so I just…cut out. I headed down the coast looking for work, looking for a place that…I dunno. Spoke to me, I guess. Ended up here. Found a place that needed an experienced mechanic who didn't just know engines but boats. It's a whole different thing, boat engines. So, I took the job and got us a place, and here we are."

"Here you are."

A silence between us. He's looking at me. Not ogling, not staring, not even really assessing or considering his next words. Just...looking at me.

I hold his gaze, meeting it with my own frank, un-flinching one. We're close to each other. I can feel him, his heat and the dense solidity of his body. He smells of my soap and shampoo, but underneath that I can still scent the sea and engine oil and diesel fuel—as if those scents are just woven into his presence.

I like it.

There's something comforting to me about those scents. Dad always smelled of oil and diesel. His hands always looked dirty, even when he'd just washed them, as if the grease was just inked into the lines and wrinkles and pores. I find my eyes going to his hands, his right hand on his thigh. Like my father's, his are large, with wide palms and long, thick, blunt-ended fingers. Without thinking, I turn his hand over to face palm-up, and trace the lines of his palm, noting the scars and calluses, the grease-inked leather of them. He could engulf my closed fist entirely within one hand.

I like his presence. I feel safe, at ease. Yet, also tense with awareness. There's a heat bubbling in me. A knowing. A needing.

He watches me trace the long, deeply etched lifeline on his palm, and his brows furrow and hear his jaw creak and crackle as if he's clenching and grinding his molars.

His hand curls closed around mine.

I stop breathing.

My skin is flushed, my pulse loud in my ears. Surely he can hear my heart drumming like thunder against my ribcage.

It's a mere moment, his hand closed around mine. I feel his calluses against my comparatively soft skin— like pumice against silk. His eyes are on mine, deep and dark and half wild, the eyes of a man who has lived his life on the untamed sea.

"Emma," he murmurs, his voice a steel file rasping against granite.

I jerk my hand free and stand up. "I have to work in the morning. I need to get to bed."

"I can sleep on the floor next to the couch," he says. "Just need a blanket and something to go under my head."

"The couch pulls out. The only issue is getting it out without waking up Riley."

He huffs a laugh. "Well that's easy. She sleeps like a corpse." He rises and breezes past me, heading for Riley. "You could drive a herd of cattle through here and she wouldn't stir." He's not even whispering.

"She decided she was tired and just…lay down and went to sleep." I smile, watching her small, peaceful face.

He nods. "Yeah, she's been like that her whole life. Even as a toddler, she'd just decide, okay, night-night time. She'd say that: 'Okay, night-night time.' Or she'd come over and put her head on my leg and close her eyes, waiting for me to put her to bed." He scoops her in his arms and cradles her as if she were a baby again. She doesn't even stir.

I pull the pillows and cushions off the couch, slide the coffee table out of the way, and pull the bed out of the couch. It's already got a clean sheet on it, so I just have to get extra pillows and a blanket from the hall closet. That done, Rory sets Riley onto the bed and covers her. She remains exactly as he placed her, still sound asleep.

I shake my head, laughing. "That's remarkable. I wish I could sleep like that."

Rory snorts. "No kidding. If a mouse farts in Greenland, I wake up."

I cackle. "Descriptive. But honestly, same. Especially in a situation like this—I have to be up in a few hours, so my mind is going to be obsessed with making sure I don't sleep too deeply, in case I were to oversleep."

He frowns. "I'm sorry."

I just wave. "It's okay, really."

His eyes hold a wealth of unspoken thoughts. Part of me wants to hear them. To hear him voice them. To know if he thinks about me the way I do him.

What holds me back? Fear? Doubt? Some of both. When you've been hurt the way I have, trusting someone again feels impossible.

To open your heart again feels like baring a target and begging someone to pierce it with an arrow. Like showing them, here, right here—this is how you hurt me. And look, it's already damaged. One more blow and it'll just shatter.

He seems good. He seems kind. Genuine. But I don't even know how to try.

What it would look like, to allow…something.

I've brought him this far into my life, and it's easy to sit with him. Close to him. It's easy to talk, to touch his hand. But what does any of that mean? Can it translate into emotional intimacy? Physical? I've told him my story and heard his. But that's just information. It's not really letting him behind the walls. And I have a feeling I'm not behind his, either.

It feels like a standoff.

I shake my head and turn away from him—we've been staring at each other in silence this whole time. "Good night, Rory."

"Night." A brief pause. "What time you wake up in the morning?"

"Usually four thirty. To work out and shower and such. But I think in this case I'll skip it and just set the alarm for six."

Another stare-down. Neither of us willing to look away, nor speak, nor move.

Finally, I duck my head and pull myself away from his magnetic pull.

My bedroom smells like him.

My bathroom is permeated by him.

My sleep is populated by a million iterations of his smile, disrupted by the rasp of his voice murmuring the two syllables of my name, a whisper loaded with an intimate weight of meaning.

5

A s EXPECTED, I WAKE UP AT 5:58 A.M., ABRUPTLY AND totally awake. I smell coffee.

Did I prep my coffeemaker last night? I must have, though I don't remember doing so.

I'm disoriented and bleary-eyed. My brain hasn't kicked on. My legs are carrying me on autopilot—first into my bathroom to pee, then toward the coffee.

I find it, one eye closed against the light in my kitchen, the other squinted half shut.

The coffee is already in a mug, being handed to me by a tall, dark, and handsome man.

Wait, what?

"Are you the coffee angel?" I murmur. "You must be the coffee angel."

His smile is slow and warm. He's sleepy, still too. I can't make sense of him. Why is he in my house? I'm still more than half asleep, and I barely even know who I am, right now.

"Coffee angel, huh? I've been called worse." He watches me sip. "I wasn't sure how you took your coffee, so I left it black. Didn't see any creamer in the fridge either. Sorry if that's snooping."

I just swallow hot, strong, black coffee and stare at him, waiting for my mind to start chugging into gear. "Mmm." It's a noncommittal sound. Vague and meaningless, more of an acknowledgment that he spoke than a real response.

Another sip.

His eyes are on mine, but then flick down. Linger at my chest, then my legs.

Why is he looking at me like that?

It makes me tingle all over, that look. Even through the occluding cloud of sleepiness, his eyes raking over and lingering on my body makes me tingle.

I slurp, not caring that it's obnoxious and rude. The coffee is hot and I need it in me now. I really need to jump-start the hamster wheel in my head.

"Not a morning person, are you, Emma?" His voice is low, a quiet bass thunder.

I shake my head. "Mmm-mmm."

"Do you even know where you are or who I am, right now?"

I shake my head again. Sip coffee. "Mmm-mmm. All I know is you gave me coffee."

"That explains a lot."

"You know the joke mug with the markings on it,

like shush, not yet, now you may speak?" I lift the mug. "If this had those markings on it, it would still be on the not yet level."

He nods. His mug lifts to his lips, tilts; his eyes, deep almost-black pools, linger on me, over the rim of his mug. Look away. Down. Up. Anywhere but me, then back to me, tripping from my face downward yet again.

I inhale steam and the scent of coffee, take a long slurping drink, and let out the sigh, finally feeling like there's some semblance of human cognition happening in my brainpan.

He's Rory, Riley's dad. He stayed here last night.

He made me coffee.

I just woke up, and he was awake already, coffee brewed, a mug ready for me.

He keeps looking at me.

Surreptitiously, I look down at myself.

And immediately blush scarlet from hairline to toenails.

That's why he's looking at me and can't seem to stop.

I'm in a pair of black hipster underwear—thankfully opaque silk rather than sheer lace, like some of my other pairs—and a short red camisole. No bra. The cami is low-cut, and *very* revealing. It's comfy to sleep in, but I'd never wear it in front of anyone. Would never, have never. It's sleepwear for me, nothing else.

I haven't stood in front of a man this undressed in *years*.

Mortified is an understatement.

I suddenly feel very naked.

The lingering glances make sense. My breasts are almost entirely exposed, the V-neck of the cami hitting just above my nipples. Like, the upper portion of my areolae are visible, darker tan half-moons.

The cami is a short one, the hem cropped above my navel. There's no support, no coverage. I suppose one could call it lingerie—I ordered an actual nightie and received this one by mistake. They sent me the correct one, but I discovered I liked sleeping in this one more. It's not *for* anyone, and I don't wear it because it makes me feel sexy or anything like that. It's just comfy. It's silky and soft. I don't like sleeping topless, even though I live alone, but I don't like feeling constricted either, and this garment offers the best of both worlds.

My half-asleep stupid self walked out wearing it in front of a man who is to a large degree a stranger.

"I, um…" I stare into my coffee, clutch my arms across my torso. "I really wasn't very awake when I came out here. I wasn't thinking." I edge sideways. If I turn around, my butt will be exposed. These being hipster panties, there's not exactly a lot of coverage over my butt.

He scrapes his stiffened fingers through his hair, gaze now aimed away from me. "I, um, sort of figured it was something like that."

"I'm sorry. I'm clearly not a morning person. I wasn't thinking."

His eyes meet mine, and I can see the war in his features as he struggles to keep his gaze on my eyes rather than anywhere else. "Would it make me an asshole if I said I'm not exactly mad about it?" He's not grinning, but I see it hidden in his eyes.

I shrug, a slight roll of one shoulder. "No, I wouldn't say that."

He licks his lips, and his attention loses the struggle, once more trailing downward from my eyes to my cleavage. He drops his head, wrenching his gaze away with a harsh sigh. "I'm sorry. You're just…you're freaking stunning, Emma."

My nerves fail me, and I flee, heading past him to my bedroom. This means turning my back to him, but at this point he's gotten an eyeful of the front side, might as well make it even and let him see the backside. My backside, that is.

Freaking stunning.

I have a confession to make.

I know he was affected by my mostly exposed state. I know this because I looked. As I moved past him, I saw very clearly the evidence that he was affected. It was outlined very prominently against the front of his shorts—which were in no way equal to the task of containing all that he is.

There was a lot of him to be contained.

A lot of him…very visibly affected by my partially naked state.

I dress in a loose, flowy skirt and a thick cardigan over a tight bra and basic T-shirt: curve camouflage. When I reemerge from my room, Riley is awake, my couch is once more a couch, and Rory is refilling his mug.

"So," I say, my tone bright and chipper. "Who's hungry?"

Riley shoots her hand up. "I am!"

"What do you like to have for breakfast? Like, your very favorite thing?" I tip my head to one side. "Aside from your dad's special famous French toast, that is."

"Do you have any good cereal?"

"Sadly, I do not. You want to know something funny? I haven't eaten cereal literally ever? My parents didn't believe in cereal. Weird, but true. My dad felt it was nutritionally empty, and in order to be able to work on the farm we had to have real food, like eggs and bacon and sausage and oatmeal. And you know something? I hated that as a kid, but now, I feel the same way."

Riley stares at me in disbelief. "You've *never* had cereal?"

"Nope."

"Not even Cheerios?"

"Not even Cheerios." I shrug. "Another strange and surprising fact about Emma Cole."

She glances at her dad, who seems content to let her handle this conversation on her own. "Dad usually eats eggs in the morning, but he only knows how to make them scrambled. He tries to make omelets sometimes, but it always ends up scrambled anyway. And I don't like scrambled. They're too…gooey. I dunno. Usually I just have oatmeal because it's quick and doesn't need to be actually cooked."

Rory rolls his eyes. "Way to throw me under the bus, Ry."

Riley makes an innocent face. "What? It's true."

"I cook for you."

"Not breakfast."

"Because it normally requires the National Guard and a full marching band to get you up in the morning, and by the time you're awake and dressed, there's not time for a six-course meal. You're...*performing* for Miss Cole today since we're guests in her home." He arches one eyebrow.

"You're being a little melon-dramatic, Daddy."

He snickers. "Melon-dramatic, huh?"

She nods, her expression sage. "Yeah. Where do you think I learned it?"

"Mel-*OH*-dramatic. Melodramatic."

"Same thing."

"Except one is a real word, and the other is not."

She sticks her tongue out at him, and he just laughs.

I clap my hands together. "So. Omelets, then?"

Riley grins eagerly. "Yes please."

I gather the materials: a carton of eggs, oil, a pan, and cheese. Riley helps me crack eggs and whisk them, and I emphasize the necessity of preheating the pan on low heat and letting them cook slowly. I don't look at Rory while I'm explaining any of this, however. I show her how to run the excess egg off the top once there's a nicely solidified layer, and then how to flip it and add the cheese to start melting while the other side cooks.

"Huh," Rory grunts. "That explains a lot."

When Riley starts eating at my island counter, I stand behind her and run my brush through her hair, then begin braiding it. A slow, simple braid. Once I've got I started, I feel Rory move in behind me. His hands cover mine, briefly, and then I let him take over the braiding. For a moment, he's towering behind me, surrounding me. Not quite touching me anywhere, but centimeters separate our bodies. I feel his heat, his solid presence. Smell him. Hear his breathing, feel it wafting warm on my neck, smelling faintly of coffee.

I'm tempted to lean back against him.

Instead, I duck out from under his arms and prepare another omelet—this one is for Rory, so I make it with four eggs, and while it's cooking, I dice up some turkey and green peppers. He hands me my mug, refilled. I plate his omelet and make my own.

There's discussion about swinging by their house so Riley can put on clean clothes. Rory makes a remark about having to stay a little late again this afternoon to finish the job he'd had to abandon yesterday due to the emergency, and I respond with an assurance that Riley and I can do some shopping until he's done.

It's all so…domestic.

It makes my heart flutter.

Ache.

Puts a flip in the pit of my stomach.

An image flits through my head—me, kissing Rory on the mouth, and Riley on the forehead, before heading out the door to work. Or maybe Riley would go with me—that's more likely.

What ends up happening is Riley and Rory leave once they've finished eating. Riley hugs me, and Rory and I exchange an awkward, eye-avoiding series of *see-you-later-thanks-no problem*.

I know he's still thinking about how I was dressed—or not dressed—this morning.

Goodness knows I'm still thinking about that too…and how it affected him…and how that leaves the fluttery, flipping weirdness in my gut feeling too hot, too melty, too shivery.

Something is happening, developing. I know it is, I can feel it. I just don't trust it.

More to the point, I don't trust myself—my heart, specifically. I like him too much, and Riley.

Things felt way too comfortable like a happy little home, this morning. That's dangerous. For him, for Riley, and for my poor, cynical heart.

Once they're gone, I clean up, gather my things for work, and head out.

My house smells like Rory.

Like someone lit a Rory-scented candle and left it burning all night, so the very walls are permeated with the scent.

I should mind it.

I don't.

All day, the mental image I had of Rory kissing me on the way out the door replays in my head:

Gathering my purse, a raincoat, and my backpack with my lunch and school materials, I would pause by the side door to give Riley an affectionate smooch to the forehead. She would lean against me in a cuddle, nuzzling me.

"Bye," she would say. "See you at school!"

Rory would be still half dressed, his coveralls and boots on, but still no shirt, the upper half of the coveralls hanging around his waist, the sleeves tied loosely in front. His heavy chest would be bare, heavy muscles furred with a scrim of black hair. It's manly and sexy, that body hair. It would tickle my nose at night, when I snuggle up to him, my smaller body incongruously the big spoon behind his much larger one.

He would hook a thick arm around my waist and haul me up against him, his grip possessive, his eyes hot. "See you later?" he would mutter, lips moving against mine, his dark eyes full of suggestion.

"Yeah," I'd breathe, and kiss him, promising what would definitely happen later. "I miss you already."

It would be a little saccharine, a lot spicy.

He'd kiss me a little too long. Until Riley would roll her eyes and groan, but it would be good-natured.

I have to shake it off, banish the image.

More than once.

Constantly.

Ugh, this is bad.

It's just a little infatuation with a sexy new guy in town. It's happened before. Maybe not a new guy, or even necessarily a single one, just a sexy dad who I'd see around the school, in the pick-up line, at plays and in the halls for parent-teacher conferences. He'd capture my imagination, and my lonely horny subconscious would do the rest. Nothing ever comes of it. I don't voice it to him, nor even let on that such a thing has even crossed my mind. Especially if he's not single.

What happens in my imagination is private and personal—not to mention fictional and harmless. You see a good-looking guy and you play through imaginary scenarios as you fall asleep, not quite dreaming, not quite awake. It's not a daydream, not a real unconscious dream. Not even a fantasy. You wouldn't want it to actually happen—the actions you take in those scenarios aren't even really *you*, nothing you'd ever actually do in real life. It's not real. It's not something you want. It's just your mind playing dumb games.

It means nothing.

Somehow, though, where Rory is concerned, it just feels…different.

Sure, some of the single dads that have passed through the school since I hired on have given me looks that have hinted at possibility. Looked at me like they like what they see. But looking is free, right? I don't act on it. I don't meet those looks with my own.

No numbers are exchanged.

But with Rory? It's just different.

And not because he's been in my home. Or because he's seen me as close to naked as anyone has since the accident.

It's something about *him*. Something in his presence, his eyes, his voice. Something in the way he looks at me.

I tell myself it means nothing more than anything else ever has.

Maybe I should put some distance between Rory and me. Just to be on the safe side.

Rory ends up not having to work late, and picks up Riley on time. I wave at him from the parking lot as Riley climbs up into his truck. It's Friday, and I have a full weekend planned for myself.

After school Friday I attend a mindful yoga class downtown. I use the mindfulness practice to put Rory out of my mind. Center myself. Clear my chakras of his engine oil and ocean spray scent, and the wildness hidden deep in his dark eyes, and the heat of his big body.

Clear it all out.

Saturday morning I spend at the farmer's market, stocking up on fresh produce and handmade soap and such. Treat myself to a fresh croissant and a coffee in the cafe at Kneads.

It's a beautiful early fall day, crisp and clear and still, a little cool but not cold, with pockets of warmth in the direct light of the sun. I strap my paddleboard to my Jeep and head to the marina. I've discovered the hard way that however warm it may be onshore, once you get a little ways out on the water, it gets *way* colder, so I dress accordingly: emergency inflatable around my waist, warm hat over my ears, thin gloves, and several layers on my torso, so I can remove layers as I warm up. I put in on the north end of Compo Beach and paddle away from shore a ways, within reach of an easy paddle should the weather change. Out here, the chop is worse than I thought it would be, the wind stiffer than it is ashore. Nothing to worry about, though. I begin working my way south, toward Cedar Point. In the distance, I can hear the shouts and yells and laughter and clack of wheels from the skate park as I round the point.

That's when the wind kicks up.

It skirls off the point and pushes me away from shore, angling me south toward open water, when I'm trying to get back to the marina. I've already logged over a mile—doesn't sound like much, until you try paddling that far on choppy seas, with a stiff headwind. And now, suddenly, what should be the last half mile from the point into the marina takes an eternity, minutes passing and my arms growing fatigued as I work against the wind. No matter how much progress I feel like I'm making, the marina seems farther and farther away.

I'm not panicking yet. It takes a lot to make me panic. Growing up the way I did, I learned early to face tricky situations calmly, to focus on the solution and worry about being scared later.

To wit: I've been treed by angry, territorial bulls, I've faced down protective black bear mamas with their cubs, chased coyotes away from the goose pens, stayed on spooked and bucking horses...it's all just part of life in the country, as far as I'm concerned. You get scared, but you figure out the solution. The shakes and the nausea and the fear are there, but you don't let yourself feel it till after you're safe.

So, I'm being blown out to open sea, and the nice clear calm sunny fall day is turning gray, and I'm not making headway, and the wind is picking up even more, and the challenging little choppy waves are turning into worrisome whitecaps. My arms are tired. My core is aching from standing and bracing for each deep stroke of the paddle. My hands hurt. Rain begins to dapple the surface of the sea, and I feel it misting on my face. I'm well insulated against it for now, but if I don't reach shore before this turns into a storm…

Solve the problem, Em.

First thing is to drop to my knees on the board. It sacrifices power from my strokes, but I'm more stable and unlikely to fall off, even with the increasing roughness of the chop. Tug my zipper all the way up and nuzzle my nose behind the collar. Pull my hat down lower. Rest my paddle across my knees and shake out my hands. The wind is blowing me south, away from shore; rather than fighting it, I cut west. Even if I'm blown steadily south, as long as I keep fighting my nose north, I'll hit land. It'll take a heck of a lot longer, but I won't exhaust myself only to end up going nowhere, like I've been doing.

The light misting of rain turns into heavier droplets that patter on my back and board, which I begin to feel through my hat. The westward shore, which should roughly be the Saugatuck Harbor Yacht Club, still seems to grow no closer, even after another half hour of shoulder-destroying paddling.

I'm still not panicking, but I am starting to worry.

Perhaps I need a new solution.

I need help. But who can I call? Ingrained in me almost as deeply as my overall strong-willed sense of independence is a resistance to asking for help. You'd think they're the same, right? Independent and strong-willed, not asking for help? Same-same.

Nope.

I'm independent in that I make my own way in life. I earn my own living. I live alone. I fix my own car, change my own oil, change my own flat. If my screen door creaks, I oil it. If my sink leaks, I fix it. Need something heavy moved? Physics, baby: find a fulcrum and a lever, or rig a pulley. I'm strong-willed in that you're not likely to change my mind on something about which I have a strong opinion, such as my capabilities, or my politics, or my moral compass.

Not asking for help goes deeper than that. You don't take your car to a mechanic for a squeaky belt. You don't ask someone to move your couch for you because you want to paint the living room. Treed by a pissed-off steer with a six-foot horn span? You don't yell for help. You climb a damn tree and wait for him to cool off and go somewhere else, and then you run like hell. In case you're not familiar with them, cows are *not* slow. When they need to move, they can *move,* and fast. So when I say run like hell, I mean like hell itself is on your heels. Because if that pissed-off 1200-pound steer with a six-foot horn span catches you, it won't be pretty. But good lord, whatever you do, you don't start howling for help.

Warring against that ingrained behavior pattern taught to me my dad and brother is a more practical sense that sometimes you come up against a problem you just can't solve on your own. If you want to overcome that problem, you may need to swallow your pride and ask for help. That's got nothing to do with my lack of a Y chromosome. It's just plain logical fact.

Case in point? I've been paddling my booty off for the westward shore for an hour, and I'm getting nowhere except farther away from land and closer to the vast gray churn to my east and south. I can see land, and unless I've been pulled and pushed way further south than I thought, I'm now even with Bluff Point. Which isn't good. I could give up the westward notion and make for Cockenoe Island, but I don't know that there's much there, if anything. I just know it exists and it's south-ish of Bluff Point. And also very far away when one is on a paddleboard.

I set my paddle on my board and pin it in place with my knee so the chop doesn't send it floating away. In addition to my emergency inflatable clipped around my waist, I have my waterproof fanny pack, in which I have my phone and a small wallet with my ID, some cards, and cash, and a protein bar. I keep an eye on my south-ward drift, getting wetter by the moment—the rain is still light, but steady. I'm not soaked through, yet, but wet enough that I'm starting to feel it even through my layers. Eat the protein bar. It adds a little fuel to my exhausted muscles, and settles my mind on the fact that I have only one real option.

I sigh, and dig out my phone.

Bring up the contact entry for Rory Kerr. Hesitate a

moment, and then two, and then hit dial with a huff of irritation at myself.

It rings twice, three times. Four.

"Hello—Emma?" His voice is muffled, distant.

"Hi, Rory, yeah, it's Emma."

"Hold on a sec," I hear him say, his voice sounding like he's at the far end of a tunnel, speaking through a thick scarf. A rustling, a silent pause, and then his voice close and clear. "There, sorry, I was outside in the yard, putting away some gardening stuff. Anyway, what's up?"

"I, um. I'm sort of in a situation."

I can feel his attention, immediate and sharp. "What do you need?"

"I thought it was going to stay nice, so I went paddleboarding."

"Shit." I can hear the understanding clarify in his voice. "Where are you?"

"Smack dab between Cedar Point and Bluff Point, being pushed out." I take a deep breath and bolster my voice, hardening it. "I just can't make headway. This weather blew in kind of suddenly and caught me off guard."

"Is this a situation where I call my buddy in the Coast Guard, or I ask my boss if I can borrow his Boston Whaler?"

I laugh. "Well, I'd really like to avoid having to be rescued by the Coast Guard, if I can help it. I feel stupid enough as it is."

"Getting you to safety is not stupid, Emma. No bull-shit: emergency, or just come get you ASAP?"

I sigh. "If you could come get me soon, I would really, really be grateful."

"Your contact in my messages is blue, which means you have an iPhone, right?"

"Yeah."

"Share your location with me. I'll be to you as soon as I can. Just hold on for ten, maybe fifteen more minutes, okay?"

I refuse to sniffle or let my voice sound small. "Easy peasy. I got it." Lightning flickers off to my left, followed several seconds later by thunder. "Although I wouldn't mind if you hurried, a little bit. I just saw lightning."

"Shit. Okay. I'm coming. Send me your location."

"Will do. Thank you, Rory."

I share my location with him, tuck the phone back into my fanny pack, shake out my hands, and resume paddling. Two strong pulls on the left side, one on the right. Keep an eye on the land ahead, gauging my southward drift. The wind is sharp and powerful now, buffeting me from all directions, it feels like. The rain is like pellets.

I refuse to panic. I asked for help. Help is on the way. Just keep moving. Freak out later. It's just wind and rain. I've been wet and cold before. Dad and Eddy and I went for a hunt way out in the deep forest late in deer season, once. A freak blizzard blew in, and none of us were dressed for that weather. God, that was miserable.

Of course, I was with them, and they knew how to build a shelter out of pine branches to block the worst of the wind and snow, and they built a fire and we just hunkered through it until it blew itself out by morning. About froze my toes off, but we made it without frostbite.

This is different. I'm alone. I can't hunker through it. If this storm hits and I'm out here on this dinky little paddleboard? I don't care to think too closely on that.

Just keep paddling.

I say it to myself, then sing it like Dory from *Finding Nemo*. Just keep paddling, just keep paddling, what we do, we paddle, paddle, paddle.

Focus on keeping my nose pointing more north than south. Don't think about how wet I am. Don't think about being cold. The shiver is nothing. Teeth chatter is nothing. I'm gonna get picked up soon. I'll get dry. I'll be safe. And I'll double-check the weather next time I go off-shore paddle boarding.

He said fifteen minutes, right? Why does it feel like an hour passes? I scan the horizon, looking for a boat. Listening. Hard to hear over the roaring of the wind and the hiss of rain.

God, the land is so far away, ahead and behind, while the open sea looks bigger than ever, closer than ever. It's suddenly easy to conceptualize the relative infinity of the ocean, when you're just a girl alone on a paddleboard, staring down rising waves. They're not just decent little whitecaps anymore. I'm ascending a wave, dipping over a peak, and sliding down into the trough. I'm soaked through. Lightning sears the sky directly overhead, and thunder booms right on the heels of the flash.

I'm not crying, you're crying.

I'm *not* crying. I'm gasping for breath because I'm exhausted, and if my face is wet, it's because it's now a torrential downpour.

I hear something behind me, off to my right. Twist to look over my shoulder, and I see a white square bobbing up over a wave—a Boston Whaler with a full pilothouse and three big outboard motors. I lift my paddle high in one hand, wave it. No sense wasting my breath shouting—it's way too loud out here to be heard.

It angles toward me, cutting across the chop. I'm rising and falling several feet at a time, and even on my knees, staying on the board requires every bit of balance and effort I have left. Which isn't much.

The boat coasts to a stop a few feet away, and I hear the engines cut down low, and then churn louder as he navigates closer. Skillfully, he pilots the Whaler to within a foot of me, and then he cuts the motors totally. Rory appears from the pilothouse, dressed in bright orange rain gear, the kind professional deep-sea fishermen wear. I dig the paddle in hard and pull for the boat, crash up against it. A wave lifts me, and then I'm being tossed backward. It's the biggest wave yet, lifting the boat like a toy, and if the boat is a toy I'm less than a speck, a piece of flotsam.

A strong hand grabs me, vise-grip strong around my bicep, and I'm flying through the air—I land with a brutally hard thud against the deck, and then the wave crashes over the boat, drenching me. I hear a clatter. My paddle? Another louder thump—my board.

I would have told him to leave them.

I can't move.

"Emma?" His voice, a rough, raspy, powerful yell against the storm—and now the roughness of his voice makes sense...he's spent his life in storms like this, shouting against the roar of the sea.

I'm in the air again. In his arms.

"Hi," I manage.

He doesn't answer. Carries me into the pilothouse, slamming the door against the elements. It's oven-hot in here. Or I'm so cold it feels that way. Rory is a huge, confident presence. He wraps a thick gray wool blanket around me, kneeling to look into my eyes.

"Got you, Em. You're safe."

I'm shivering, my teeth are chattering. I know my fear—now that I'm safe, it's more outright terror than I'd even realized—shows fully on my face. I can only nod.

"R-R-Ri...R-R-Riley?" I stammer.

"Home." He's at the helm, pushing the throttle forward and twisting the wheel to bring us about. "She's got a bowl of popcorn and a Disney movie. She knows the neighbor's phone number by heart. Wasn't about to bring her out in this shit."

"S-s-ssss—"

"Can it with the apologies, Em." He's snapping at me, but not out of anger; his eyes concerned as they find mine. "Worried as hell, getting out to you. You're way the fuck out here, you know?"

I wipe my face with the corner of the blanket. "I couldn't get any closer. I've been paddling since..." I have to pause to breathe, to contain the sobs trying to escape. "I don't even know how long I've been out here. Hours."

He frowns. "Hours?"

I nod. "I thought I could make it. I just kept getting pushed farther and farther."

"Not your fault. This shit wasn't on the radar." He stands in a wide stance, easily braced to balance against the pitch, one hand on the wheel, the other on the throttle. He glances at me, casts a gestural look and a lift of his chin. "There's coffee."

I follow the direction of his gaze, and spy an antique, battered green Stanley thermos in the small sink. I pour a little bit into the silver cap and blow into it so the steam hits my face. Take a sip—it's scalding hot, and what Dad calls cowboy coffee: so thick, so black, and so strong that you could almost float a horseshoe in it.

It tastes like home.

Rory watches me take a sip. He makes a surprised face. "This may sound sexist or something, but most girls won't drink my coffee."

I laugh. "I think by now it should be clear I'm not most girls, Rory."

"No indeed, you certainly are not."

"My father grew up on a horse ranch, son of the ranch foreman." I sip, breathing the scent and savoring the bold, bitter coffee. "He says he was taught to make coffee by old school cowboys, meaning in a percolator over a campfire. If you can't chew your coffee, you made it wrong." I laugh. "Which means I've been drinking plain black cowboy coffee since I was eleven." I raise the thermos cap. "This is just right."

"Sounds like there's some overlap between cowboys and fishermen."

I eye him, thinking. "Wouldn't have thought so until I moved out here, but yes. There's a certain rough-edged capability that you share with my father and his friends."

He chuckles. "Rough-edged capability." He reaches toward me, and I pour a little more coffee into the cap and pass it to him. "You make that sound almost like a compliment, Emma."

I shrug. "I guess it is."

"You guess, huh?" he says, grinning. "But you're not sure." He slurps a big mouthful of coffee and hands the cap back.

"With you, it is," I say. "My dad is a different story."

He eyes me. The question, the curiosity is in his expression, but he says nothing. Not pressing, willing to listen and equally willing to let me pass on it.

I sigh. "I have a complicated relationship with my family, my dad especially."

"Complicated relationships I understand," he says.

I don't elaborate, and he doesn't say anything else. We're approaching the marina, now, and I watch as he skillfully navigates the boat into a slip, easing it into place despite the dramatic pitch and roll, even in the sheltered waters of the marina. He cuts the engine and jogs to the bow, tying it off with hand-blurred speed.

He comes back for me, hand extended, and I attempt to stand up.

Attempt being the keyword, here. I send the signal to my muscles indicating that I would like to stand up now, please.

Nothing.

He pulls and I make it a few inches off the seat.

I fall back, laughing. "I think I'm broken," I say. I'm laughing and joking, but it's covering up for the fact that I'm in agony. Every muscle aches and burns.

A bone-deep chill is setting in.

He frowns. "Is that a joke, or are you actually injured?"

I try again, and this time I force myself to my feet; I groan, wobble, and my legs nearly give out. Only through sheer force of will am I able to remain standing. My shoulders, arms, and core are ravaged.

Rory's eyes narrow. "You are not okay, are you?"

I wince as I lurch a step toward the exit of the cabin. "I'm f-f-fine."

He releases my bicep and gives me space. "Ayuh—you can make it to your car just fine, and safely drive home as well, in that case."

I reach the door, and fall against it, bracing to remain upright. I'm shivering, still wrapped up in the thick wool blanket. My clothing is soaked through, heavy and sodden—it feels like I've been mummified in icicles.

I'm actually shivering so hard my teeth hurt from chattering.

I honestly doubt I could make it off the boat under my own power.

I hang my head, hating with every fiber of my being

the admission that's ripped from my clattering teeth. "N-no. I need help."

He shakes his head. "You already called me for help, Emma. My services as a knight in shining armor don't end at the rescue itself."

I glare at him. "I don't need a knight in shining armor, Rory. Or, in your case, a knight in orange rain slickers."

He just gazes at me evenly. "Everyone needs help once in a while, Emma. No shame in it."

I huff, and force myself upright, away from the door. "Not me. Just get me to my car. I can make it from there."

He's near once more, and I can smell him, his engine oil-and-brine scent. His arm goes around my waist and holds me against his body. His palm rests against my forehead. "You're feverish."

I grit my teeth. "I'm fine."

He betrays frustration with a raspy bark of laughter. "Stubborn woman. You are not." He opens the door of the pilothouse, dousing us both in a torrent of sideways-blowing rain and surf-spray. Scoops me in his arms, moves through the door and kicks it closed. "I'm taking care of you, now, Emma." His tone brooks no argument.

And honestly, it feels good to be carried. I don't quite relax, but I come close.

He carries me to his truck, a ten- or twelve-year-old red F-250. Sets me on my feet but keeps an arm around my waist as he opens the passenger door. His hold on my waist is, thus far, friendly rather than intimate. He deposits me on the passenger seat. The cab of the truck smells like him. There's a case of motor oil on the rear bench, and an unopened bag of pork rinds. He swings up into the driver's seat, hands me the thermos, and starts the motor with a low rumble. Turns the heater on, aiming the vents at me.

It feels good, but it's only a surface warmth, whereas the chill I feel is in my bones themselves. I shake, shiver. Ache. Burn. I feel the fever kicking into high gear. My brain is foggy, sluggish. My muscles ache so bad even the simplest of movements cause pain. Such as breathing.

My eyes close—just for a second.

"Emma?" His voice on my right. "Let's go inside."

I'm woozy. I try to function, but no words come out and I can't even manage to twitch my fingers. The best I can do is a pained, exhausted grunt.

He huffs a laugh. "I got you."

I'm airborne. Rain spatters on my face, my scalp.

"Door's locked," he murmurs.

"Keys," I mumble. "Fanny pack."

"Don't know if I can hold you and get them, sweetheart. Don't have enough arms."

I fight for one last surge of functionality. Fumble with the zipper of my fanny pack and find the keys. The world is dark and gray and wet. We're at my side door. My house is a mid-century ranch with a detached garage and a kitchen entrance on the right side, classic and standard and instantly familiar. I unlock my door and push it open, and then sag back into his arms.

The door closes behind us, and the sound and cold of the rain vanishes. He carries me to my room. Hesitates.

"You're soaked through, and now even that blanket is wet. I set you on your bed, you're gonna have a wet bed."

"Bathroom."

His boots echo on the tile, and he sets me on the closed toilet lid. "You really need to get out of those clothes, Emma. And a shower to warm you up."

I'm cold and shivering, but burning with fever at the same time. "Need help." I meet his eyes. "Everything hurts."

He nods. "I've got you."

First, he shrugs out of his slicker jacket, then he removes the blanket from my shoulders and tosses it aside—it hits the floor with a plop. Shoes first, then socks. He hesitates. Eyes meet mine. Whatever is going on between us is not platonic, and even though he's helping me out of kindness, undressing and helping me shower is crossing a line.

But there's no two ways about this—I need to get out of the wet clothes and I need to warm up in a hot shower, and I can't do these things on my own. I'm too weak, too feverish, too tired.

I smile at him. Try to make it flirty. "Just get me naked, Rory."

He lets out a slow hiss. "Emma, dammit."

"I need help, Rory. And besides—you already saw most of what I've got to offer the other morning."

His hands clutch my calves, a quick tightening, and then release. Slide up my legs to my waist. I lift my hips, and he peels my skintight, thick Spandex-and-Lycra leggings down. They stick at my butt, and he has to tug to get them to roll down past my buttocks. They come free with a wet suction sound, and then they're off and splatting on the floor. I'm immediately colder with the air on my wet skin, but somehow, the absence of the wet clothing also feels better. He unzips my outer shell, unclips my fanny pack. Peels the next layer off, and then I'm down to a sports bra and my underwear.

His eyes flick over me, and then away. He reaches into the tub and twists on the hot water. Once it runs hot, he adds cold water, tests it, adds a little more. "That should be good."

He helps me stand up, and his eyes meet mine. "Last layer."

I nod. "It's okay, Rory." Standing up is hard, even with his hand on my waist steadying me. I can't help but lean against him; he's solid, so warm.

He licks his lips, nervousness showing in his eyes, the set of his features. His fingers curl under the strap at my back, lifts. My own heartbeat crashes hard. I can't say I haven't daydreamed / fantasized about this moment with Rory—albeit, not quite like this. The bra catches at the front. A hesitation, and then his fingers slide under the strap, around to the front. His knuckles brush my breasts as he lifts the undergarment up and off, and now I'm topless. Cold. My nipples, already pebbled, harden to diamonds as his eyes rake over my bare chest.

He squeezes his eyes shut and drops his head.

"Rory." I touch his jaw, cup it in one hand. "It's *okay*."

He shakes his head. "I just—"

A shiver wracks me. "I'm naked. You're a man, and

unless I miss my guess, you're as attracted to me as I am to you."

"Doesn't excuse that I can't keep my eyes to myself."

I laugh. "It kind of does." I touch his chin, nerves and need warring in me, both losing to necessity. "You don't need an excuse. You're allowed to look."

"I don't want you to think I'm taking advantage of you when I'm supposed to be taking care of you."

I hold on to his shoulder with one hand and struggle with my underwear with the other. I manage to get them down around my thighs before I lose my balance, overcome by weakness from the ordeal and the shakes from the post-adrenaline rush and delirium from the onset of the fever.

He catches me, and helps me get the underwear the rest of the way off.

I'm naked.

I want to be aroused by the heat in his eyes as he looks at me—his gaze, now, openly scours my body from head to toe, taking in every line and every curve and every detail.

I grip his hand hard for balance as I step into the shower, under the hot spray. He moves to let me go, and I shake my head, do not relent in my grip on his hand. "I can barely stay on my feet, Rory."

His eyes close briefly. "Okay. I got you."

He stands beside me outside the tub, his hands now on my slick naked flesh at my belly and shoulder blades. I sway, and he keeps me upright. I rinse my hair, letting hot water sluice away the cold. Scrub my skin. After a few minutes, the once-hot water begins to feel less hot, and then lukewarm.

The minuscule amount of strength I have left is quickly evaporating.

"I'm ready to dry off and lie down," I murmur.

He twists off the water, one hand on my back keeping me from swaying backward as he snatches the dry, clean towel off the rack beside the shower. He wraps it around me, covering me, scrubbing to soak up the water. Another from the rack, which he uses to gently blot my hair.

His touch is sweet, soft, and clumsy.

I haphazardly twist my hair into the towel, but the one around my body hangs open; I don't have the energy to care. "Need to lie down."

He tugs the towel closed and presses me into his side, his arm slinging over my shoulder, hand on my hip. It feels nice. I want to be touched by him. To touch him.

But right now, my primary need is to sleep.

Leaning against Rory, I head for my bed. He pulls back my comforter, and I climb in, shedding the towel in the process. I feel his eyes on my body as I lie down. Then, I'm covered by the warm weight of the comforter, and my eyes are shutting. I feel him add the fleece throw blanket I keep folded across the foot end.

His palm touches my forehead. "You're burning up, Emma."

I'm sliding into sleep. "Mmm."

"I don't think you should be alone."

"Riley."

His weight presses on the edge of the bed beside me. "Would it be alright if I bring her here?"

I flop my hand out, and it finds some part of him. Leg, maybe? "Thank you," I mumble.

"I'm going to go get Riley. We'll stay here with you until you're better."

"Mmm."

I feel him rise. Feel his presence leave. Faintly, I hear the side door open and close.

My last thought as I topple into a feverish sleep is that he's seen me totally naked, and I haven't even seen him without a shirt.

Seems unequal.

6

I HAVE NO CONCEPT OF TIME.

I have a vague impression of Rory, hovering over me. Checking my forehead. Sitting on the bed next to me, helping me sit up enough to coax some water into me.

Hurting all over.

Hot, and cold. Nauseous, achy, cotton-headed.

Riley at the door, big dark eyes concerned.

Hours pass; or is it days?

Rory, coaxing me to drink more—not water, something semisweet. Electrolytes.

Chills. Shivering, shivering, chattering. Can't get warm, even though I'm weighed down under what must be almost every blanket I own.

Rory again.

More to drink, spilling it down my throat, between my breasts. He dabs it away.

I'm sweating, blazing heat billowing through me. I kick off the blankets.

Rory comes in. "Oh," he stammers, startled. "You're, um—the fever broke."

"So hot," I mumble.

"I know. But that's good." His eyes look everywhere but at me—I'm still naked.

"Thanks for taking care of me, Rory," I whisper.

His eyes find mine, finally. "Yeah, of course."

"How long was I out?" I ask.

He is determinedly only looking at my eyes. I ought to cover up, to spare him, but I'm too hot, pouring sweat from every pore. "It's Monday afternoon, so all of Saturday and Sunday. You slept most of Saturday, and you were in and out Sunday and this morning."

"Monday?" I ask, panicking. "My students!"

"I called the office and told them you were sick."

I close my eyes. "Well, that's gonna start the rumor mill."

"I know. I thought about that. But it didn't seem like there was anything else I could do. I told them you had a really bad fever and were unconscious and would be out for a couple days at least. Donna at the front desk called me earlier and said they have a sub for you through Wednesday."

I open my eyes again; he's staring fixedly out the

window. "I don't think I'll ever be able to thank you enough, Rory." I touch his hand, and he flinches in surprise at the unexpected contact, then meets my eyes. "You saved my life, and then spent your whole weekend and today nursing me back to health." A thought occurs to me. "You had to have missed work today, too."

"Don't even worry about that, Emma," he says. "My boss understands. Plus, I bought myself a little leniency with that whole at-sea repair fiasco. He owed me one after that."

"Riley is at school?"

He nods. "I drove her in. She's worried about you."

I squeeze his hand. "Well, I'm feeling much better now, thanks to the A-plus nursing."

I'm still sweating like I just got off my Peloton, but I drape the flat sheet over my lap and press it against my chest. He relaxes, and his eyes go to mine again.

"I didn't do much. Sat with you. Got you to drink some electrolytes."

"You stayed with me when I needed you," I say. "I won't forget it."

He huffs a laugh. "You threatening me?"

"With payback plus interest," I say, smiling. "For real. Thank you."

"It was no hardship." He turns his hand to face our palms together.

"Because you got to see me naked?" I quip.

"Because I like you—I care about you." He holds my gaze, allows a smile across his lips. "But getting to see you naked was…" a pause. "You're extraordinarily beautiful, Emma."

"Thank you."

"Although, I must say, I'd much rather see you naked in other circumstances." He pauses again, licks his lips, eyes roving my face.

"The kind of circumstances where there's touching involved?" I say.

He nods, shrugs, dark, deep brown eyes piercingly hot and refreshingly frank. "Ayuh." He lets out a breath, rubs the pad of his thumb over my knuckles. "But, I, um—I would like to take you out. First. On a date."

I arch an eyebrow and tug the sheet higher up my chest; I pin it in place with my arms, and the covering effect is somewhat diluted as the flat sheet molds to my breasts. "Are you asking me out, Rory Kerr?"

He nods. "I am." His eyes flicker downward, then back to my face.

"I'm sweaty and sick and must look like a haggard old witch."

He snorts. "I don't mean today, Emma. At some point. When you're feeling better." He bobs his head to the side. "Maybe this is just establishing the grounds to actually ask you out later, when you're feeling better."

I shake my head. "I'm just laughing at your timing. You ask me out when I'm at my literal worst. I feel about as sexy as a walrus."

He leans back and chortles. "You're funny, Emma."

His laughter makes me feel gooey and warm inside. In a good way.

Laughter fades to a grin. "I mean it, though. I really want to take you out on a date. When you're back to a hundred percent."

"I would like that."

"You would?"

I nod. "Of course. I like you, too, Rory."

He smiles, and I smile back. There's a lot of smiling.

I lie back into my nest of pillows—they feel icky and clammy from my sweat. "I should try to rest. I think I'll be okay from here."

He nods. "You're sure? I can stick around a while longer."

I shake my head. "I'm okay now. I'll just rest. Maybe take a shower and eat something at some point." I squeeze his hand once more, then let go. "I really appreciate what you've done for me, Rory."

He shakes his head. "Of course. You ever need anything, just ask. Okay?"

"I mean, I literally owe you my life, so…same for you."

He shakes his head again. "You've already been there for me in major ways, Emma. You took care of my daughter when I couldn't."

I smile. "But who's keeping track, right?"

He laughs. "Right." He stands up, shoves a hand in his pocket—he's wearing faded jeans and an old T-shirt. "Well, I'll let you rest. I'm glad you're on the mend, now."

"Me too." I laugh. "Mainly, though, I'm glad I didn't die out on the water."

He makes a face. "You nearly did, though, so that joke's a little on the nose."

I snort. "No kidding." I close my eyes and breathe out a sigh. "I don't think I've ever been so scared in my life. Or so glad to see someone as I was you."

"That was a hell of a storm. It's honestly miraculous you stayed on the paddleboard like you did." He shakes his head. "You never cease to impress me."

"Why? Because I was dumb and got myself into trouble?"

He shakes his head. "You couldn't have known. I've literally spent my entire life on the ocean, and I wouldn't have predicted that storm. It blew up out of nowhere. It wasn't on the radar—I know, I looked. I was thinking of taking Riley out for a sail after I finished my work in the garden, but by the time I was done it was clouding over and then you called." He rubs the back of his neck. "So don't get too hard on yourself. I'm just glad you called me."

I sigh. "I should've called sooner. But in case you didn't realize, I'm a little stubborn."

He holds his finger and thumb a tiny sliver apart. "Just a little." He backs into the doorway of my bedroom, pauses, waves at me. "Well, get some rest. I'll see you soon, okay?"

He leaves, and suddenly, my house feels empty.

By the end of Tuesday, I'm back on my feet. Still so sore I can barely move my arms, and walking is a tricky proposition. But the fever is gone and I've eaten and showered. I call Donna to tell her I'll be in class tomorrow.

"I'm glad you're feeling better," Donna said. "We all missed you. I think that's the first time off you've taken since you started here."

"I'm rarely sick," I say. "But when I am, I'm *really* sick."

And cue the interrogation in...3...2...1...

"So, Rory Kerr called to say you were sick. I didn't know you two were an item."

"We're not." Maybe if I keep my answers short and terse, she'll get the hint.

"He called from your phone, though. And it was pretty late Sunday evening." Heavy implications in her tone of voice.

"We're friends—I'm friends with his daughter."

"I see." A pause. "He's a very attractive man. I may be happily married these forty years, but it doesn't mean I can't appreciate a fine-looking man." Hint hint, wink wink.

"He is handsome," I agree.

She sighs, audibly comprehending that I really don't want to talk about this. "All right then," she says. "Keep your secrets."

I think Donna Bellanger just quoted *Lord of the Rings* at me.

"No secrets. Rory and I are friends. I got sick and he helped me out."

"Mmm-hmmm." She doesn't believe a word of it. "Well, we'll see you tomorrow?"

"Yup. Goodbye, Donna."

"Bye, now."

Wednesday is difficult. I can tell I'm going to be unable to do any kind of workout at all for at least another week, maybe longer. I might possibly be able to manage some nice, slow, restorative Yin yoga—*maybe*. Mostly, though, even walking is hard. Carrying my purse feels like I'm doing farmer's carries for distance.

I can't stop thinking about Rory. It's worse than ever.

It's complicated, though. Yes, he saw me naked. Yes, he's attracted to me. Yes, I'm attracted to him. We're both single. I'm not his daughter's teacher so there's not even any kind of possible overlap there to complicate things.

I'm just a very wounded person. I like him, I want him, and he seems trustworthy, but overcoming my reticence to let him close after what happened with Trace… seems impossible sometimes. The hardest part about my history with my ex-husband is that it wasn't even a betrayal. He didn't cheat on me, he didn't beat me. He loved me. We were happy. We had a future. And then he got into a car accident, and through no fault of his or mine, it was all just taken away.

Unlike some girls I've known, I don't keep tabs on him via social media. I don't know if he's still single, if he remarried. If he recovered totally, or if there are other side effects or symptoms from the brain damage. I don't know anything about him—I haven't spoken to him since the day I walked out of the courthouse when our divorce was finalized. As part of the divorce proceedings, I requested that my surname revert back to my maiden name, so when the judge signed off on the divorce, I was once again Emma Cole.

I haven't looked back. I haven't heard from him, either. I honestly spent the first year or so looking over my shoulder, waiting for him to show up and beg me to take him back.

Hubristic of me, perhaps. But before the accident, Trace worshipped me. He acted like being married to me was the greatest thing that could ever have happened to him. He'd tell everyone he married way up. I never felt that way—I loved him totally, and felt every bit as lucky to have a man as kind and considerate and romantic as Trace. He brought me flowers on the way home from class at least once a week. Took me on dates—even when we were broke AF college students, he'd scrounge up enough money to put together a picnic on the quad. Something, anything, just to make me feel loved.

I was ready to have his babies.

Then, bam.

Gone.

No rhyme or reason, no medical explanation other than how little we truly understand the human brain and psyche, or cognition and personality really work. I mean, sure, we understand a lot of the structure of personality development from a psychological standpoint, but the actual *how*, the mechanics of how it happens inside the brain? Nah. They have theories and guesses and maybe even where in the brain it happens, but not how. You're a sperm cell and an egg, and somehow, you turn into a human being. Don't tell me it's not magic.

What's just as opaque, then, is how damage to the brain works. How it heals, or doesn't.

Trace woke up from that coma, and he was a different person. To me, at least. I watched him with his parents, his friends…he was the same old Trace. With me? My Trace, my husband was gone.

It's not fucking fair, and I'm angry about it.

It's not men I don't trust. I'm not hesitant about getting into something with Rory because I think he's going to betray me.

It's the universe I'm pissed off at.

Life.

God.

Whatever. I don't know and I'm not sure I even want to know. I just know "It" took Trace and my marriage away, and left me broken.

I put on a good act, maybe.

I can flirt. I'm confident in my body, in myself. I have a lot to offer.

But deep down? I'm terrified of letting anyone close again. If I were to let someone close again, like I did Trace, and I lost him too? I'd be done. Over. Shattered. Irrecoverable.

Can I even try?

I don't know.

I can't even pretend.

God, I'm so pathetic that I can't even let myself have a fling, a one-night stand, or a friend with benefits.

Because at the core of me, I'm a romantic. More to the point, I'm a demisexual.

Meaning, sex is inextricably bound to my emotions. I can't just *sleep* with someone simply because my eyes and brain find him attractive. That's inconsequential. My brain goes, *hey, a hot guy. Cool.* Done. There's no desire. I don't think about him naked. I don't fantasize about ripping his clothes off and riding him like a penny pony at the grocery store.

Those fantasies I have, about the attractive men around school? They're not sexual fantasies.

Well, they are. But they start with a strong emotional bond being formed first. That strong emotional bond creates trust and vulnerability. Which creates a sense of safety and security. Which allows the fragile little pilot light of my sexuality to ignite.

My sexuality is kind of like solid-state rocket fuel—stable, with an absurdly high ignition point. But once it's lit? It's wild, white-hot burn.

I trusted Trace. I grew up with him. We were childhood friends, best friends going into middle school. By high school, we were hyperaware of each other as members of the opposite sex, but still best friends with a lifelong bond. Then, at a Halloween party sophomore year, we sampled some spiked cider, got a little tipsy, and I kissed him.

WHOOOOMPH.

Ignition.

I craved him from that point on. Needed his touch every moment I could get it, in whatever form I could get it. The burn only intensified as kissing led to making out, to getting handsy, to having sex…to developing an ongoing sexual relationship which grew as our love grew.

The burn never lessened, never dimmed. Never faded.

It was cut off.

Doused abruptly.

I haven't so much as felt a glimmer of a spark with anyone since.

Until Rory.

But…I'm afraid.

I'm afraid I'll develop feelings for him, and the spark will light, and he won't love me the way I crave to be loved. Or it'll be taken away. By a hurricane, perhaps. Or an accident with the nets, or…any number of things.

It's a conundrum, because I feel the spark crackling inside me, threatening to ignite the burn. I want it. I want that again—I miss it. I miss the connection, the emotional thread weaving us into a single entity. I miss the closeness. Cuddling in the afterglow.

I miss the orgasms, yes. But those I can give to myself, and I do—regularly. It's not the same, of course. How could it be? But I can get an approximation of that with a vibrator and a vivid mental fantasy; I can't get an approximation of that special, magical, genuine emotional bond, not with any amount of mental creativity.

What am I supposed to do about Rory? I'm reaching a point of no return.

7

I SEE RILEY AFTER SCHOOL ON WEDNESDAY, AND SHE
very sweetly asks if I'm feeling better. She
regards me a little strangely, though, as if she has
a question to ask me, but can't figure out how to ask
it, or if she should. I don't press her on it, though. I
expect to at least have a quick chat with Rory as he
picks her up, but he's on the phone. He waves at
me, phone clenched between his shoulder and ear,
distracted. Unhappy, even, possibly.

I let it go.

It's harder to let it go when days pass and I barely
see him, except for a quick wave from the truck as he
picks up Riley, on time more frequently.

I consider texting him if something changed.

If I did something to offend him. If—if, if, if. A
thousand ifs run through my mind, in ever more

desperate attempts to explain his abrupt and unex-
plained distance and silence.

I don't text him.

I just wonder and try to ignore my misery.

A week after the incident, I'm close enough to one
hundred percent that I get back on the Peloton—I haven't
taken a week off of it since the day I got it. Apparently,
it's something like an addiction, because I don't feel totally myself without my morning rides.

Every time I see Rory in the truck, now, he just
looks…upset.

I consider asking Riley what's going on—but I have
a set-in-stone policy regarding never involving a child in
adult relationship issues. Call it a rule borne out of childhood trauma—my parents squabbled like cats and dogs,
and sometimes, when it got serious, they'd pull Eddy and
me into it. I hated it. Then, when I became a teacher, I
saw divorced parents use their children to wound each
other, and I saw how it affects the child—uniformly neg-
atively—and this only reinforced my view.

So no, I'm not pumping Riley for information on
what's happening with her parents.

Also, I haven't seen as much of Riley lately as I'd
like—Rory has been picking her up on time, and I've
only gotten a few minutes here and there.

I miss our afternoons together.

I miss Rory.

October swings around, and with it cooler weather.
Leaves turn.

I begin to wonder if I imagined things with Rory—if

I was mistranslating my own attraction to him as his attraction to me. Your mind can play funny tricks on you, you know?

I decide perhaps it's best if I put Rory out of my mind. Something clearly happened, and I'm not going to go chasing rainbows.

8

SATURDAY MORNING, BEGINNING OF NOVEMBER. I'M AT odd ends. It's a chilly day, and my workouts throughout the week were all intense, so I planned on taking the weekend easy, not doing anything too strenuous. There's a yoga class later this evening I was planning on going to, but that leaves the rest of the day for me to fill. And for once...I don't really know how to fill it.

In lieu of anything truly interesting, I'm aimlessly browsing Netflix for something to watch—and so far, finding nothing. An embarrassment of choices, but nothing which interests me.

Go figure.

I'm about to settle on a late-90s thriller when my doorbell rings. I'm not expecting anyone, obviously, so I'm a little stumped as to who could be ringing my doorbell at ten on a Saturday morning. I'm in my lazy loungewear: loose sweatpants, tank top, and a cardigan. My hair is piled high in a loose, frizzy bun. No makeup. No bra, no underwear. I'm clutching a mug of coffee; my fourth, but don't judge me.

I pull open my front door, and there's Riley. Rory is behind her, on the second step, looking embarrassed and uncomfortable.

I open the storm door and kneel to pull Riley into a hug. "Hey, girl! I missed you! Come on in."

She clings to me. "I've missed you much, Emma."

I glance at Rory as I stand up, holding the door for Riley to scamper in. "Hi." It comes off a little cold, but he did sort of ghost me.

He shuffles, one hand clenching and unclenching, the other scraping his usual ball cap off and passing through his messy dark hair. "Emma, I—" He huffs. "Riley missed you. Begged me to let her come see you."

"Riley missed me, huh?" I arch an eyebrow.

Give me something, Rory. Please?

He drops his head. "She has a whole thing planned. I told her you might have plans."

"I don't." I sweep a hand inside. "Come in."

He grabs the storm door from me and I retreat inside rather than allowing him to pass too close to me. I'm still affected by his presence—tingly, nervous, giddy, anxious, overheated. But also annoyed, hurt, and confused. Maybe even a little angry.

Riley is on my couch, feet swinging. She's dressed to be outside: jeans, heavy boots, a sweatshirt, a jacket, thin knit gloves, and a matching knit hat; I recognize the knitting as the work of Alice Bowers, a local who sells knit goods at the farmer's market.

"Do you like cider and donuts and hayrides, Emma?" she asks, everything from her face, her tone, to her body language hopeful. "We're going to a cider mill and I want you to come. Please?"

I blink. "Um. Yeah, I—yeah. I love cider and donuts." I grin at her. "And you know, when I was a teenager, my first job off my parents' farm was giving hayrides at the local cider mill. So yeah, safe to say I like hayrides."

An awkward, tense silence. Riley looks from Rory to me, as if sensing the tension. "Daddy, I'm hot. I'm gonna go put my coat and stuff in the truck. Okay?"

This is said with a significant look at Rory.

I almost laugh at her transparency, but manage to stifle it. Rory just nods, and she scampers outside, shucking her coat, hat, and gloves. She walks with exaggerated slowness, kicking her feet, dragging her heels. Clearly, trying to give us enough time to talk.

"So. A cider mill." I arch an eyebrow. "Does she mean her and me, or the three of us?"

He swallows hard. "The, um—the three of us."

I wait.

And wait.

He huffs. "I'm sorry, Emma."

"For?"

"You know—vanishing on you."

"You did sort of ghost me, Rory."

"It wasn't ghosting you. It's just—" He shakes his

head. Yanks his hat off and scratches his scalp. "It's complicated."

"I feel like it can't be that complicated."

"Maybe not complicated, but...hard to talk about."

"Did I do something? Last time we talked, you were asking me out on a date. Then nothing for over a month. I admit I'm pretty confused." I've never pulled punches, and I'm not about to start now. "And, honestly, more than a little hurt. And I feel like I deserve an explanation."

He nods heavily. There's a long silence. "Mindy called me." His voice is thick.

"Mindy, your ex-wife? The one who abandoned you and Riley?"

He nods again. "Yeah."

"She called you?"

A nod. "Yeah."

"Out of the blue? What did she want?"

Another long, hard silence. "Visitation."

"No." I stare at him. "No!"

He nods, then shakes his head with a bitter sigh. "Yeah. I ignored her first call. And the second. And the third. I ignored her voicemails. Her texts." A hand tugging in his hair. "Finally, I got sick of it. She was insistent. Begging me to call her back. And when I did, she told me she just wanted to give me a heads-up that she was going to be asking the judge for visitation. Maybe even partial custody."

"Where does she live? Why does she want back in your lives now, after so many years of total silence and absence?"

He gives a gruff sigh. "I don't know any of that. I wish I did." His eyes are bitter and sad. "I don't know what to do. I don't want to see her, I don't want to talk to her. Nothin'. I don't want nothin' to do with her ass. And I certainly don't want to put her back into Riley's life, only to have her vanish again. Riley's effectively never known her. She doesn't remember her at all."

I let the silence breathe a moment or two. "So...I understand all that, and how hard it must be. But...why didn't you call me, or come in and talk to me? Let me know that you had stuff going on. I wouldn't have pushed you for details, Rory. I think you know that. Even a text would've been better than nothing at all."

"I'm messed up about it, Emma. I'd gotten as over her as I could." He turns his eyes to me. "But then she shows up, or—not shows up, like, I haven't seen her in person yet. But I get all mixed up just thinking about her. And it didn't seem fair to you to drag you into any of that."

"Any explanation is better than none," I say.

"I know." He searches me. "I apologize. I didn't handle it right."

I glance out the storm door: Riley is playing with the red, gold, and yellow leaves gathering on my lawn, picking them up and scattering them, pushing them into piles and rolling through them.

"So you're only here now because Riley begged to see me?"

"No, I..." He shakes his head, not quite looking at me. "I wanted to see you, too." A pause. "Honestly, it's been miserable, not talking to you, not seeing you. Leaving things the way we did. I still don't know what—or...or how to—" he breaks off with a rough hiss of frustration. "What I'm doing, with you. Especially now that Mindy's trying to get back into the picture. It could get messy."

"I don't know what this is either," I say, gesturing between him and me. "I have my own holdups, Rory. I like you, but I'm not sure what I want. Or...maybe it's more accurate to say I'm not sure what I'm capable of, at the moment. After, you know, what happened...with Trace."

He nods. "I get that. I'm not assuming you and me are...a thing. Or that something is happening. I'm not assuming anything." He huffs in frustration. "How do I even...express any of this? I *like* you. I'm attracted to you. I enjoy being around you. I would like to spend more time with you. But...after Mindy, it's hard to—" he breaks off with a wordless growl and shake of his head, abandoning his attempt to encapsulate his feelings.

I can't help but soften. "Rory, I understand. Completely and totally, I understand. Because...I feel the same way. It's hard to even wrap my head around how I feel, because it's complicated. So I get why you're having trouble expressing it. I don't know that I could do any better, honestly."

His eyes meet mine, and he laughs, a gentle snort. "I'm glad you get it."

"So, where do we go from here?"

He shrugs. "Baby steps, maybe?"

I hesitate. "I guess if there's anything I'd want you

to understand, it's that I'm not worried about you having issues with your ex. Like, if we—you and me—were to…turn into something. Or whatever. I'm not…threatened. Exes are part of life. It doesn't bother me, as long as you're open and honest about what's going on. If you were to rekindle things, or something, just tell me. Don't hide it. Don't play games. Just tell me, and allow me to handle myself like an adult. Because I can and I will."

He barks a cynical laugh. "There will be no rekindling. That's a guarantee. I can forgive a lot. But vanishing on me? Walking away from her daughter without so much as a goodbye or an explanation? No, there's no going back from that, even if that is what she wants. Which, from the voicemails and the brief conversation we did have, it doesn't sound like that's the case. I don't really know what she does want, though, or why she'd reappear like this, years later. I'm not sure I want to know. I don't know that I'm willing to let her back into Riley's life. But…she's Riley's mother—can I not? Does Riley deserve to have her mother in her life, if she's genuinely making an attempt? I don't know. There's no rulebook or guidebook for any of this."

I push a wisp of hair behind my ear. "I can't say I know the right answer. If she's genuine about wanting to see Riley, I suppose it would make sense to give her a chance. But I also understand the hesitancy to give her that chance, considering the circumstances under which she left."

He chuckles. "Some help you are."

I shrug. "You don't seem to be asking me for my

advice, formally speaking. But even if you were, I don't know that I'm qualified to give you advice on something like this. I'm not a mom, you know?"

"But you know kids."

I nod. "True."

"So as someone who deals with children professionally, what should I do?" He holds my gaze.

I sigh a laugh. "Stability and consistency are super important to kids. It would be detrimental to her emotional health if Mindy were to show up and get involved for a few weeks or even months, and then vanish again." I pause, thinking. "But, on the other hand, not having her mother in her life at all, ever, or any other positive female role model…well, that's not good either."

"So which is the lesser of the two evils?" he asks.

"Well, that's not a simple question. But, knowing Riley as I do, I know she's a sweet, smart, well-adjusted young lady. It's clear you're an incredible father, and she shows every sign of being loved and nurtured." I tip my head side to side. "So if you're asking me what I think you should do?"

"I am." He touches the back of my hand with his fingertips. "I value your opinion, Emma."

"I'd say first talk to Riley. Feel her out. Does she have any questions about her mom? Does she know Mindy is making advances? She's old enough that having a conversation with her about the situation is beneficial. Make it clear she has agency in this. If she has zero interest in, essentially, meeting Mindy for the first time, then I'd strongly consider going with her decision. But if she's unsure or open to the idea, start small. Supervised visitation. I really don't know the laws on it, but I think unless it's clearly unsafe, I don't know if you even can, legally, refuse to let Mindy see her. But then, she also did voluntarily give up all rights, so it may be different in that case." I sigh, rubbing my nose. "It's complicated, Rory. But either way, start small, as much as possible. Feel it out. Try to determine if she's really interested in seeing Riley and being a presence in her life, or if she's just, like, curious about Riley but isn't planning on actually being involved."

He nods. "That's in line with what I was thinking." He sighs, a bitter, frustrated sound. "I just don't want to even lay eyes on her. Just hearing her voice, talking to her—it messes with my emotions."

"I completely understand," I say.

"I guess if anyone could, it's you." He squeezes my hand. "So, do you want to come with us?" He drops his eyes, then meets mine again. "I would like it if you did."

I look at our hands, his atop mine. I let out a small breath, allowing myself to feel the shiver of eagerness at the minute contact. "Yes, I would very much enjoy that. Let me just get dressed."

He smirks. "I think you look fabulous just as you are."

I stand up and do a flouncy model pose, exaggerated and silly, hip popped out, one knee turned in, flashing jazz hands. "I know, ri-*iii*-ight?" I adopt a ditzy accent. "I call it hobo chic. It's all the rage."

He cackles. "Hobo chic. You're funny." He stands up and heads for the door. "I'll wait outside."

"I won't be long."

He shrugs. "We're in no hurry."

I dress quickly in a matching bra and underwear set—even though I have no plans to let him see me like that... again—my favorite jeans that fit just right and flatter my hips, backside, and thighs, and a long-sleeve cashmere sweater under my leather biker jacket. A beanie hand-knit from alpaca wool by Alice Bowers and my battered but beloved Doc Martens finishes the outfit. I feel cute, presentable, and dressed for the weather. Some color on my lips and cheeks, mascara, and eyeliner, with my hair braided and draped over one shoulder, under the hat.

In all, I'm able to go from hobo chic to cider mill ready in less than ten minutes. Not bad, overall, I'd say.

The cider mill, Beardsley's, turns out to be a little over half an hour away, outside New Haven. It's cute, quaint, and delightfully pastoral. There's a corn maze, fresh pies, acre upon acre of apple trees. The air is redolent with fall—apples being processed into cider, a subtle bite of cold, a faint scent of leaves burning. It's busy, clusters of families picking apples, couples leaning into each other with mugs of hot cider and bags of donuts.

"We pick apples and have cider and donuts here," Rory says, as we park and head for the U-Pick apple area, "and then we go for a hayride at another place not far from here." He shoves a hand into his jeans pocket. "We could just do it all at the other place, but…sometimes you do something one way and it just becomes the way you do it, even if it's not exactly logical, you know?"

I grin and extend my hand to Riley. "Traditions rarely make sense." Rory takes her other hand, and I have to focus hard on quashing the yearning in my gut for this to be real, to be more; neither of us is ready for that. "My family back in Colorado has a weird Thanksgiving tradition. No one is quite sure how it even started, but I went back last year and they were still doing it. When I was a kid, it was a really big deal in our family, all the cousins would come over and everything. Grandma, who's passed on now, God rest her, would make not one, not two, not even three, but FOUR pumpkin pies. Grandpa and Uncle Will would go out while the pies were cooling and catch a cow. Usually, the orneriest, crankiest heifer they could find, and for the younger cousins, they'd get a calf or a yearling. The tradition is they'd have a mini rodeo. Whoever could stay on the cow longest, wins, and the winner gets a whole pie to him or herself."

Rory stares at me. "That sounds…dangerous."

I laugh. "I mean, I guess? The only time I can remember anyone ever getting actually hurt was when I was… ten? Twelve, maybe? Nicky, my…second cousin? First cousin once removed? I don't know. My aunt and uncle's son's son. A little older than me, thirteen or fourteen at the time. He decided he wanted to be a real rodeo star, and the heifer Grandpa and Uncle Will had in the corral wasn't good enough. So Nicky went out and tried to rope an honest-to-god steer."

Rory arches an eyebrow. "I don't see that going well."

"It did not," I say with a laugh. "He managed to actually rope the steer, bless him, but what he failed to comprehend is how much skill it takes to control a roped steer, not to mention strength, and how much it depends on your horse. Nicky was riding a trail horse older than he was."

"I don't know the first thing about horses."

I laugh. "It means it was an old horse that wasn't trained to do anything but easy rides on trails it knew. It wasn't a cutter, like a horse meant for roping and stuff like that. Totally different. I don't know fishing, but it seems like it's fairly analogous to trying to run a net from a zodiac."

His eyes widen. "Did he survive?"

I snort. "Barely. The steer tossed his head and took off, and Nicky didn't have the sense to let go of the rope. The horse went one way, the bull went the other, and Nicky was airborne. Thank god he landed in a big old pile of mud and manure." I sigh. "Of course, Dad, Will, and Grandpa had to then go catch the steer and get the rope off of it before it hung itself. Nicky had to sit at the kids' table the rest of Thanksgiving."

Riley looks up at me. "Did you ever win a pie?"

I arch an eyebrow. "Did I ever win a pie? Young lady, you happen to be looking at the reigning Cole Family Thanksgiving Pie Ride champion. My best time is twelve seconds, and no one has even gotten close." I grin. "I won more years than I didn't."

He frowned at me. "You stayed on a cow for twelve seconds?"

I smirk. "Well, I'll only tell you this because there's no chance of my family finding out, but I cheated, kinda. That year they picked Loo-Loo, who happened to be my favorite heifer. She'd let me ride her all the time. I had her halfway trained at that point, but no one knew it. And with anyone but me, she was actually pretty mean."

"You can train a cow to be ridden?"

I tilt my head to one side. "Usually? No. But Loo-Loo was special, and I had a special bond with her. But then she had a calf and that ended. It was fun while it lasted, though."

Riley is starry-eyed. "You have the coolest stories, Emma."

Rory laughs. "I was thinking the same thing."

We spend over an hour wandering the orchard, filling a bag for me and another for Rory and Riley. Once we have our bags filled, we head into the shop, get cups of mulled cider and a bag of donuts, and find an empty picnic table. The air is crisp and cool, and the cider is piping hot. Riley is sitting as close to me as she can get, while Rory is on the other side of the table.

"You tell a story now, Rory," I say.

He polishes off a donut, washes it down. "Um. Mine aren't as cool as yours."

I roll my eyes. "Nonsense."

He grins. "Fine." He tilts his head to one side. "I punched a bear, once."

I frown, arch an eyebrow. "And yet, here you are, alive and without any obvious scars."

He snickers. "Yeah, we startled each other. I was eighteen, it was fall, and I was supposed to be on the boat with Dad. I'd been telling him for weeks that I needed a day or two off—he never rested, never took a day off. Not ever. Not once in all the years he was alive, I don't think, did a single day go by that he didn't work the nets. And I was like, that's all well and good for you, Dad, but I don't want to spend every waking moment of my entire life on the boat, fishing. He acted like I'd told him, in Ancient Greek, that I was a giraffe and wore women's underwear on my head. He literally didn't seem to understand the words. He was just like, no, son, we fish. It's what we do. We're fishermen." He shakes his head. "So, I snuck off the boat early, before he woke up, and headed into town. Got myself a nice leisurely breakfast at the diner, and took a long hike into the woods."

Riley is listening to her dad, frozen, as if hearing him talk about himself before she was alive was blowing her mind. "Well, I was a fisherman, okay? Not a woodsman. I didn't know what I was doing. I didn't have a compass, or a canteen, I had no idea where I was going. I had no idea what to do if I came across a bear."

I laugh. "Rule number one of dealing with bears: don't punch them."

He nods, laughing. "I know that *now*. I suppose I knew that then. Like, it's just common sense. But like I said, we surprised each other. I came out into a clearing through some brush. I was looking down at myself, picking sticks out of my shirt and burrs off my pants, and I look up, and there's a bear literally two feet away. As far from me as I am you, across this table." He gestures from me to himself. "I nearly walked into him. He was on his hind legs, and he was snuffling and looking at me, and making bear noises. I yelled in shock, and he yelled back. I don't think he was swiping at me, but his paw came toward me, right? And I just…reacted. I socked him right in the ear. Like in *Fight Club*, right? It must have taken him by such surprise that he dropped to his feet and ran off."

I laugh, shaking my head in disbelief. "That sounds like something from a bad comedy movie."

"It felt like it!" He says. "The timing of the whole thing was just…pure comedy. I nearly walk into a ten-foot-tall bear, and I yelled and he yelled and he waved at me like, hey bro, I was here first. Only I don't speak bear and it looked an awful lot like he was wondering if I'd taste good, and then I hit him and he was like, what the shit was that? In the ear? Why the ear?" He glances at Riley. "Oops, sorry, Ry. Shouldn't have said that word in front of you."

Riley just rolls her eyes. "Dad, come on. Like I haven't heard you say worse than that."

He frowns, but it's hiding a rueful smirk. "Way to throw me under the bus, there, Ry."

She makes an innocent face. "What? I have! When you're working on the truck, you say all kinds of bad words. Especially when you can't get a good angle on a screw or whatever."

I laugh. "Not being able to get a good angle on the screw will make anyone say bad words."

It's all too easy, with them.

We get more cider to go, and head to the other farm for the hayride. It's crowded on the wagon, and a cold wind has picked up. Riley ends up on one side of Rory with me on the other. I'm dressed warmly, but Rory seems to radiate heat, and I find myself leaning into him. He's a hard wall of male muscle and presence and bulk and heat. He smells so good, a familiar barrage of scents that make me feel at once at home and intoxicated—the ever-present scent of motor oil and grease, soap, fabric softener, and somehow, a hint of the sea, as if the smell of the ocean spray is as imprinted on the fabric of the man as motor oil is.

Anyone else, the scent of engines might be a turnoff. But for me, it's just the smell of men, of home, of constancy and familiarity. I don't have the best relationship with my family anymore, but those early weekend mornings in the pole barn with Dad and Eddy, watching them tinker and turn wrenches and wriggle underneath and change ratchet heads…those are good memories.

I lean closer. The creak of the wagon and the soft grumble of the wheels over the gravel as we head for the trail…chatter of voices, Riley turning this way and that, trying to see everything at once—Being here with them like this feels…like a memory I've not yet lived.

I know this moment.

I expect it and welcome it, when his arm casually lifts and wraps around my shoulders. I nuzzle in against his side, and meet his eyes. His expression asks if it's okay, and my response is to rest my head against him.

Riley is watching.

She has a smile on her face, a self-satisfied one.

She knows what she's doing, I think.

The cider mill date, if indeed that's what it was, ends with a hug from Riley on my front porch, wherein she extracts a promise that she'd see me outside of school again soon. Rory and I hug, awkwardly. It nearly turns into a kiss—you know how it goes…hug, pull away, pause with faces a little too close.

Drown, briefly, in the urge to kiss…

I pull away first. Back up, nervously twisting the end of my braid in my fingers. "Um. Thank you. For today. I had a lot of fun."

He removes his hat with one hand and immediately replaces it with both hands. "I, uh—I had a lot of fun. We both did, didn't we, Ry?" He glances at his daughter, who's watching us with hawkish intensity.

"Uh-huh." She glances up at Rory. "Are you guys gonna make out or what?"

Rory cackles with abrupt force, and then glares down at her, going from hilarity to sternness with whiplash speed. "Riley Kerr!"

She shrugs with exaggerated innocence. "What? I was just asking. It looked like you might kiss."

"If we did, it wouldn't be in front of you," he says, arching an eyebrow at her. "Now go get in the truck, peanut. I want to talk to Emma alone for a minute." When she's climbing up into her booster in the passenger seat, he turns back to me. "I'm not sure if I should apologize for that, or not."

"Not if you're asking me." I smile at him. "She's not wrong, you know. There...there was a little moment, there."

"Was it my imagination, or did you pull away first?"

I shake my head. "It was me. I...Rory, I..." I glance past him at Riley. "I don't want to put the cart before the horse. And I don't want to hurt or confuse Riley. You know?"

He nods. Ducks his head and sighs. "I do know. And honestly, I have to admit I'm grateful you're more sensible than I am, clearly." He lifts his head, and his deep, dark brown eyes bore into mine. "Because I would have kissed you. I wasn't thinking. About you, or Riley, or anything." His eyes go to my lips. "I was thinking...your lips look so red, and delicious. And that you smell so good."

I'm flustered, my heart beating a trillion miles a second. "Rory..."

He's barely breathing. His eyes are on my mouth. He's leaning toward me. Falling forward, in increments. "Yeah?"

I put my hands on his chest—I'm not sure if I'm holding him back from closing the inches between us, or simply touching the firm broad warmth of his body; both, perhaps. "I want to kiss you, too. But...I'm scared."

This makes him blink, straightening away. "You're scared? Of me?"

"No. Of kissing you."

He shakes his head, gaze searching. "I don't understand. What are you scared of?"

"Not wanting to stop. Getting lost in…in you. In us. In kissing. In wanting more."

"And how is that a bad thing?"

I swallow hard. "Because I get attached easily and quickly, Rory. And…and my heart still feels…fragile. You have Riley to think about. And now your ex is coming around, and…and…" I shake my head, claw my fingertips into the meat of his chest, and then back away into my front door. "I'm so mixed up, Rory. I like you. I'm attracted to you. But I can't…I can't do just a little bit. I'm not…I'm not that type of person."

He frowns at me. "If you're under the impression that I'm after—I don't know…a quickie, or a casual hookup or something, then you're grossly misunderstanding me as a person."

I shake my head. "No, that's not what I mean."

"Then I'm totally confused."

"Me too," I say with a laugh. I sigh and sag back against my door, swiping my beanie off my head. "I can't just kiss you. Or just…like you. Just…date you a little. I'm an all-or-nothing kinda gal, Rory. And I'm not sure I'm ready for everything, you know? But also I'm scared of never being ready. And…I'm just so complicated, okay? I need to more than like you if I'm going to have everything with you."

He sighs, a growling noise. "I'm no less confused, Emma."

I wipe my face with both hands, sighing a laugh. "Have you ever heard the term demisexual?"

He shakes his head. "No. Like, partly sexual? How does that even work?"

"I'm not sure I can make sense of the origins of the word for you, but it means I have to have a strong emotional connection before I can feel sexually open and attracted to someone."

He eyes me. "But you said you're attracted to me."

"I am. But in the sense that I find you to be a physically attractive person." I huff. "And I want to kiss you. To…I don't know. Feel things. To let myself feel things. But I can't."

He nods understandingly. "Yeah…I'm lost."

I laugh. "Me too."

"What if we just take it slow and one step at a time?"

"What's the next step, then?" I ask.

"You come over to our house and Riley and I will make dinner for you?" He takes my hands in his. "We just…keep getting to know each other. Slow and easy."

I nod. "I'd like that."

"So…dinner tomorrow? Six o'clock?"

"Tomorrow, huh? Not next weekend?"

He grins. "Why waste time?"

I can't help but grin back. "Sure. Tomorrow at six. What should I bring?"

"Just beautiful you."

"I'm bringing something. Salad or dessert, you choose."

"Dessert. A salad I can do. But I have no imagination when it comes to healthy treats. If it was just me, I'd go without. But Riley's just a kid, you know?"

I grin. "I'll bring something delicious."

He brings my hands up to his face. "And in the meantime, I'll make a promise to you—until you tell me otherwise, the only kiss I'll give you will be this…" He kisses my knuckles, slowly, from the far end of one hand, lips touching and moving, across to the other side.

My heart is galloping, my mouth is dry, and for a moment I find myself wondering if maybe we have more of an emotional connection than I realize, because that was…decidedly arousing.

"Okay," I whisper, as he releases my hands and steps away.

"Okay," he repeats, grinning at me, as if he can read my flustered mind, confused heart, and mixed-up body.

Before I can say or do anything else, I wave at Riley, turn on my heel, and flee inside my house.

My knuckles tingle.

My stomach is tight, and within, butterflies do loop-the-loops.

My hands are shaky.

And nothing even happened.

9

I DRESS UP, THIS TIME.

A knee-length, figure-hugging, short-sleeve maroon dress, a chunky-knit cardigan with huge wood buttons, and calf-high leather boots with cream wool boot socks folded over the top of the boots. For the first time in a very long time, I brush my hair out and leave it down, give it a gentle spiral away from my face.

I've made a cheesecake, decorated it with fresh strawberry quarters, and drizzled melted chocolate over it. It looks divine, I must say—or perhaps decadent is the better word.

At 5:30, I text him: *Address?*

He responds immediately, sharing his location as a pin on the native map application—their house is across town, near the marina.

Me: *Got it, thanks. Will be there soon.*

He pings back a moment later: *This is Riley. Daddy is cooking he says he needs all of his thumbs. I cant wait to see you again! Are you bringing a dessert.*

I snap a photo of the cheesecake on my counter as a reply, and receive approximately eighty-seven party emojis in response, which has me laughing all the way to the car.

The drive is short, thankfully, which doesn't give me enough time to overthink myself into an anxiety attack.

Or an aroused tizzy.

Or some weird combination of both.

Too soon, and not soon enough, I'm pulling into the driveway of a lovely Craftsman with white vertical siding and black roof and trim. It has a deep porch with a pair of white-painted rocking chairs on one side of the porch and a built-in porch swing on the other. It's properly a Connecticut fall, now, cool and crisp, sometimes even downright cold. The street is lined with spreading oaks turning half a dozen shades of red and orange. The white-brick chimney spews a thick plume of white smoke. I hear children laughing somewhere, a few doors down. A dog barks playfully. A leaf blower hums from the next street over.

Rory and Riley's front door is open, and through the glass storm door, I can see them in the kitchen. They're dancing together, Riley on Rory's feet, both of them laughing. I can hear the music through the glass, Louis Armstrong singing about a kiss to build a dream on.

For a moment, I'm dizzy with a possible future: I'm just home from running errands, with my man and my girl dancing in our kitchen, waiting to welcome me home with a kiss, to sweep me into the dance with them. Louis on the radio, a glass of wine on the counter, a fire roaring, something delicious in the oven.

I shake my head to clear the vision. Shut off my Wrangler and descend, gather my cheesecake from the passenger seat, and head up to the porch. Hesitate at the door.

I have a moment of doubt—if I knock, if I go in, it's a step toward that vision.

I want it, but I'm scared of it.

More accurately, I'm afraid of walking into that vision and having it too stolen away from me. The fear of having my joy kindled and dashed yet again has kept me isolated and lonely for three years. It's kept me from accepting dates. It's forced me out of first kisses. It's had me running in a panic from what would have been a one-time hookup while at a teacher's convention in NYC last year.

He was hot, he was into me, and no names needed to be exchanged. I couldn't do it. I couldn't even enter the hotel room with him. I apologized and ran like Joseph from Potiphar's wife, leaving him with a hopeful hard-on and the keycard in the slot and a very confused expression.

That was the last time I got even close to a man with anything like romantic or sexual intention, and I still laugh at myself for thinking I could have gone through with that.

I'm frozen on the front porch of Rory's house, eyes closed as nerves rifle through me, as fear of being alone forever wars with my fear of being hurt again the way Trace hurt me.

I hear the storm door rattle and creak open. "Emma?" Rory's voice, warm and deep. "You okay? You didn't knock."

My eyes fly open and I bring a smile to my lips. "Hi, yes. I'm okay. I just…" I shake my head. "I'm fine."

He's so freaking handsome.

No hat, today. He's wearing a pair of khaki chinos, barefoot, with a baby-blue short-sleeved polo shirt. The sleeves are stretched around his huge arms and tugs tight over his thick chest, hanging loose around his trim waist. It's tucked in behind a brown leather belt, untucked everywhere else. He's made a valiant attempt to tame his hair and beard—his hair is longish, draping past his ears and curling around his collar and sticking to his beard just underneath his earlobes. His beard is curly and bushy, but glossy and brushed and smelling of cedar and pine. I'm tempted to bury my nose in his beard.

His eyes hold mine for a moment, and then make a slow, blatant perusal of my body, from head to toe and back up to my face. "You're so damn gorgeous, Em," he murmurs. His hand lifts, drifts to my shoulder, tracing the knuckle of his forefinger against the fall of my hair. "Really like your hair down like this."

I smile. "And I like you without a hat on."

He scrapes stiffened fingers through his hair, which messes it up—and makes it even sexier. "It gets in my face at work. But I don't like barbers and I sure as heck can't cut it myself."

"No barbers for you, huh?"

He laughs as he ushers me inside. "Nope. Went to a barber shortly after…after I was first single, and got a nasty-ass hack job. I ended up going to one of those cheap chain places and getting it buzzed all over, and I haven't touched it since." He grins. "I look terrible with a buzz cut."

I shake my head. "Yeah, I can't picture it. You have great hair." I can't help myself—I tuck a lock of his hair behind his ear. "I, um. I could cut it for you, if you want."

He arches an eyebrow. "You could?"

I nod. "Mom used to cut Dad and Eddy's hair for years. Then she developed arthritis in her hands, and couldn't. My cousin Dana is a licensed cosmetologist, and she taught me how to properly cut hair." I roll my eyes grin. "I discovered the hard way that the only reason Dana taught me was so the men in the family would get their haircuts from me instead of bugging her."

He looks at me—we're standing just inside the front door. "I mean, if you're offering, I'd take you up on that. At some point."

I just want an excuse to run my fingers through his hair. "I'm not a professional, you understand. And it has been a while."

He digs his phone out of his back pocket and swipes rapidly through his photographs. "Feel free to laugh. I took a picture just to record for posterity what has to be the worst haircut in history."

He hands me the phone, and the first thing I notice is that he's noticeably smaller all over—at least twenty pounds of solid muscle skinnier. The second thing I notice is that his haircut in the photograph is exactly as bad as he's claiming.

It's somewhere between a mangled attempt at a woman's pageboy and a mullet, but it's uneven all over, bangs dangling past his eyebrow on the left and up near his temple on the other, and not even cut on an obvious angle along the way.

"Did you offend the barber before they took the scissors to you?" I ask. "I mean, I feel like you'd have to be trying to cut hair that badly."

"It was off-island, at a shop I'd never been to before. I even looked them up online and requested the stylist with the most mentions. I asked for a haircut. She asked what kind. I said I dunno, just shorter. Whatever you think will look best." He laughs. "She had me facing away from the mirror, and when she was done, she turned me around and whipped the apron off me, like voila, my masterpiece. I'm not a talkative man, necessarily, but nor am I exactly taciturn, you know? But that shit left me literally speechless."

I hand him his phone back. "No wonder you don't trust barbershops."

He shrugs. "I guess I just use the term barbershop. It was actually a salon, or whatever. Mostly for women, but I asked when I booked it if they do men too, and they said yes. I dunno, I just…I couldn't believe what I was seeing. I asked if she was joking, because if so, I wasn't laughing. I paid her and told her if that's her idea of a good haircut, she needed a new line of work. I even left the most scathing review possible without using curse words. Which is the only time I've ever left a review online."

I cackle. "You left a bad review online?"

He nods. "I sure did. I believe I included the words 'hack job' and 'abomination,' and the picture I just showed you. I figured my embarrassment may help others avoid my fate."

I grin at him. "Well, I can't promise you a Hollywood caliber cut, but I can guarantee it won't be so bad you have to buzz it afterward."

He pockets his phone. Something beeps, in the kitchen. He doesn't seem to notice, his eyes lingering on my face, my hair, flicking down to my cleavage and back up. My dress doesn't feature a plunging neckline, doesn't show much skin, but it is tight and molded to my frame.

"Dad?" Riley calls from the kitchen. "The food?"

He jolts. "Crap, I gotta take the chops out." He spins on his heel and hurries into the kitchen, yanking oven mitts off the island and onto his hands. He opens the oven and pulls out a large cast iron pan, which he sets on a hot pad, and then goes back in for a baking tray lined with foil. I smell pork chops and broccoli.

Riley comes running, then, and I realize she'd likely intentionally waited until Rory and I had finished talking to come greet me.

Hopeful little matchmaker, that one.

She reaches for the glass dish in my hand. "I'll take this. Does it go in the fridge?"

I let her take it. "Yeah, that's fine." I snicker. "Are you excited to see me, or my cheesecake?"

Her pause is telling. "You?" She breaks into laughter. "But also, cheesecake."

"I mean, not to toot my own horn, here, but that cheesecake *is* gonna be pretty epic."

Rory straightens from where he was checking the internal temperature of the pork chops. "Did someone say cheesecake?"

I laugh. "You didn't see it in my hand when we were talking just now?"

He ducks his head, hiding a grin. "I was more focused on, um...you."

I hold his eyes. "You were more focused on me?" I give a significant glance down at myself, glance at Riley—who is busily rearranging the fridge to make a spot for the cheesecake—and then give a little jounce to the girls. Which definitely draws his gaze. "Or on...*me*?"

I barely recognize myself, in this moment, flirting with him like this, so blatantly, so salaciously. It sends a thrilling little tingle down my spine.

He closes his eyes, and I know he's valiantly attempting to not think about me as he saw me after the storm. He swallows hard. "Your hair," he growls. "Your long, beautiful, thick, lustrous brown hair. That's what I was focused on."

"Uh-huh, right," I deadpan.

I mean, I may or may not have chosen this dress in particular because of how it flatters my figure. Knowing he'd look, and hoping he'd like what he sees.

He sighs. "Caught me." He meets my eyes. "Can't blame me, though, can you? You're just...breathtaking."

I give him a gentle smile. "I'm teasing you, Rory."

"Daddy doesn't have a sense of humor," Riley says,

without looking at us from where she's finally found a place in the fridge for the cheesecake. "He says he put it down one day and forgot to pick it back up, and hasn't ever been able to find it since."

I laugh. "Here's the funny thing—my dad was the single most serious and unfunny person I've ever known. He could watch the funniest thing to ever happen and not even so much as crack a smile." I've talked about my past and my family more since meeting Riley and Rory than I have in years. Since leaving Colorado, certainly. "I made it my mission in life to make him laugh."

"And did you?" Rory asks.

I nod. "I did. Once. I could make him smile, occasionally. A couple times I made him give a little snort of restrained amusement. And one time—one glorious, memorable occasion—I made him actually, legitimately belly laugh. And as far as I know, no one has heard the sound before or since."

While this conversation is happening, Rory is plating the food—a pork chop for each of us, a helping of seasoned and baked-crispy broccoli, and a simple tossed salad on the side...in legitimate, honest-to-goodness wooden bowls.

"Tell the story, Emma!" Riley says, fixing herself a glass of ice water.

Rory sets the plates on the table, eying his daughter. "I think we've begged enough stories out of poor Miss Emma. She's probably sick of it, by now."

I wait for Riley to choose her seat, and take the one opposite here, kitty-corner at the small, round, four-seat table. "Honestly, it's the opposite. I haven't thought about my childhood in a long time. Lately, most of the memories that come up in my mind have been…the not-as-funny ones. So it's pretty nice to recall the more pleasant ones." Rory is at the fridge, hesitating over something. "Emma, I wasn't sure what you'd like to drink. I, um, I do have a bottle of wine that someone gave me a while ago. If you'd like."

"I'm really not picky. Ice water is fine. If you would choose to drink a glass of wine with me, then I would accept one. But if you'd rather not, I'm absolutely okay with that."

He gazes at me evenly for a moment. "When I told you I don't drink, it's not because I can't handle it. It's not that sort of situation for me. So if you want one, it won't bother me."

I smile at him. "Rory. You're overthinking this. Ice water is just fine, thank you."

He seems to breathe a sigh of relief, and I think I made the right choice. He would have had some with me, *for* me, but I don't think it would have done him any favors. And for me, alcohol has always been a once-in-a-rare-while thing, for reasons I typically choose to not think about. And certainly wouldn't talk about in front of Riley.

"So, the time I made my dad laugh," I say as we dig into dinner—it's delicious; the pork chops are crispy with seared seasoning on the outside and tender and juicy on the inside, the broccoli is just right, flavorful and baked with herbs and parmesan cheese. "Our farm growing up had a little bit of everything—we owned horses and raised chickens and we had some pigs, but our primary source of income was horses. Dad was a breeder—he owned several very high-end studs, which just means male horses whose sole job is to make baby horses, because he's got the best genetics. He sort of got it into by accident—he won a stud in a game of poker, and made enough money studding him out that he was able to buy another stud, and that became his business. So we didn't own a huge horse ranch with hundreds of heads of horses. We owned a couple dozen, and he'd breed and train them, sell most of them and keep the best ones. But we also raised cattle to sell, and we lived off beef we owned, plus our chickens and our pigs."

I wave my fork. "All this is just to set it up. If you've never been around pigs, you have to understand them a little. And by pigs, I mean hogs. Not the cute little mini potbellies that people have as pets, but big ol' hogs that can be hundreds of pounds and are smarter than dogs. They also smell *awful*. If you raise hogs, you keep them far, far away from your house and your other animals, because they're just…gross. Amazing, intelligent creatures, but so stinky. Well, me and Eddy would take turns for who had to feed them every day. We both hated it, so we'd take turns. And you had to be extra especially sure to latch and lock all the gates behind you, because those hogs were wicked smart and liked to escape. And if they escaped, they'd make all kinds of trouble. Dig up the garden, wreck fences, eat all the cattle feed, chase the chickens and eat their food. It'd be a mess. So locking up afterward was super important. Well, one day, Eddy forgot to latch the gate."

"Uh-oh," Riley says.

I nod. "Uh-oh is right. He left it open, and next thing you know, you've got a dozen hogs running wild, each one the size of a large dog and four times the weight. They were into *everything*. The feed in the barn, the chicken yard, the house, the garden. It took us hours to get them back into their pen, and that alone was a wild time. Chasing a pig ought to be an Olympic event. Despite being up to six hundred pounds, those suckers are *quick*, and they can turn on a dime." I laugh, remembering. "Anyway. All of us spend half the day rounding up the stupid hogs, finally get them all in, and head home to relax. And what do we find rooting in Mom's flowers? Goober. Most of our hogs we didn't name—we raised them for meat and to sell, so we didn't name them. But Goober was…unique. He was the biggest hog I've ever seen in my life, and he was flat out crazy, and dumber than a bag of hammers. I told you pigs are smart, right? Like, border collie smart, generally. They have memory, and personality. Well, Goober got an extra helping of size, but the trade-off was his smarts. As in, he didn't get any. He'd sit on his hind legs like a dog with his face up against fence post, and just…yell. He'd make the most godawful racket you can imagine, and if you've never heard a pissed-off pig, thank your lucky stars because it's a terrible, terrible sound."

"I had no idea pigs were like that," Rory says.

"Me either," Riley chimes in. "So what happened to make your dad laugh?"

I sigh. "I thought I could get Goober into the pen on my own. So I start yelling and clapping and trying to get him to get out of the flower bed. He just looked at me like, girl, I don't know who you're yelling at, but I ain't moving." I laugh. "Well, that set off a battle of wills, and everybody else stood back to watch."

Rory shakes his head, chuckling. "I admit, sometimes I have a hard time reconciling this tough, stubborn, half-wild, animal-taming farm girl version of you with the sweet, smart, kind schoolteacher version of you."

I grin. "Because I've done my best to cultivate that schoolteacher persona. But deep down, I'm really still the farm girl. Much to my eternal chagrin. I just can't seem to leave the farm behind, no matter how long I've been away or how far I go."

"So who won the battle of wills?" Riley asks. "You or Goober?"

I shake my head. "Me, eventually, but not before Goober made it plain he was not going to go quietly. Now, he was dumb, and weird, and crazy, but he was a sweet pig. Not all hogs are sweet, some can be down-right mean, being so smart. You really have to be careful around hogs. But Goober wouldn't hurt you. He just didn't listen. So I was behind him, pushing him out of the flower bed. Or, trying to. It was like trying to push a fully loaded dump truck up a hill. He was all of four feet tall at the shoulders and weighed almost seven hundred pounds. That's as much as a small horse. And he didn't want to go. He liked those flowers. Peonies, apparently, were his favorite treat. So he was munch-munching, and

I was yelling and screaming and pushing, and smacking his behind, and he was like, "Who? What? Who there?'" I give my best Goober impression—deep, slow, and dumb. It makes Rory snort and Riley cackle. "Finally, I did the one thing I knew would make him move. I got Dad's old fishing pole and tied his actual most favorite snack to the end of the line: donuts. Goober *loved* donuts. That's not a joke. If you went to the pigpen with a donut, he'd come running, and he'd dance around and snort and beg for it every bit as pathetically as a dog in the kitchen. So, I did my best cartoon character impression. I climbed up on his big old back, and I hung the donut in front of him."

"You did not," Rory says. "Really?"

I nod. "I swear I did. Dumbest thing I've ever done, too. See, riding a pig is...darn near impossible, let's just say that. You think riding a bucking steer is hard? Try staying on the fat slippery barrel back of a seven-hundred-pound pig running for donuts."

I spread my arms wide apart like I'm hugging an imaginary redwood. "You can't sit on him like you would a horse, you have to lay on his back and hold on like this. Only, I was also trying to hold on to the fishing pole and guide him into the pen. So I'm holding on to Goober with one arm and both legs, and I'm screaming bloody murder because he's running around at top speed and he's yelling because he wants the donut and he's not running in a straight line because I can't keep hold of him and the pole at the same time, but I also refused to fall off or let go. So I'm on the back of this crazy hog who's running wild all over the yard chasing a donut that's swinging in circles, and it was just this absolutely bonkers situation."

I pause, laughing at the memory. "Dad was laughing so hard he was bent over double. I did a double take when I realized it was Dad laughing like that, because like I said, no matter how silly I was or how funny the joke was or anything, he'd barely crack a smile. And here he was laughing like crazy. Made the whole wacky adventure worth it."

"And that's how you got Goober into his pen?" Riley asks.

I shake my head. "Nope. I fell off. I went one way, the pole and donut went another, and Goober, of course, went after the donut. I threw the donut, fishing pole and all, into the pen. He followed, and Dad closed the pen."

"Why didn't you just tease him with it and then throw the donut in there in the first place?" Rory asks.

I laugh. "An excellent question, and one I only thought of *after* the fact."

The rest of dinner is just as fun. After dinner, we play a few rounds of Old Maid. Riley is ostentatiously not asking about dessert, and I think Rory and I are playing an unspoken game of seeing how long she'll go before finally breaking—or maybe the game is to see who can make her break first, I'm not really sure. We play cards more and more slowly, take longer and longer to play our hands. I excuse myself mid-round to the bathroom, and walk with exaggerated slowness. Rory fills his water glass but with the faucet only open a quarter of the way, so it's barely a trickle.

After the third hand of Old Maid, Rory looks at me with a barely suppressed smirk. "You know what I haven't played in the longest time? Scrabble. Three is plenty for that."

Riley, whose gaze has been longingly darting to the fridge since before we even finished dinner, looks stricken with panic. "Scrabble? Can't you play that after I go to bed?"

Rory nods, only just managing to hide his smirk. "Hey, that's a great idea. Good night, squirt!"

She looks at him as if trying to decide if he's joking or not. "Dad."

"Riley?"

"Come on."

"Where are we going?"

She rolls her eyes. "Dessert? The cheesecake?"

Rory finally breaks into a guffaw. "Oh my goodness, I plumb forgot about dessert."

"Me too," I say, "I was just so full from that amazing dinner, it slipped clean out of my mind."

Riley's gaze flicks from her dad to me and back. "You guys are being mean."

Rory slides out from the table and goes behind her chair, tickling her until she writhes and screams with laughter. "That's for saying I don't have a sense of humor."

She huffs, when he finally stops tickling her. "You've been teasing me this whole time?"

Rory tweaks her nose. "Sure have, peanut. And it's the most fun I've had in a long time."

She glares at him. "I'm pranking you back. Just you wait."

He arches an eyebrow. "You said I don't have a sense of humor. The thing about forgetting it was a *joke*, you big dork."

"I *know* that, *Dad*," Riley snarks back. "I was *teasing*."

"And Emma and I were teasing you back."

She shakes her head seriously. "You should never tease about dessert. Some things are sacred."

I cackle. "Oh my goodness, Riley, where do you get this stuff?"

"It's cheesecake! You know how long it's been since I've had cheesecake?" She pauses for effect. "Never! That's how long! I've never had cheesecake!"

Rory snorts. "Oh stop, you have to. You had a slice of chocolate swirl cheesecake the size of your head when we took that trip to Hartford, remember?"

She glares. "Yeah, *two and a half years ago*. That's forever, when you're just my age."

Rory laughs. "Fine, fine. Cheesecake time." A glance to me. "Would you like to do the honors?"

The cheesecake is amazing. I have to reassure Rory several times that it does not contain any sugar or artificial sweetener or processed flour.

Rory allows Riley to have a small second piece, but puts his foot down when she pleads for yet more. I tell her I'm leaving the rest and she can maybe have more another day, if she's good.

She brushes her teeth, and puts on pajamas—shorts and a tank top—and asks if I can tuck her in.

I do, of course, and I feel the wall separating me from my desire for the vision I saw before I got out of my car crumble a little bit. If it's an emotional connection I need, this is the way toward it. Riley. I want it, but I'm scared of it. And to be honest, the fear runs deeper than I allow myself to even really recognize.

I read her a story, *Uni the Unicorn*, by Amy Krouse Rosenthal.

By the time I'm done, Riley is half asleep. I have to resist the urge to kiss her on the forehead. "Good night, Riley."

She smiles without opening her eyes. "This was the best night ever."

"It's definitely on my list of top ten best days ever for me."

"Really really?"

I tuck a lock of hair behind her ear. "For realsies."

A pause. "Emma?"

"Hmm?"

"Do you like my dad?"

Eeeep. Tricky. "Um, yeah, I do. I like him a lot."

"No, like...*like* him."

I sigh. "Riley..."

"I want you to." She blinks her eyes open and looks at me, direct and earnest. "Sometimes I have dreams about you and Daddy being married and you're my mom and I wake up and it's not real and I'm sad."

"Riley, I..." I swallow hard. "That's...I...that's a little complicated to answer, sweetheart."

"Daddy really does have a sense of humor you know."

My heart cracks a little. "I know that, Riley. I knew you were kidding when you said it."

"He doesn't have any friends. He just goes to work and takes care of me. But when you're around, he's... different. And I like it. And *I* like you. I want you around all the time."

The crack widens. Gooey stuff seeps out of the crack. "Riley..." I really, really, really don't know how to handle this conversation. "All I can do is make you this one promise, okay?"

She nods against her pillow, eyes half closed, blinking slowly as she resists sleep to listen to me. "Okay."

"I will always be your friend. No matter what. I like you for you. I was *your* friend first. Because I like the person that is Riley Kerr. And whether your dad and I... um, I don't know. If we—if there's—something, or if not, I'll still be your friend. Okay? That's my promise. You and me? BFFs."

She smiles, closes her eyes. "I guess that will have to do for now." Her smile is teasing. "But I still hope you and Daddy could be together. That'd be the best thing."

"You don't make it easy to disagree," I whisper. "And neither does he."

I can't resist it anymore. Just this once. I kiss her on the temple, and a flash goes through my head—the future that wasn't, and the future that could be.

I click off the lamp beside her bed, pull the covers a little higher, and soft-step out of her room.

And find Rory leaning against the wall beside her room. He'd clearly heard every word.

His gaze as it finds mine is a tumult of emotions.

I close her door with a quiet click of the latch catching.

I find myself, as I turn away from the door toward the hallway, face to face with all six feet and four inches of Rory Kerr, his broad chest lifting and lowering heavily. Looking up at him, I see the pulse in his throat racing.

My mouth goes dry. His eyes are burning, wild and fraught. Desire, conflict. Pain, need.

He steps into me, and I catch up against the wall beside her door, where he'd been leaning moments before. I'm imprisoned within the thick iron bars of his arms. His palms brace against the wall, and his body blocks off the world and radiates heat and wild masculine power. His scent is all around me.

"I promised you the only kissing I'd do is to your hands," he growls, his voice a low, quiet rumble. "Never wanted to break a promise so badly in my life."

"Rory, I…she was asking about…us. You and me. And I didn't know what to say."

"I know. I heard." He touches his forehead to mine. Every cell in my being throbs, jangles with electric need, with the hot pulse of tension searing between Rory and me. "Just gonna come right out and say I was standing out here on purpose, listening to your conversation with her. Not gonna apologize, either. She's my daughter."

I press my palms flat against his chest. Not pushing him away, nor stopping him from getting any closer. "I know. I'm fine with that."

"You handled it…better than I could have, probably."

"I just didn't want her to think that if something

happens between you and I and then it didn't work out that she'd lose me too." I blink hard. "That's what I'm most afraid of. Or, one of the things. Hurting her."

His brow furrows. He closes his eyes as if holding himself back only with great effort. Slowly, he drops one hand from the wall beside my face, takes my hand in his. For a moment, he holds my hand against his chest. Then, slowly, he lifts my hand to his lips. Touches his lips to the center of my palm.

Kisses, delicately.

I groan, and my eyes close.

I can't.

If I kiss him, right now, I'll start falling.

I almost laugh—because, haven't I already started the tumble?

"Rory?" I hear my voice, and it's a low, breathy whisper.

"Mmm." His eyes pierce mine.

"You promised…"

He growls as if in pain. "I know." He exhales heavily, and begins swaying away from me, as if pushing a thousand pounds up a hill. "I'm sorry."

I wrap my hand around the back of his neck. "You misunderstand me." I pull him toward me, pushing away from the wall and settling up against his big hard body. "*You* promised."

I lean in, closer and closer, till I can feel the hot huff of his breath on my lips.

"But *I* didn't."

10

I LIFT UP ON MY TOES, AND I EXHALE THE LAST OF MY
doubts—for a moment, at least, my need for physical
affection and closeness wins out against my fear of
rejection, abandonment, and pain. I know, even in this
moment, that I'll play hot and cold with him later, that
I'll freak out and panic and confuse the hell out of the
poor, sweet, sexy man.

But right now, I just need to kiss him, to be touched,
to be surrounded by heat and muscle and protective shel-
tering bulk.

My lips touch his.

He huffs a quick, relieved sigh as our mouths fuse.
The sigh of relief turns to a growl of…amazement?
Wonder?

God, his mouth is soft. He's so hard all over—his
shoulders under my palms feel like mountains of granite,

his chest is like an anvil, his arms and legs like tree trunks. His skin is weather-roughened, leathery. But his lips? Warm and welcoming and eager and soft.

For a moment, it's me kissing him. I'm lifting up on my tiptoes and my hands rake over his shoulders and delve into the feathery softness of his hair and I'm hungrily mating my mouth to his and inviting him to take over.

And then, he does.

It happens at the moment when his sigh of amazement that I'm kissing him turns to a growl of need.

It's like a switch is flipped. Off to on. Me kissing him flips the switch on, and while I'm kissing him it's a fluorescent light bulb flickering as it warms up. Then the bulb is fully lit—he growls, and I'm no longer kissing him...he's kissing me.

He leans down, pressing in harder, deepening the kiss. My hands roam the hard mountain roads of his shoulders and I open my mouth for him and taste his tongue as it lashes mine, slithers into my mouth.

Want—want—want. Need pulses in me.

It's so rare to feel such hot, powerful, driving desire. It's an uncommon thing, for me. Even with Trace, knowing him, growing up with him, growing into a love with him over time, I wasn't typically a girl who burned hot, sexually. It was a slow burn, a simmer that would suddenly and somewhat unexpectedly boil over.

Something about Rory Kerr, though, has brought my simmer to a full rolling boil—it's unexpected and honestly kind of confusing.

I'm in my head, again.

I don't want to be.

I push away the tangled skein of thoughts trying to take over, and dive back into physical sensation.

His hands on my cheeks, cupping, grasping with gentle power and restrained strength; his body against mine, his chest flattening my breasts, his hips nudging mine; his lips scouring my lips, his tongue demanding and eager.

I feel him.

Just feel, Emma. Just feel.

It's okay.

For this moment, it's okay.

At that moment, he pulls away, and his hands drop from my face to my waist. "Em? Feels like I lost you."

I shake my head, biting my lip. "No, I...no."

"Em, it's okay. If you're not ready."

I rub my hands on his chest. Shake my head. "Sometimes, what I want, what my body wants, get confused by my stupid, frantic, overthinking brain."

He cups the back of my head, and I lean against his body and look up at him as he stares down at me. "So physically, you want this."

I nod. "I do. I really, truly do."

"But your brain is saying..."

"My brain is a jumbled-up ball of chaos and anxiety and irrational fears."

"Like?"

"Like a bunch of thoughts that are in no way conducive to getting back to kissing." I touch his lips with my fingertip. "Which, by the way, you're really, *really* good at."

"And what about your heart? Where does that fit in?"

"Somewhere in between my head and my body. I'm scared. I've been hurt and I don't know that I'd recover if it happened again. But I'm lonely and tired of being alone and I want companionship and I want—" I close my eyes and pause, biting my lip, and then I just let words topple out, pell-mell and impulsively truthful. "I want to be held. I want to be kissed. I want to be loved. But I want...god, Rory, I also want things I've never had before. Wild, irresponsible, crazy passion. I want to be swept off my feet. I want to jump headfirst into something fun and physical without necessarily having my heart all the way bound up like I was before. I don't know, Rory. See? I'm a mess. My brain is spinning a million miles a second and my heart is going crazy and my hormones are on *fire* right now. I feel like a powder keg. One little spark, and—kaboom. And I kind of want to go kaboom. But I'm scared because I really really like you, like I *like* you like you, and I'm really attracted to you and you're a really incredible kisser—"

He slams into me, abruptly silencing me with a rough kiss. I bump against the wall with a loud thump, and then he's pinning me beautifully in place and towering over me and crashing into me. His mouth is wild and insistent.

He lowers at the knees and his hands cup my backside, and then he's lifting me effortlessly. I react instinctively, wrapping my legs around his waist and clutching his face and devouring his kiss with hot need flaring through me.

He carries me and his stride is long, eating the space with hungry steps. His foot cracks against a door, and then I sense darkness around us. Another few steps and I'm toppling backward and downward into the mattress. I don't have time to even register this before he's on me again, kissing me with maddened intensity, and I can only egg him on. I claw at him. Rip at his shirt, tug and pull and yank until he huffs a laugh, pauses in kissing me just long enough to rip it off one-handed—which, holy hell, is *so* freaking hot. I can barely make him out in the darkness of his bedroom. Just the outline of his body, his sexy, powerful physique. I reach for him, palm his chest and under his arms to his back. Pull him back down to me.

He has other ideas.

He hovers over me, kisses my mouth, once, briefly, and then his mouth descends to my clavicle, and I gasp as his tongue slicks over my collarbone and his lips stutter down the slope of my cleavage. He kisses the upper swell of my breasts, but his hands, meanwhile, gather the hem of my dress. Push it upward. I lift my butt, allowing him to drag the dress upward even as his mouth kisses lower and lower. I'm trembling—with arousal and wild anticipation...and fear.

What if I panic, and cut this incredible experience short?

What if he changes his mind?

What if he's not actually attracted to me? What if he's attracted to me, but just to my body?

What if he only wants to get into my pants, and once he's gotten that, he'll be done with me?

What if I fall for him, but he doesn't fall for me?

What if I'm too scared to really open up for him, and I doom what could have been a life-changing relationship?

"You're in your head again, Em," he murmurs.

"Scared."

"Of what?" He pauses, my dress up around my belly, exposing my black lace bikini cut underwear.

"It's a long list."

His breath is hot on my breasts. I tremble, and tingle. My core aches, throbs. "Do you want to stop?"

"No," I breathe. It's the truth. In this moment, at least, I want this more than I'm afraid of what comes after. "Don't stop."

He kisses my left breast, from the top of the swell slowly down to the neck of the dress. Tugs the neck down, exposing more. Another kiss. Tugs lower. Then the other side. I tangle my fingers in his hair. His body is a big hard wedge between my thighs.

He wiggles lower, and his hands push my dress up higher. Kisses my belly, which I suck in concave at the touch of his lips. Kisses higher—diaphragm, just beneath the underwire of my bra.

A pause. I can feel his eyes on me. Assessing, asking. I scratch my fingernails down his spine, but I can't quite reach his buttocks, so I settle for scratching and massaging and exploring his broad back and wide shoulders and curling my fingers into his hair and cupping his scalp and palming the back of his head.

He presses my dress higher, and I lift my head and shoulders off the bed. He accepts the invitation for what it is, yanking the dress up and off. Oh god, oh god. I was naked in front of him before, but I was too weak and sick to care. It wasn't an erotic moment. Not like this.

He groans and kisses my ribcage, the valley between my breasts. Up, and his lips find mine. He's everywhere, his body pressing mine into the bed, and his mouth is hungrily moving on mine, and our kiss is soaring into abandoned fury. I want to kiss him until I'm nothing and nowhere and no one but mouths mating. Except, I am more. I am my body's need for his touch. My breasts ache for his hands, his mouth. My nipples pucker, beg to be bared, to be kissed. My sex pulses for his touch. I ache for release—for a release I didn't give myself.

More.

He slides his hands under my back, hunting for the clasp of my bra. Instead of wasting words, I reach between my breasts and undo the front clasp, and my breast spring free, swaying to either side. Immediately, his mouth leaves mine and he sinks down, and he cups my breasts in his hands. His touch is reverent. His mouth is worshipful.

I ache, ache, ache. My core throbs. My sex is wet and I want more and more.

I gasp as his mouth laves my nipple, flicking it with his tongue until it's so erect and hard it hurts. He growls, a sound of pleasure as his hands knead my breasts and his mouth licks and kisses my nipples. I arch my back, bolts of ecstasy zinging through me, arcing from the tight hot barbs of my diamond-hard nipples down to my sex, making my clitoris throb in time with my slamming heartbeat.

I need to be touched.

I need release.

I've never needed it so badly in my life. Never have I felt so aroused, so afire with need. So beautiful, so sexy, so wanted.

"God, Em," he murmurs. "So sexy. So responsive."

"R-responsive?" Feels like an odd thing to say.

He flicks his tongue over my nipple, and I flinch with my whole body, a little whimper escaping. "Like that."

"Oh," I huff. "I'm just—" I cut off with another gasp when he pinches one nipple and suckles the other. "So... I'm so—oh god. I'm on fire. I need...I need more, Rory."

He cups my breasts in his hands and kisses downward, between my breasts to my diaphragm, to my navel, to the waistband of my underwear. Oh god oh god oh god, I'm crazed with need and nerves. He kisses my skin above my panties, and then, like he did with the neckline of my dress, he teases kisses downward and tugs the elastic down with each subsequent kiss. My fingers knot in his hair, but I'm powerless to stop him. I don't want to. Don't dare. If he stops, I might never feel this need, this bravery again.

He kisses my hipbone. His fingers curl under the elastic. I gasp, a shuddery inhale—my lungs fill like a balloon, abruptly pierced with a surprised shriek as he tugs my underwear down. My hips obey his command, lifting. Lace scratches past my buttocks—he leans away, draws them off, and I'm utterly naked, and his mouth is hot on my belly, and my thighs quiver and my belly curls inward. His lips browse lower. I'm breathless, anticipating.

My mind asks a question: when was the last time anyone has pleasured me the way Rory is about to?

Did Trace ever?

I shake my head and groan, viciously shoving away the train of thought. Get out of your damn head, Emma Cole.

"Em?" His voice, concerned, questioning.

I shake my head again, this time less violently. Caress his head, his hair, trace the shell of his ears. I draw my heels closer to my buttocks, close my eyes—scrape my fingers into his hair and apply the merest downward pressure.

He rumbles a laugh, complying with my silent, subtle plea. His soft wet warm lips touch my skin below my navel, and then the delicate, intimate crease where sex meets hipbone. "You want it?"

I feel his eyes—my own fly open and meet his deep wild brown gaze. "Please, Rory. *Please*."

His shoulders nudge open my legs, and he kisses the tender silken flesh of my inner thigh, caresses from knee to sex as he positions my leg on his shoulder, knee hooked over. The other leg, kissing and placing. I feel the hot huff of his breath on my damp seam, and then a single finger drags over my clit and I jump, gasping.

"Sensitive, aren't you?"

He traces my slit again, and I arch, writhe. "God, yes. God yes, so sensitive."

Another slow, delicate touch. "So I should be very…very gentle?"

I can't even gasp, so breathless does his touch leave me. "Tease…teasing me."

"I'm not. Unless you want me to." He gentles his touch more, until it's barely a feather brushing over my flesh, a breath.

Up, and down. Up and down. Pausing at the top to press a tiny amount, a soft circle. Down again. Barely counts as touching.

"Rory—please. Don't, please. Don't tease. It's—it's been too long, and I want it too badly." I gasp as he slides the finger into me, slowly plunging inside my sex. "I just want you to—I just want to…I want to come, Rory. I want to feel—I want to feel good. I don't want to think or feel or be afraid. I just want to feel good with you."

"It's been a long time for me, too, Em. You're so incredible, so sexy, and I just want to…savor you."

Savor me?

Oh god.

His mouth closes over my sex, and his tongue slides between the lips and touches my clit, and I cry out, and my hips lift. Then, he slides a second finger into me, spreading me a little, and his tongue circles me, once, twice, three times.

I'm on fire.

I'm gasping.

Hips tilt up, surge against his mouth. I'm shaking all over. So fast? I've never come this fast, before. It usually takes a while.

But Rory is nothing like anyone or anything I've ever experienced. He touches and kisses my body like I've been his forever.

His tongue flicks and darts, licks and circles, and those two fingers move into me, withdraw only to plunge back in. Faster. I whimper, and then cry out louder than ever.

"Sssshhh," he whispers.

"I…oh god, Rory. I don't know if I can be quiet." I grit my teeth around another whimper. "It feels too good."

I fumble over my head and find a pillow—just in time. He twists his hand to face palm up, and his fingers curl against me on the inward slide, and that just does something. It makes my hips jerk, and I shriek into the pillow. And then, as I'm jerking and shrieking, he suckles around my clit and his tongue flickers against me and I lose myself in a scream, bury it into the pillow.

He assaults my sex, then, as I scream. Fingers plunge in and out, and his tongue circles, and I fly up the face of a mountain—climbing swiftly toward a climax. Faster and faster, flicking and kissing, suckling and circling, fingers squelching in and out, and my hips are flying, gyrating against him and I have no control over my body. He owns me, in this moment. Dominates my movements. A kiss, and I jerk. A circle of his tongue, and I cry out. He knows when to slow, to bring me away from the edge. just for a heartbeat, and then he renews the frenzy of his tongue and lips and fingers, until I'm at the peak and scream-ing into the pillow and writhing against his mouth. My legs are hooked around his shoulders, and I'm lifting off the mattress. He devours me, taking me to the edge and throwing me over.

I bite down on the pillow as a scream unlike any other rips out of me, a primal scream of pure orgasmic abandon.

Beyond the edge of climax, I can only shake and gasp, shiver and writhe and tremble helplessly as he licks every last drop of pleasure out of me, until I'm limp and whimpering, a puddle of amazed, incredulous woman.

I'm panting for breath as he lets my legs down from his shoulders and kisses his way up my naked body, nuzzling my breasts until I gather him up to me. I smell myself on him. Taste my own essence on his beard as I kiss him. Wipe at his beard and kiss him again.

If I'd thought an earth-shattering orgasm beyond compare would sate my arousal, I was wrong. It only served to light the wick of the powder keg that is the desire and need within me. I roll against him, feeling the hot firm flesh of his torso with my hands, pressing against him with my body, flattening my breasts against him and writhing.

Kiss him desperately.

Lean into him and fumble for his fly. His hands are on my ass, in my hair, and his kiss is equally as desperate, as hungry. He pulls me closer, and I'm halfway astride him as our kisses clash, warring for supremacy, fighting to determine who's the more frantic. So far, I'm winning. I rip at the button of his jeans, and then the zipper. I need him. Need him more than I've ever needed anything.

I get his jeans open, yank at them. His hips lift, and I fight with the jeans and his underwear. Frustrated, I mewl an irritated sound. Abandon the fight and just thrust my hand under the waistband of his underwear and grasp him.

I groan out loud as he fills my hand, a thick hard hot column of throbbing manhood. He matches my groan, and releases me long enough to wriggle and shove and kick until his jeans and underwear are off and flopping away. I can't get enough of his body, now, greedily rubbing my hands over his tree-thick thighs and hard belly, and then I wrap both hands around his erection, stroking him.

"Oh god, Emma," he hisses. "Ohh god, the way you touch me."

I am burning with desire. It ravages through me, charring away any reticence or hesitation or self-consciousness or fear I may have had. I just want him. I clutch his erection, twist a slow downward stroke and pull away from kissing his mouth to taste his pec, and then his belly. He arches his back and gasps, gathering my hair in his hand. I touch him everywhere as I kiss toward his sex, scouring his chest and abs, thighs and sides. Cup his balls and curl hands around the shaft again, eager and shameless. I take him in my mouth and taste his essence pooling at the tip, and a hard, rough groan rips from his throat, rumbles in his chest. I swirl my tongue around him as I stroke his length, and then kiss the tip and slide twisting strokes downward as I caress his sac. He arches, cries out a ragged groan.

"Emma, god, Em, oh god." His teeth are gritted, muting the volume of his voice.

He bolts upward, lifting me bodily. I'm astride him, suddenly, and his mouth slashes against mine and his tongue spears into my mouth and his hands clasp my ass. Oh god, oh my lord, he's nestled against my opening, huge and thick, sticky with pre-cum. I sink against him, no thought in my entire being but that I need him. Right now.

"Rory," I breathe, reaching between us to grasp him, clutching him and guiding him into me, spreading my lips open with his broad round head, teasing and nuzzling, and then I sink lower with a low shaky moan, and he allows me to control the speed of the thrust, letting me take him inch by thick, stretching inch, until I'm fully impaled on him and shaking with the burning beautiful size of him and gasping breathless whimpers, because he's just barely too much for me to handle, just too big enough to be perfect.

I can't help but laugh, a hysterical laugh. "Oh my fucking god, Rory," I breathe. "Oh my god."

"Are—are you okay?"

I fall forward against his chest and surge down on him, hiding my moan in his shoulder. He meets me, driving upward, filling me in a single slow thrust that drives the breath out of me and the climax through me. I feel it building, the ache in my core. He moves, takes over, grasping my hips and lifting and lowering, dragging me down against him as he drives up into me.

This isn't gentle, but it's not rough either. It's slow

and forceful, passionate and intense. I cry out again, sinking my teeth into his muscle and groaning. He matches my groan, and our motions synchronize.

Faster.

"Oh god, Em...Em, you feel so good. So tight, so wet. Fuck, Em." His voice is ragged, and his dirty words rile me up even more.

"Rory!" I slam down on him, ass meeting his thighs with loud slaps. "Rory, holy shit, Rory! Ohmygod don't stop, don't stop, ohh god you're incredible."

The intensity builds and builds until we're moving with frantic abandon, bodies meeting with clashing grinding slapping. I've never felt this good.

I come with a scream that he devours with a kiss, swallowing it. "Rory!" I scream. "I'm coming, Rory, I'm coming, oh god oh god..."

He drives into me, speed slowing as the force of his thrusts increases. "Em—Emma, Emma, I'm gonna come. Right now, I'm—oh god, Emma."

Rory Kerr, this man. He fills me, stretches me. He's made me come until I'm cross-eyed with it.

He feels so good, bare inside me. Too good.

A different kind of scream rips out of me. "Don't!" I gasp, terrified. "Don't come! I'm not on birth control!"

I bolt forward to get him out of me—he slides free of me with a wet slap, and he's curling forward to half sitting, cursing through gritted teeth.

"Shit!" he snarls, every muscle of his body tensing into rock. "I'm sorry, I'm so sorry—"

Even in the darkness, I can see the raw tension and

downright pain as he hauls himself back from the edge. I can feel it in him. Hear it in the rough scrape of his breathing.

I can't let this end like that. I can't, I won't.

"Rory, let me." I slide down his body so I'm sitting on his thighs and grasp him in both hands.

He shakes his head. "I'll be fine, you don't—you… oh god." His eyes are slits, dark gaze glittering in the dim light. "Emma, you don't have to." He says this even as his body responds to my touch.

I don't answer. I just stroke him. Caress him. No teasing, no playing. I just caress his beautiful manhood until he's writhing under my hands and his hips drive upward, tilting and rocking. The more desperate his movements, the slower and gentler my touch, until my strokes are one-handed, grazing, long and slow from tip to root to tip in a smooth glide, while I caress his balls with the other, slow and gentle and soft. Until finally—perhaps a minute, maybe two after I began—he's breathless and groaning and his movements are ragged and helpless.

"Emma," he growls, drawing the syllables out into a groan—*Emmmmmaaaaaa*. "Oh god, oh fuck, please."

I don't know what possesses me, in that moment. I've done it once before and didn't like it, and never did it again. But with Rory, in this moment, I don't even think. I just act on impulse. As I feel him reaching the edge, feel his balls tensing and his shaft pulsing and his stomach going concave as his hips drive up, I bend over him and take him into my mouth. I suckle around the head and lick the opening with a swirl of my tongue, and I squeeze his sac and stroke the heavy thick pulsing erection until I taste his release.

He tastes salty, bland, with a slight edge of something almost sweet. Thick. Hot.

I like it.

More so, I like the vanquished gasp he makes, the raw, ragged sigh of a man who's so overcome by pleasure that he can't even growl or curse or any of those other manly, masculine noises of enjoyment.

I draw it all out of him, every drop, every pulse, every shift of his hips. I tongue him and swallow each spurt, stroking and caressing and squeezing.

When he goes still, only his chest rising and falling with ragged, destroyed gasps, I give the very tip, leaking a little still, one last lick.

He hauls me up to his chest. "Emma, I'm sorry. I wasn't thinking. I shouldn't have—"

I touch his mouth. "Me too. I wasn't thinking either. It's okay, Rory." I nestle closer. "We pulled out in time."

He tightens his arm around my shoulders. "I should have…protected you better. I just wasn't even thinking. I was so…crazy with…you. With how beautiful you are, how sexy you are. How good it felt to be with you. And I just…spaced out on protecting you."

"It was both of us, Rory. I'm at fault, too. I was just as crazy for you. So don't hog all the blame, okay?" I find his hand and tangle our fingers. "I really, *really* enjoyed it. All of it."

"I'm usually a better protector than that." He seems

to be taking this pretty hard. It's honestly…sweet. Melts my heart even more.

"I know you are, Rory. I don't doubt you for a single second. We just lost control. We're adults, and it's been a long time for both of us."

"A long time, yeah," he murmurs. "A real long time."

"Are we sharing about it?"

"Up to you."

"Since before the accident. He…my ex-husband, Trace. He'd been super busy for several weeks before the accident, and so was I. We basically only saw each other at night, to sleep, both of us too tired for anything else. So…it was probably a good two months before the accident. Which was more than three years ago, now." I think, for a moment. "Probably closer to four years, for me, since the last time I was with a man."

"You never…dated, or anything?"

I shake my head. "No. Not for lack of trying. I'd go on dates and just…freeze. I got up to a hotel room with someone once, but panicked. The thought of letting anyone that close again just…froze me. And most people just never stood a chance. They couldn't engage me, you know? Like, I've been shut down. I push people away. I don't even have any women that I'm close to, much less men."

"Yet here we are," he says. "What's so different about me?"

I laugh. "I don't know, Rory."

He chuckles. "I think I'm insulted, actually."

"No, no. I do know, Rory. You're…kind. You make

me feel safe. You're so, *so* sweet with Riley. I think it's her, to a degree. I see how you are with her, and I know if you're that sweet and patient and protective with her, that I can trust you." I wander his chest with my hand. "Plus, you took care of me. You rescued me, and you took care of me at my weakest. Taking advantage didn't even cross your mind. You're funny. You're capable." I inhale softly, feeling things deep inside me crackling, melting, falling away. "There's also just something…familiar. You're nothing like my father, so it's not that, nothing weird like that. Just something…familiar. The thing about my father that made me feel safe, you have."

He swallows hard. "Emma, I…" He sounds…choked up. "You are safe with me. I promise."

"I know."

"Things were rough between Mindy and me for a long time before she left. So, for me, it's been…good lord. Almost five years. Riley was just a baby the last time Mindy and I…" he trails off, and he doesn't need to finish it. I'm glad he doesn't. "It was bad. Quick, cold, and not at all…" he trails off again. "I dunno. It was just bad. She was checked out, hated our life, hated the island, hated the isolation, hated the cold, the rain. And I knew I couldn't give her what she wanted, never would be able to, and that just made me feel like shit, so I was in a dark place too."

A long pause.

"We coexisted for a while after that. A year or so. But we never shared a bed again, even to sleep. She spent nights away frequently, with other guys, I'm sure.

Off-island. The trips got more frequent, and she stayed gone longer. Then she just never came back. And since then, my sole focus in life has been Riley. Taking care of her. Making a living." He tilts his head to look at me. "Until you, I honestly never even thought about women. I was lonely, of course. Been lonely for a long damn time. But Riley has been everything I need, emotionally. Until I met you, that is. You just…" he breathes out sharply. "You make me feel alive in a way I don't think I knew was possible." A laugh. "Before tonight, I mean. Now? Alive isn't even the right word. I could fistfight a grizzly."

I laugh. "Please don't. I like you the way you are. Namely, alive."

"Hey, I got away with it once."

I laugh. "Sheer accidental luck."

Quiet, then. Not sleepy, just…relaxed in a way I've not felt in years.

If I ever have.

I hear the door creak open. "Daddy?" Riley's quiet, sleepy voice. "I had a bad dream."

"Okay, Ry. I'm coming."

"I'm scared." Her voice is so small, so quiet.

I put my lips to his ear. "Go."

He scrambles out of bed and puts on his underwear in record time. Scoops Riley up in his arms and whisks her back to her room. I can hear him whispering to her.

Then, I hear him sing. His voice is rough, not quite melodious and certainly not good, but it's low and quiet and soothing. He sings "Hush Little Baby," but he clearly knows none of the words. He just makes them up as he goes. "Hussh little baby, donn't say a word, Daddy'ss gonna buy you a mockingbird. And if that mockingbird won't sing, Daddy's gonna buy you a...better bird."

And that's the moment.

That's when I know.

And it scares me shitless.

11

B Y THE TIME RORY EMERGES FROM RILEY'S ROOM, I
have my bra and underwear on.

"You're leaving?" he asks.

I hold my dress in my hands. "Yeah. I think it's best,
don't you?"

He sighs. "I mean, I don't like it." His hair is wild
and messy, tangled around his eyes and ears and sticking to his beard. "You leaving right now, this soon after
we were together, it just feels…too casual. And that's
not what this is for me and it's not what I want—it's not
how I want things to go."

"I know, Rory. But Riley…" I twist the dress in my
hands. "Are you ready for her to see us together? For me
to be here when she wakes up?"

He stabs his fingers into his hair, swiping it backward.

"I mean, it doesn't feel like an exaggeration to say she loves you."

"And I love her back. I do. But...that isn't really what I asked."

He pinches the bridge of his nose. "No," he whispers. "I don't think I'm quite ready for her to see us like that just yet."

My head is winning. The heat of passion is subsiding and all the fears and ingrained panic and doubts are swarming back up. Was this a mistake? Did we just complicate this nascent thing between us?

"I should go," I murmur.

Rory must have a sixth sense. Or an ability to read me more accurately than I'd thought possible.

"Em."

I duck my head. Shake it. "I need to go, Rory."

He crosses the room. His hands go around my hips and hold me, forehead touching mine. "Emma. Am I wrong in feeling like you're starting to freak out?"

I huff a laugh. Shake my head. "No, you're not wrong."

"Why? What are you freaking out about?"

I blink hard. "Everything."

"Talk to me, Em."

I roll a shoulder. "It's just my stupid brain."

He takes my dress out of my hands, orients it, and holds it open over my head. "Arms in."

Numb with anxiety, brain beginning the spin-out I knew was coming, I comply. Arms in, and the garment settles onto me. He smooths back my hair with his hands.

Takes my hand and tugs me out of his room and into the kitchen. He guides me to a stool at the island. He withdraws a bag of decaf coffee, starts a pot to brewing. While it's brewing, he moves behind me and begins massaging my shoulders and upper back. His touch is firm but gentle, browsing the upper surface of my muscles for knots and using his thumbs, knuckles and palm heels to loosen them. He doesn't say anything, and I let my head loll forward, a long low groan slipping out.

Most "massages" I've been given—of the personal, nonprofessional variety, I mean—lasted about sixty seconds and did precisely nothing to relax me. Rory works on my tense shoulders and neck for nearly ten minutes.

I groan again. "Coffee smells good."

"Want some?"

I nod. "Mmmm. Please." I watch as he pours us each a mug and sits beside me. "This *is* decaf, right? I watched you make it, I know, but if I have caffeine at this hour, I'll be up all damn night."

He huffs a laugh. "Same. So yeah, it's definitely decaf. I made regular late at night by mistake once—not something I care to repeat."

I sip—and sigh with pleasure. "You make such good coffee."

His laugh is deep with amusement. "You are, very literally, the first person who has ever said that."

"I like my coffee like I my men—" I start.

"Dark and bitter?" he quips, finishing for me.

"I was gonna say hot and strong." I laugh. "Are you, though? Bitter, I mean."

He sips. "Sometimes, yeah. More than I'd like, to be honest." He's quiet a moment. "Don't get me wrong—I live for my daughter. Everything I do is for her. I wouldn't change a thing. But…being thrust into single father-hood the way I was…yeah, I get a little bitter about it, sometimes."

"It's understandable—and I *do* understand. I mean, shoot, I get bitter about how things happened with Trace, you know? Like, I can't really get mad at him. He wasn't at fault for the accident, and he didn't ask for it. He didn't cheat on me, or just sort of randomly decide he didn't want to be with me anymore. It really tortured him, I can tell. But something about what happened to his brain just…changed him somehow. So it's no one's fault, which makes the bitterness even worse. Because I can't even get mad at him."

Rory tilts his head to the side. "Well, I guess I've got it easier than you, then, because I can be mad at Mindy."

"Speaking of whom—what's the latest on that front?"

He sighs heavily. "There's a hearing next week. She's petitioning for visitation."

"Have you talked to Riley about it?"

He shakes his head, a small, miserable gesture. "I don't know how."

"I'm not a parent, I'm not even her teacher, and I'm certainly no family counselor. I'm just someone who cares about…well, both of you. But Rory, you can't blind-side her with this. She's too precocious for that. If she was less aware, less *self*-aware, if she was less mature, or younger, it would be different. But if that hearing results in Mindy getting visitation rights and Riley suddenly has to go to the library to have a visit with her mother—whom she's essentially never known—and she has no time to get used to the idea? That could really shake her, Rory." I stare into the swirling black liquid in my mug. "I know I'm probably way overstepping here, I just—"

"No," he interrupts, gently. "No. You're not. I know I need to talk to her." He swallows hard. "I just don't know how. I don't even know what I want. Should I contest her request? Or would that be depriving Riley of a chance to know her mom?"

I reach out and rest my hand on his forearm. "Only you can decide that."

He laughs bitterly. "I know. Trust me, I know. But I don't know what's right." He covers my hand with his. "Tell me what you think. I'll make my own decision, but Emma, I really value your input."

"Have you met with her? Mindy?"

He shakes his head. "I'd rather cut my arm off with a hacksaw."

I wince. "Yikes."

A rough sigh. "Sorry, that was probably uncalled for. I just…don't want to see her. I have nothing to say to her."

"You're angry, and that's okay. You don't have to apologize to me for your anger. I just ask because I feel like if you met with her, you could assess where she's at. The question really is, number one, whether she's safe to be around Riley? Does she seem sober and stable? If she does, that would lead to question number two—what's her intention? To get to know her daughter because she's feeling regret or something similar? Or is she broke and lonely and trying to get to you via Riley?"

"How am I supposed to know?"

"Are you a bad judge of character?"

He laughs. "I hooked up with her. Calls my judgment into question, I'd say."

I huff. "Are you being fair to yourself?"

He shakes his head. "No, not really. She changed." A thoughtful pause. "Well, really, I think she just realized she'd bitten off more than she could chew. Being with me in the summer when weather is nice and we were all infatuated with each other was one thing. Being together in the worst of a Maine winter? With a baby? While I'm gone working more often than I'm home? That's a whole other bag."

Another long pause.

"She was never toxic. She wasn't an alcoholic or addict. She just…wasn't ready to be a wife and mom. She wasn't ready for me, for Riley, or for the life we had. Instead of working with me to figure out a solution, though, she just bolted. Maybe I was struggling with things, too. God knows I definitely carry my share of the blame for what happened. But I didn't run."

"You don't have to convince me of anything, Rory."

He sighs. "I know. I guess I've just not really thought about any of this in years."

"Meaning, you've never really dealt with it."

He nods, sighs a rueful laugh. "Yeah, that's probably true."

"Meet with her, Rory. Just feel out the situation. If you need, I can be with Riley."

He just looks at me. "Why are you so amazing?"

I laugh. "I'm not. I just like Riley." I grin at him. "And you."

"So what you're saying is, you like her more than me?" he asks, laughing.

"I like you different but equal, how about that?" I lean close to him, murmur quietly. "And Rory, I *really* like you. A *lot*." My voice drops to a whisper, my stomach flipping as I speak a truth that makes my insides squirm. "I'm not an oral sort of girl, Rory. I don't…it's not something I…" I duck my head, cheeks burning. "I've only done that once before, and I didn't like it. With you, I…I was doing it to you before I even thought about it. And…I liked it. I…I enjoyed making you feel good."

He sighs, a low, slow, rumbling growl in his chest, a very primal, bear-like sound. "Emma, that was…unexpected. Appreciated more than I could even begin to put into words, but so unexpected." A laugh, a shake of the head. "Everything about today was unexpected, Em."

"Because I said I wanted to take things slow?"

He nods. "And because I do too. Or, I did. I don't know where tonight leaves us. But…Em, please hear me very clearly when I tell you I am *not* a casual sex sort of man. This isn't that. At all."

My throat is hot and tight. "I know." I hold his gaze. "I don't what this is either. Not unwelcome, and…definitely something I want to keep exploring with you."

He sighs in relief. "I'm glad to hear you say that. I was half worried you'd tell me it was a mistake."

"Unplanned, yes. A mistake, no." I laugh. "We clearly have chemistry."

He matches my laugh. "Um, yeah."

"So, we probably should...um...plan for things to happen again in the future." I take his hand, twine our fingers together. "The issue is, I can't and won't do birth control. The hormones are just...no good for me. They mess with my emotions and make me gain a ton of weight and I just...no. I hope you understand."

He squeezes my hand. "All good. I'll take care of it." He hesitates. "I just don't have any condoms because I haven't been with anyone in so long. And while I have been hoping that you and I would eventually reach a place where we have a physical relationship, I wasn't anticipating it happening so soon."

"I wasn't either." I still can't quite believe what happened. What I did. How it felt. I need some time alone to process. "I...I'm glad it did, though."

His dark eyes search me. "You are?"

"Yes, Rory." I run my thumb over a small, thin, white scar on the back of his thumb knuckle. "You present an anomaly, for me. I told you, I just can't—or haven't been able to—throw myself into a sexual relationship unless I feel emotionally connected. I've tried, and the thought of exposing my body to someone I don't know, don't trust, don't have a connection or bond with? I just couldn't do it. And you and I are...well, there's something. It's just sort of starting, I guess. But something. And yet, I'm so attracted to you, physically, that it throws me off. I've never felt this way for anyone before, physically." I swallow hard. "Not even Trace. Maybe in some ways, especially not him. We were…comfortable together. Things were…good, physically. But it was all I knew, so I had no frame of reference. And then you come along and…god, you just…it feels like you set me on fire. In a good way. Scary, and weird, and disorienting, but good. Because I feel alive. I feel…seen. I feel connected to my sexuality for the first time in a very, very long time." I close my eyes and let it all keep tumbling out. "I think…I think Trace and I were complacent. And not very…intense. He was, um—" I shake my head. "You don't want to hear about this."

"If you want to share it, I want to hear it."

"Rory."

"It's important to you. And it would help me know you, and understand you. So I want to know. But it's your personal, private business, your past, and it's your choice to share it. Just like it's utterly and totally your choice and only your choice to not go on chemical birth control. It's got nothing to do with me." He pivots on the stool to face me. "I'm not threatened by your past, if that's what you think. I don't need the intimate details of your past sex life, but talking about the history that has shaped you into who you are now is important. And it won't scare me off or make me uncomfortable hearing about it."

He wiggles his coffee mug, a silent query if I want more, and I nod, hand him my mug.

"I guess I'm just realizing things about my past, my-self, as I get to know you." I bite my lip, shrug. "And especially with how things happened tonight, I'm realizing things about Trace, and our relationship." I pause to formulate the thoughts into words. "Trace and I were each other's first, and up until things ended, only. So, you're my only other partner. He and I were together for six years. So it's not like I'm inexperienced. But…with you, it was just…different. I mean, you're totally different people and one could argue that I'm not the same person I was, then. God, it's hard to put this into words. I…you…I couldn't *not* touch you. Kiss you. I *needed* you. There was no thinking about, no overthinking it. No examining my feelings. It was instinctual. And you clearly felt the same. I've never had that—I've never wanted someone so bad and never been so badly wanted that we just ripped each other's clothes off and didn't even stop to think. In the past, it was…habit. Ritual, almost. Part of being a couple. Desire was there, and I don't have any specific memories of not…enjoying it." I chew on the inside of my cheek, and then let out a hard sigh. "But with you, tonight? I felt like if I didn't kiss you, didn't touch you, didn't…*taste* you—if we didn't…" I shake my head. "For lack of a better word, if we didn't *fuck*, right then, I would have just…died. Exploded. And I don't use the word fuck lightly, or to minimize the emotional connection I am starting to feel with you."

He grips his mug in a tight fist. "Emma…I can categorically state that I've never in my life lost all control like that. I was…just…crazed for you. It felt like I was…

high, almost. I've never done any hard drugs, but it felt like I was just…yeah, high." His eyes drop, and I can tell he's holding something back.

"Rory, whatever it is, just say it."

He nods, but still hesitates. "I guess it scares me a little. Or, a lot, maybe. How intense my need is for you. I feel like any second, you could look at me funny or sway those hips just so or…or just…anything. And I'd lose all control. I'd just snap and…attack you. Rip your clothes off and just—" he cuts off, shakes his head. "At the risk of sounding like some tawdry romance novel…every moment I'm around you, I feel like I could just ravage you senseless."

I swallow hard and focus on breathing. "What's scary is that that doesn't scare me. The opposite, if anything." My heart is crashing, racing. I'm hot all over. "What scares me is that I'm sitting here and I'm telling you to…not hold back. Give in. Scare me. Do your best, or your worst, or whatever. It scares me because I don't know what this is, in terms of boxes or labels, or what the future is. I don't know if I'm capable of giving you my whole heart, and it scares me because I still want you to…to just…not ever hold back."

He lets out a shuddery breath. "I don't know if you really understand what you're asking for, Emma."

"Rory, I don't know if you understand what you've done." I clench my hand into a fist to stop it from shaking. "I very well might be the one doing the attacking, is what I'm saying."

Silence.

"The real question is why should we hold back?" Rory's gaze bores into mine.

I shake my head. "I don't know. The only reason I can think of is that you and I may not work out, as a couple, and I'm worried what that would do to Riley."

"Why wouldn't we work out?"

"I don't know. But that, more than anything, is what I'm scared of—having this amazing physical chemistry with you and then losing it."

He lets out a sharp breath, like a balloon being punctured. "I guess that's valid."

I set my empty mug down and push the stool away from the counter. "I should go."

He stands up with me. "I admit, it's tempting to look for reasons for you not to."

Despite my best intention to walk away, I'm drawn to him, inexorably, like steel shavings to a magnet. I find myself settling up against him, hands on his shoulders, breasts flattened against his chest, hips to hips. "I know," I whisper.

His hands close around my waist and slide down to cup my backside. "This is not helping."

I huff a laugh. "Making it…harder?"

He groans a laugh. "Oh good lord, Emma."

I rest my cheek against his. "Sorry. Bad puns aren't like me. But as I said, you do something to me."

His hands tighten on my bottom. "If you don't go, I'm gonna do something to you."

"Is that a threat?" I breathe.

"Yeah, it is."

"I meant to leave. I got up to walk away, and instead, here I am. I don't know what's wrong with me."

His lips find mine. "I don't know either, but I like it, I must admit." He squeezes my butt again. "You have such a fantastic ass, Emma."

I moan at his words, his touch. "In about ten seconds, one of two things is going to happen. One, I'm going to rip your clothes off and do something wildly inappropriate to you, right here in the kitchen. Or two, I'm going to be a good girl and go home. Because a lot has happened and I really do need time to think about it all and process it."

He growls, a low grumbling sound of frustration. He picks me up, settles me with my thighs clamped around his hips. His mouth finds mine, and he walks with me.

Oh boy, here we go again.

Only, instead of back into his room, he carries me outside onto the porch, and his bare feet tromp quietly across the porch and down the steps, pad silently across the grass to my Jeep. He kisses me all the while, pausing, kissing, pausing, kissing. Pressing me up against the door of my Jeep, hands under my butt, he kisses me until I'm frantic with arousal and gasping for oxygen.

"You went the wrong way," I whisper.

"I know." He steps away from the door. Holds me one-handed and opens the driver-side door. Deposits me into the seat, behind the wheel. "I must be either an idiot or crazy."

"You took me to my car instead of to bed," I murmur, gazing up at him. "I'd say you're an idiot."

"You said you need time to process."

I swallow hard. "I do."

"So do I."

I press my thighs together. "Did you have to turn me on before sending me away, though?"

He leans into the doorway and his right hand curls behind my neck, pulling me in for another, hot, searing kiss that leaves me shaking and boiling with renewed arousal. And he doesn't stop.

"Rory," I murmur. "What are you doing? What's your plan, here?"

His left hand slides up my thigh, under the hem of my dress. I part my thighs for his touch, and gasp as he traces a finger over my soaked seam. He doesn't answer in words—this is his answer. So I respond. I kiss him back and arch my back and let my thighs fall open. His mouth pauses in kissing me, hovering over my lips as he slips his fingers under the gusset of my underwear and into my slit. His touch gathers my essence and he smears it up onto my clit, and as I whimper, he resumes kissing me, ratcheting my arousal higher with every touch of his lips to mine, every tangle of tongues. His touch on my sex is deft and gentle, providing me precisely the right amount of pressure and circling speed to bring me to the edge of climax within seconds. I'm shifting on the seat, gyrating, hips driving, and my lips on his lose their seal, the kiss fumbling as gasps turn to whimpers.

I'm delirious with arousal. I barely understand it when his touch slows—I only know he's stopping when I need more. I only know compliance when he tugs my underwear off, hips lifting to let him yank them free. I only know ecstatic relief when I feel his mouth on me, tongue spearing into my channel and then laving upward, lapping at my sex and licking away the essence that is positively dripping out of me. Then his mouth is on my clit and his tongue is circling and oh lord he has fingers inside me too, and I'm being thrown off the edge into a crushing climax, my thighs clamping around his head and my hips lifting, shoving myself against his mouth and shrieking through clenched teeth as I come and come and come.

He licks me gently down from the climax until I'm shuddering and so intensely sensitive I have to push him away.

He stands up. His beard is wet from me. He looks very pleased with himself.

I stare at him—I'm turned sideways on the seat, one hand death-gripping the steering wheel, the other clutching the headrest. I'm falling half out of the Jeep, dress pushed up.

"Holy shit, Rory," I gasp.

He wipes at his beard. "Good lord, you taste so good." He has my underwear balled in his fist. "I could eat you out for hours."

I swallow hard. "I could let you." I tangle my fingers in his beard and pull him to me, smelling myself on him, tasting myself on his tongue as I kiss him. "My turn?"

He shakes his head. "Nah. Next time."

I blink at him. "So you're gonna turn me on, give me an orgasm, and then expect me to just leave?"

"Yup."

"Rory."

He just smiles at me. "Go process, Emma."

"Next time, I'm gonna…" I shake my head. "I don't know what I'm gonna do, but I promise you, it'll leave you brainless."

"I'm looking forward to it more than you know."

I let him go, and he stands up—the fly of his jeans is bulging outward. "Rory. Let me take care of that for you."

He shakes his head. "If I let you do that, I'll bring you back inside and let you help me out for about thirty seconds, and then I'll be inside you, and we still don't have condoms." He holds my hands in his. "I'll be fine, I promise. Till next time."

I look up at him. "Promise me one thing."

He nods. "Any promise I know I can keep, I'll make."

I can't help reaching out to cup the bulge. "When I leave, go inside and take care yourself. And think of me. Okay? Think about how I finished you, earlier." I feel bold, a frisson of arousal from the post-orgasmic glow still rippling through me. "Think about my mouth on you. Taking you. Swallowing every last drop."

He grips the edge of the door and breathes hard. "*Fuck*, Emma."

"Or, you can just let me do it for you again. Right here, right now." What's come over me? Who is this bold, wild, blatantly sexual woman?

He leans in, kisses my mouth, and takes two long steps backward away from me. "The hardest thing to do right now is tell you to go. But it's the right thing. Because I know I won't be content with your mouth, Em. That feels incredible, don't get me wrong, but it's not what I really want, what I really need—which is you."

He doesn't give me a chance to respond, but walks backward away from me toward his house. Reaches the bottom step, and lifts his hand in a wave.

I swivel to sit properly behind the wheel—my head still spinning, and now my heart spinning as well, and my body pulsing with unsatisfied desire.

I shut my door, turn the engine over, put it in reverse, and back out of his driveway.

It's not until I'm halfway home that I realize he still has my underwear.

Inexplicably, I find that unbearably hot.

There's something for sure wrong with me.

Even more inexplicable is that I don't even care. There's a phrase I've heard, but never understood or felt myself, until now: if this is wrong, I don't want to be right.

12

WATCHING RILEY FOR THE HEARING IS TRICKY. It's a late hearing, the last one before the courthouse closes, so she came home with me after class.

She's…off. And as with most kids, getting her to talk about what's bothering her isn't an easy thing to do. Kids hold on to things. They have trouble knowing if they should talk about it, what to say, what not to say, and for all her precocious intelligence and maturity, Riley is still just a kid. So I don't push it.

She's quiet and reserved instead of her usual wild, talkative energy. I suggest a tea party and then a movie, and she just shrugs. So we skip the tea party. I make her hot cocoa and give her my favorite blanket and let her turn on whatever she wants—some YouTube streamer who makes crafts for dolls. I sit with her and grade writing assignments.

An hour has passed and I haven't heard from Rory, and Riley is just…silent.

I set my papers aside, pick her up and settle her on my lap. She stiffens at first, and then snuggles up against my chest. I just hug her.

"I'm confused, Emma," she says, eventually.

I pause the TV. Kiss her forehead. "Do you want to talk about it?"

"My mom is back."

"I see. And how do you feel about that?"

"That's why I'm confused. I don't know." She sniffles. "I don't remember her. But I always wondered what she was like. What it would be like if I had a mom. Like, not just a mother, but…a *mom*, you know?"

Such painful wisdom from someone so young. It hurts my heart. "Oh, honey. That's hard," I whisper.

"I guess I…I guess I was hoping you and Dad would… be together. And maybe, someday, I would be able to call you Mom. But now my actual mom is back, sort of, and I guess she wants to see me. But I just…she's not really my mom. I don't even know what she looks like."

"Your dad and I are…figuring things out." I hug her tight. "But no matter what, you know that I love you, okay? I do. No matter what happens with me and your dad, or your mom, or anything, you're in my heart."

She nods. "I love you too, Emma." A pause. "I just…I have questions and I don't know who to ask."

I sigh. "Sometimes, kiddo, there aren't any answers.

Sometimes, even adults don't have the answers. If you want to ask me, I'll do my best to answer them, and at the very least, you've gotten to get the questions out, even if there aren't any good answers."

"Like, do I have to call her Mom? Or can I call her Mindy since I don't know her and she's not really my mom? What if she leaves again? Why is she back now? Why did she leave in the first place? Where did she go? Did she leave because of me? Was Daddy mean to her? What if she's back for good? I want you and Daddy to be together, not her."

"Whoa, that's a lot of questions." I have to be very careful, here. "I think I can say pretty definitely that no matter what happens between your dad and me, he won't be getting back together with...um, Mindy. I think that's as solid of an answer as there could be. As far as what you call her, I think you should talk to your dad about that, but for me, and it's not up to me, but just my opinion, I think you'd call her Mindy. She's essentially a stranger to you. She's your mother, and she's expressing interest in seeing you. That's good, right? I don't think it's my place to talk about why she left, where she went, or anything to do with her relationship with your dad—you'd have to ask him about that stuff. I don't think your dad was mean to her, though. He's just not a mean person. And I don't think there's any way of knowing if she's back for good."

"Do I *have* to see her?"

I wince. "I, um...I kind of think you do, if the courts

say she can see you. Till you're older, at least. Once you reach a certain age, you have more of a say."

"That's what I thought. Kids don't get to decide anything for themselves."

I laugh. "Well, that's usually because kids don't have the perspective and experience to make the best decisions for themselves."

She's not amused. "I just…it's confusing. Why come back now? What does she want? If she wanted to see me, why did she leave?"

"I wish I had an answer for that…and honestly, I think your dad is wondering the same thing."

"Am I allowed to ask her that?"

I hesitate. "Um, well? I guess I personally feel like you have a right to ask her just about anything you want. But as always, you should talk to your dad."

She shrugs, a small, miserable gesture. "It's hard to talk to him about it. He gets…not mad. Just…upset. He doesn't like it."

"I know. It's not an easy situation for anyone." I swallow, hesitate. "You know, it's probably not a very easy or simple situation for Mindy, either."

"So I have to be *nice* to her?" She says this is as if it leaves a bad taste in her mouth.

"Yeah, it's probably a good idea."

She huffs. "I guess I can try."

There's a knock on my door, then.

"Come on in, Rory!" I call.

My front door creaks open, the storm door opens and

slams closed, and I hear Rory's distinctive heavy tread. I twist my head to look over my shoulder at him.

And gasp.

He's in a suit.

His beard is trimmed, brushed, and neat. His hair is, well, as unruly and too long as ever, but he's done his best to tame it. The suit fits him like a glove—if anything, it's too small around the shoulders and arms and thighs. It's dark charcoal, with a white shirt and a pale blue tie. His eyes look black, deep…and exhausted.

"Wow," I breathe. "Rory, you look…gorgeous."

He just huffs a laugh and falls to the couch beside us. "Thanks." He tugs at the knot of the tie. "I feel like I'm wearing a costume. I had to go buy this today. I hate it so much I think I'm gonna return it."

I laugh. "Don't. You'll need it again, I think. And plus, you do look really, really hot."

Riley twists on my lap and gives me a look. "You think Daddy is…*hot*?" Her nose wrinkles as she grapples with the foreign concept.

"Yeah, I do."

"So when you told me you guys were figuring things out…"

"I asked if she likes me, check yes or no. And she checked yes."

Riley rolls her eyes. "Nobody does that anymore, Daddy."

"Oh."

Riley scoots off my lap and onto her dad's. "So? What happened?"

He leans his head back against the couch. One arm goes around Riley, and the other hunts between our thighs for mine. I take it. Hold tight. "She got visitation," he says, his voice tight. "One hour, supervised, every other Saturday."

"Did she tell the judge why she came back?" Riley asks.

Rory lets out another harsh sigh. "She said she regrets leaving the way she did, especially where you're concerned, but that she just couldn't handle life on the island anymore and wasn't prepared to take you with her, that it wouldn't have been the best life for you, that I offered the better future. But now, she wants a chance to reconnect and get to know you better."

Riley is silent. "Oh." She frowns. "I…I don't really understand what that means."

"It's a bullshit excuse, that's what it means," Rory says.

"Rory," I scold.

He sighs yet again. "Sorry, pumpkin. I shouldn't have said that. She seemed genuine about wanting to reconnect with you, I'll say that. How long it'll last, I'm not sure."

"Did you talk to her?" I ask.

He shakes his head. "Not yet. I was going to talk to you about that. The first visitation is next Saturday. I was going to message Mindy and meet with her before the visitation, and I was hoping you could hang out with *this little monkey* while I talk to her." He squeezes Riley and tickles her and kisses the top of her head as he says, "this little monkey."

"Of course."

He glances at me. "That's the week before Thanksgiving. You don't have plans?"

I bob my head to one side. "I'll head to Colorado the day before Thanksgiving and come back the day after."

"So you're not staying there for any real length of time."

I shake my head. "No, not really. My relationship with them is a little…strained."

"Oh. I'm sorry."

"Don't be. It's just life. It's fine. Or, it will be." I shrug. "So, what will you two be doing?"

"We'll do our own little thing. A turkey in my smoker, a pie from the store since I can't bake. Watch movies all day."

"Sounds like a perfect way to spend the day," I say.

"Well, my folks have both passed, and I never even met Mindy's, so it's not like we have a lot of family to spend it with. So for the last several years, it's been just us chickens." He shoots me a look. "You, um…would you want to come over before you leave town?"

We haven't had a chance to see each other since our little…evening together. We texted some, after school, and chatted as he picked up Riley, but I've had a lot of work to do getting the kids caught up before the break. And, honestly, a little time away from him to get space from the intensity of what happened that night was necessary.

It has only served to heighten my feelings, though.

I miss him when I'm not with him.

I miss Riley.

I miss his touch.

I wake up in the middle of the night with my sex soaked and fragments of wet dreams spinning in my head—his mouth on me; his fingers in me. And god, those glorious, incredible, earth-shattering moments where he was bare inside me, plunging and thrusting.

God, I want him.

But I want him in my life, not just…in my body.

Our lives could merge so easily, so seamlessly.

What's holding me back?

Fear. I know it.

I'm afraid he'll be taken away from me, like Trace was.

It's hard to admit and come to terms with, but Trace was my forever. I had it all planned out. Babies, and the white picket fence and everything.

And then, through no fault of mine or his, it was just…gone. Erased.

"Em?"

I shake myself out of the spiral of thoughts. "Huh?"

"Lost you, for a second." He frowns at me, rests a hand on my shoulder. "I asked if you want to come over before you go to Colorado."

"Yes," I say, immediately. "I really, really do."

Riley squeals in glee. "Can you make a dessert?"

Rory huffs and frowns. "Riley Kerr. We want her to

come over to spend time with us, not because she makes the best treats."

She rolls her eyes at him. "Well *duh*. But homemade treats are *way* better than nasty old store pies."

I tweak her nose. "How about I come over early and you can help me make the treats?"

She's so full of eager excitement that she can't contain it. "Yes! Oh my goodness that would be *so* much fun. Daddy won't let me bake on my own."

I laugh. "Well, I think that's prudent. But I'll teach you my ways, and maybe someday you'll be an even better baker than me."

Rory sighs. "That will be fun, huh?" He gives her a gentle shake. "Well, Ry-Ry? You ready to go home?"

She shakes her head. "No."

"Yeah, me neither. But we gotta. You need a bath."

"Do we *have* to go?"

His voice hardens, just slightly. "Riley."

A sigh. "Fine." She leans in to hug me. "Bye, Emma. Thanks for talking to me."

"Any time, kiddo."

Riley scampers off to put on her shoes and coat, and I walk them to Rory's truck. He starts it and buckles her into her booster, then pauses outside the driver's door.

"You don't have to bring or make anything, Em."

I laugh, rub his chest. "Well no, I don't *have* to. I *get* to. I love baking. And I think I'm going to love it even more with Riley helping out."

"We tried baking cookies once. It was…a disaster." He huffs a laugh, shaking his head.

"I can imagine." I hesitate. "You should talk to Riley. About all this stuff with Mindy. She has a lot of questions and concerns that I think you need to address. She's having a hard time with some things."

"I can't get her to talk," he says. "I have tried."

"Try again. Just…I guess reassure her that there are no bad questions and that nothing between you and her is going to change."

He nods. "I'm glad she opened up to you." A sigh, rubbing his face with his hands. "I honestly don't know how I ever got along with her without you."

That makes my heart clench, squeeze, and flip, makes my gut twist and my blood pound and my emotions go into a flat spin.

I don't have an answer for his statement. I just stare up at him.

"I really, really want to kiss you right now, Em." His voice is deep, quiet, husky.

"I really, really want you to," I answer. "But…what about Riley?"

He makes a pained face. "I think there's enough going on in her life, I'm not sure I want to confuse her with us being a thing just yet."

I nod. "I know. And I agree." I bite my lip. "I do know that she wants us together, though. She told me today that she had this idea that you and I would get together and eventually she could call me mom." I study his reaction. "She was wondering if she has to call Mindy mom. I told her I didn't think so, but she should talk to you. I hope I didn't overstep."

He shakes his head. "Nah. If she's asking you questions, you gotta answer something, right?"

"Yeah, I guess. I just don't want to tell her one thing and have you disagree. You're her dad." He twists the end of my braid between his thumb and forefinger. "So, you, umm, understand and agree about not being…open… in front of Riley just yet?"

"I do." I cover his hand and meet his eyes. "But I…I wouldn't mind if we found some time to be alone."

"I've been literally dreaming about you," he whispers, and then his voice drops even quieter. "Sexy dreams. About you."

"You wake up thinking about me?" I ask.

"Every night."

"What do you do about it?" I ask, my eyes conveying my arousal.

"You know what I do about it."

"Maybe I don't. Or maybe I just want to hear you say it."

He closes his eyes, then opens them and stares into me as if willing us to be alone so he can show me instead of telling me. "You want to hear me say that I jerk off thinking about you? That I think about getting you naked and eating you out till you scream my name and being inside you?"

I let out a whimper. "Yeah, Rory, that's exactly what I want to hear." I shake all over, tremble like a leaf. "Because…I touch myself and think about exactly those things, too."

He groans. "Shit. Now I'm gonna think about you touching yourself."

"You're welcome," I say with a smirk.

"I should get her home," he says. "Before I kiss you anyway."

"Okay," I say. "I'll even make it easy on you and walk away first." I turn away, and he grunts.

"At least this way I get to watch you walk away."

I laugh, and put a little extra swish to my hips, just for him. I pause at my door and turn back, wave at them as they back out of my driveway.

I wait till they're gone, and then I go inside, and I wonder what it means that my physical desires are, for the first time in my life, overruling my emotional fears.

Am I being stupid for floating along with whatever my body demands with Rory? Should I be trying to slow us down?

He asked it first, though: what reason do we have to slow down?

I know, intellectually, that at some point I just have to jump off the diving board and back into the dating pool. Meaning, I'm going to have to trust someone, eventually, and just hope that I don't get destroyed again.

I was in a very dark place for a long time after Trace told me he'd fallen out of love with me, or whatever actually happened. Depressed, angry, bitter, and resentful. That's when I found yoga, Peloton, and weightlifting. Getting in touch with my body and losing myself in physical exertion allowed me to get out of my head, away from my broken heart. I may have gone a little overboard, for a while. Riding twice a day, or riding in the morning and then going to the gym to practice deadlifting, snatching, pressing, and squatting. Or riding and yoga. Or sometimes, on a really bad day, all three. Sometimes, it felt better to be so sore I could barely move than have to feel the agony of knowing the man I loved was gone. That he wasn't dead, but our relationship was.

I shut down, emotionally.

I faked it, for the kids. I was there for them. Open and patient and loving—I'm a great teacher, and I love my kids. But as soon as they were gone, the smile vanished, the energy faded, and the facade of a happy Emma Cole crumbled.

At some point, I realized I wasn't faking it anymore. I wasn't happy, but I wasn't miserable anymore. And I didn't need to work out two or three times a day to survive the day. I wasn't thinking about Trace almost at all.

I had moved on.

But I hadn't started living again. I didn't know how to open up to anyone. I'd started to think something inside me was broken.

I'd never love again.

I'd die a celibate old maid with a dusty hoo-ha.

Then I met Rory, and my worldview exploded. The things I'd thought were impossible, the parts of me I'd worried were dead and broken came alive again.

And now they're more alive than ever.

What started as a flicker of attraction for a hot dad from school has morphed into a roaring, burning inferno of unquenchable need—one I really don't know how to deal with.

I just...*want* him. All the time, and in the worst way. I want him alone. I want to climb his body like a tree. I want to...god, I want things that even thinking about make me blush.

I ignore the ache in my core for as long as I can, after they've left. I clean up, tidy the kitchen, vacuum—chores to distract myself.

But I'm thinking about Rory—it's so bad that I find myself vacuuming the same spot on the rug by the couch over and over again. My mind replays our night together.

Ripping each other's clothes off.

Kissing, touching.

His mouth on me. Oh lord, that's something I could get used to—Rory wanting to pleasure me like that. It happened once in a while, in my previous life. But Rory does it as if *he* derives pleasure from it.

I need to stop thinking about Rory. About sex with Rory. About his mouth between my thighs, his tongue driving me to blissful delirium.

I turn on a show, and pretend to watch it. I honestly don't even know what I'm watching. People with British accents making cakes.

My phone chimes. I snort awake, realizing only as I do so that I'd dozed off. My phone reads 11:43 p.m.

Rory: *thank you again for taking care of my girl, today.*

Me: *Of course, it was my pleasure. I really do love that girl.*

Rory: *and that means more to me than I can say.*

A minute, later—Rory: *WYD*

Me: *lol text slang from Rory Kerr? Strange.*

Me: *I'm watching TV. But, not really actually watching it, TBH*

Rory: *then what are you actually doing?*

Me: *Honestly? Trying to distract myself from thinking about you.*

Rory: *I mean, if you want to think about me, I'm okay with it. I'll just be over here with a very vivid mental image of you, naked, in bed, thinking about me and giving yourself an orgasm.*

Never in my wildest dreams or fantasies have I ever considered sexting. Because that's totally what this is.

Me: *you would not be very far from the truth.*

Rory: *what would you say if I suggested you make it the truth?*

Me: *I'd consider it, but only if you do too.*

Rory: *I'm in bed already. Couldn't sleep.*

Me: *Do you sleep naked?*

Rory: *Not usually. Underwear. You?*

Me: *Am I in bed, or do I sleep naked?*

Rory: *Yes*

Me: *Lol. No, I'm on my couch, and I usually wear a T-shirt and underwear to bed. Actually, you saw me in my usual "pajamas" when you stayed the night at my place, that one time.*

Rory: *I got a hell of a hard-on, when you walked out wearing that. You were mostly asleep so I don't think you noticed.*

Me: *Oh, I noticed. It was, um, HARD to miss.*

Rory: *oh*

I'm smiling, laughing. God, he makes me feel good. Bold.

I float into my bedroom and close the door. Above my bed is a ceiling fan with a dimmable light—I flick the fan on to stir the air and make it nice and cool in my room, hardening my nipples inside my bra, as intended. Dim the light.

I'm embarking on another wild, daring first—sending photos of myself to a man. I've never taken a photo of myself in any state of undress, let alone sent it to a man. I've never had reason, or opportunity. But I'm so worked up, so wild with need that I don't even think twice about it before lying down on my bed, still fully clothed in my work outfit—dress slacks and a button-down, mismatched comfy underwear and plain, supportive bra.

I snap a selfie of myself on my bed, fully clothed. Send it without a second of hesitation.

Next, a short video—slowly, teasingly unbuttoning my blouse. Let it fall open. Send.

The next short video shows me undoing my slacks. It's a little awkward, trying to remove your pants one-handed while recording yourself and trying to look sexy doing it. I feel like I managed as well as could be expected.

Now clad in just my mismatched undergarments, I send him a full-body selfie, lying on the bed, hair loose and wild around my shoulders.

Me: **Want more? Reciprocate.**

Moments later, I receive a photo of him in bed. He's covered from the waist down by a blanket. Hand under his head, eyes piercing and dark, his beautiful body hard and muscular.

Next is a video of him with the blanket off, baring him in nothing but a pair of black briefs.

Rory: *your turn*

I sit up, record myself reaching behind my back and unhooking my bra. It sags open, and I remove one arm, switch my phone to the other hand and clutch the bra in my other. Hesitate, with an expression that I hope is sensual. Keep it pressed to my chest while tugging my arm free of the strap. Another moment of hesitation, for effect. And then I drop it, baring myself for him.

My pulse races, slams in my throat and ears.

Send.

Rory: *I'm already shirtless.*

Me: *I mean, it IS your turn. Show me yours, and I'll show you mine.*

A minute or so later, a short video comes through from him. As it starts, I can see that he's tenting his underwear. Straining against the fabric. His thumb hooks into the waistband at his side. He teases for a minute, pulling the elastic away without lowering it, or revealing anything. And then, ohhh lordy, and then he pulls the underwear away and down, exposing his erection. He lifts his hips, the angle tilting as he brings the garment past his butt, and then he kicks them off. The camera pans up to his face, showing his grin, a little goofy, clearly either embarrassed or unsure if he's doing it right.

Me: *I've never done this before.*

Rory: *Thank fuck. Me neither.*

Me: *You're so freaking hot, Rory. I wish I was there. I'd explore you with my mouth again. I liked that. I want to do it again.*

Rory: *I dream of that. I wake up with a hard-on. I fall asleep and as I'm drifting off, I think about it. About you with your mouth around my cock.*

I bite my lower lip hard, but I'm too aroused to stop. I consider how I want to proceed? Fingers? A toy? Maybe a little of both? I fetch my favorite device from the drawer, a Lelo clit stimulator. I set it beside myself and start a recording. Stare up at the camera, picturing Rory above me. Imagine it's him I'm staring at. Remember with tremulous desire the way his mouth felt on my sex. Pan the camera down to capture my fingers stealing between my thighs. Gasp at the touch, swallow hard and quake as I circle my clit. I'm quick to rise, bringing myself to shaking, hip-thrusting spasms within seconds. Then I remove my fingers, biting my lip hard as I stare into the camera.

"Rory," I breathe. Take the vibrator and turn it on, touch it to myself. "I wish this was you. I wish it was your mouth."

I gasp as the vibrations sear through me, sending me to the edge almost immediately. I hit a button, and the vibration pattern changes from a steady buzz to a high-low alternation—*BVVVVVVVVVVvvvvvvBVVVVVVVVVvvvvvv.*

"I...Rory, I want you. I wish it was you." I whimper as the precursor of the orgasm sizzles through my sex, making my belly tense and my thighs clench, my buttocks squeezing to lift me up off the mattress. "I wish it was your cock. I want you. I want you inside me." My mouth is running away from me. "I want your cock inside me. I want your cock in my mouth. I want to taste you as you come. I want to come together. Holy shit— oh god. Oh god—"

I break off as the orgasm swells through me, wordless moans and whimpers and gasps and shrieks rippling one after the other, my hips gyrating, thrusting. As the climax peaks, my mouth locks open and I'm breathless, eyes closed, hips flexed upward and my whole body trembling.

I wonder if I managed to keep the camera trained on me as I came.

The orgasm fades, relinquishing its grip on me. My butt settles back to the bed and my eyes open. I'm panting, sweating.

"Your turn," I murmur.

End recording. Send.

Set the vibrator aside and catch my breath. Take it into the bathroom and wash it, dry it, put it away.

My phone chimes.

His video begins with his fist already around his erection. He stares up at the camera, like I did. His fist moves slowly, at first. Strokes downward. Grips the base in a tight fist, then loosens and glides upward. Again. Still slowly. I watch greedily, remembering viscerally how he had filled my hands. So thick, so long. The veins soft and stuttering under my palms. He strokes himself steadily, his speed increasing gradually. I can almost feel him in my hands again.

Oh god, I'm on fire all over again, watching him and wishing it was my hands on him instead of his own. My fingers go to my sex as I watch, and I bring myself closer and closer to the edge as his speed increases until his fist is a blur. His belly curls in and I can see his thighs bunching as he clenches them. I can imagine his toes pulling back toward his shins. He grunts—I hear his breath huffing through clenched teeth.

"Em, fuck. Wish it was you." His voice is low, a breathy growl. Faster, then. Harder. Fist gripping tightly, jerking himself almost angrily. "Fuck. Gonna come, Em. Picturing you. Your mouth. Wishing it was your sweet mouth on me instead. Ohhhhh…*fuck*, Em. Fuck. Em, god, Emma…"

The blurring speed of his fist on his erection stops abruptly. Squeezes around the head, just the tip protruding above his fist. He jerks, his whole body torquing as he comes with a teeth-clenched grunt. Cum spurts out of him, laying in a thick white stripe over his belly, and then he slowly, tightly strokes downward. Another grunting spurt of seed puddles with the first, striping higher yet, onto his diaphragm. Again and again, fist slowly grinding down and back up, he comes and comes, until there's a pool of seed on his belly. I hear his breathless panting.

I come with him, a hissing whimper escaping my lips.

The camera pans back up to his face. "It was better when it was your mouth." He reaches to the side and comes back with a wad of Kleenex, wipes at the pool on his belly. "Now what, Em?"

Me: *that was hot, Rory. I really enjoyed that. I came again, watching you.*

Rory: *Can I just say I'm surprised, pleasantly*

surprised, but still a little surprised that you wanted to do this with me? I would never have figured you for the sexting type.

Me: *that's because I'm not. At all. I've never so much as flirted via text. Never taken a naked selfie, or even one where I'm partially clothed. Certainly never recorded my-self...doing THAT.*

Rory: *me either, all around. It was hot, though.*

Rory, a moment later: *I can't wait until we can be alone together again. The things I'm going to do to you, Emma Cole...you'll definitely dream about them.*

Me: *You make me want things, Rory. You make me feel bold enough to do things I never imagined I'd ever want to do, much less feel confident enough to actually go through with.*

Rory: *Like what?*

Me: *Like...I don't even know. Pull you into a closet and fuck you. Go out in a dress without panties just so you can do things to me whenever and wherever you feel like it.*

Me: *I can't believe I just sent that to you. But I mean it.*

Rory: *Holy shit, woman.*

Me: *Told you. You do something to me. I don't under-stand it and it scares me. But I'm going with it. I don't know where it's leading us, what it means, what will hap-pen. I just know I'm...I don't know. I can't help it. I can't NOT want you and I can't NOT give in to all the things I want to do with and to you. Two double negatives. Sorry lol but you know what I mean.*

Rory: *Yeah, I know what you mean.*

Rory: *I'm about to fall asleep.*

Me: *Same*

Rory: *Good night. Thank you.*

Me: *Good night to you, too. Thank you for what?*

Rory: *This. Doing this with me. I feel lucky AF to be able to see this side of you.*

Me: *You're sweet. I'll talk to you soon. Okay?*

Rory: *The question is when will I see you?*

Me: *Saturday, at least. Maybe sooner.*

Rory: *Sooner is good. I like sooner. Especially if it means I get to kiss you.*

Me: *Kiss me where?* I add the winking/tongue-out emoji, so the hint is broad and unmistakable.

Rory: *Everywhere you'll let me. For as long as you'll let me.*

Me: *As if I'd stop you.*

Me: *The only reason I'd stop you is so it could be my turn.*

Rory: *Would it be forward of me to buy condoms?*

Me: *I'd be annoyed if you didn't. Maybe even put one in your wallet like when you were a horny teenager.*

Rory: *When I was a horny teenager, I kept them in the glove box of my truck.*

Me: *I guess I'm just feeling…unpredictably horny. I've never felt this way and I've never had this kind of relationship before, so I just don't know how to…anticipate anything.*

Rory: *what kind of relationship is this? Asking for a friend.*

Me: *I don't know. A physical one. An intensely sexual one. Not just physical or sexual, mind you, but…yeah.*

Rory: *correct me if I'm wrong but It feels like we're entering territory that would be better explored in a face to face conversation.*

Me: *Very much so.*

Rory: *I'm going to say good night and actually sign off, then. But…I'll be dreaming of you. Naked.*

I snap one last selfie of me from the waist up, naked in bed, eyes heavy, a satisfied, flirty smile on my face. *You'll be dreaming of me as I am, then. Just like this.*

Rory's selfie back is waist up too, but shows a hint of the V leading down to his manhood.

Me: *Good night, Rory.*

Rory's only response is a sleepy emoji, the one with the Zzz.

I fall asleep thinking about him.

About how the real thing is so much better than sexting. But in the absence of his physical presence when we can't be together, it's as good a substitute as I could ask for.

The only issue is, it doesn't do anything to sate my suddenly ravenous sexual appetite.

The opposite, if anything.

13

I HANG OUT WITH RILEY AT HER HOUSE ON SATURDAY, while Rory meets with Mindy. It's weird being in his house without him, but I do my best to focus on Riley, and not letting my mind wander. She's clearly nervous for the visitation to follow, so I do my best to distract her.

We bake.

I start simple: chocolate chip cookies. We crank up my favorite baking playlist, a mix of 80s dance hits, movie soundtrack hits from the 80s and 90s, some current pop tunes, and some of the requisite early 2000s alt-rock and pop hits. It's a great playlist to crank up and jam out to while making a mess in the kitchen, and make a mess we do.

The cookies go in the oven and we clean up. She's quieter, now, and I gradually turn the music down. She's aimlessly wiping at a spot on the counter, but clearly isn't seeing what she's doing.

"Riley?"

She sighs heavily. "I'm nervous. Maybe even kind of scared."

"About what? I mean, your mother, obviously, but what in particular has you scared?"

A shrug. "I dunno, the whole thing. What if she doesn't like me? What if I don't like her? What if I *do* like her and then she leaves again?" She lets out a shaky breath. "I just really, really wish *you* were my mom."

My heart cracks. "Riley, honey. I love you, no matter what, okay? Your dad and I are...figuring things out. It's complicated adult stuff, and I'm still figuring it out myself, so I can't really say much else. But you and me?" I hug her. "We're golden. I'm not going anywhere."

"Okay." She squeezes me tight, and then backs away. "We'd better finish cleaning up before Daddy gets home. He's weird about the kitchen being clean."

I laugh. "Good to know."

We're a whirlwind of cleaning as the kitchen fills with the scent of chocolate chip cookies baking. We finish getting the kitchen tidied up just as Rory walks through the side door.

"Hi!" I say, my voice bright. "How'd it go?"

His face is tight, unhappy. "Fine, I suppose."

Riley's eyes go wide. "Daddy?"

He slumps into a stool at the island, tossing his keys onto the counter. "Hi, pumpkin." He picks her up onto his lap and hugs her.

"What's wrong?"

He shakes his head. "It's just hard and weird, seeing Mindy after all this time." He tweaks her nose. "Nothing for you to worry about. We should go, soon, though. Your visitation is in twenty minutes."

"Why didn't you have me meet you with her?" I say. "Would have saved you coming back across town."

He shakes his head. "I thought about it. But I guess I wanted some sense of…separation."

"Of?" I prompt.

He looks at me. "Past and…future."

I sigh and come up behind him. Lean against him. "Rory, I appreciate it. But it's not necessary." I lower my voice. "If I'm going to be your future, I also have to be your present."

"Oh, you're a present alright," he murmurs back. "One I'd really like to unwrap right about now."

I laugh. "Later."

He sniffs the air loudly. "I smell something delicious."

Riley is at the oven, watching the timer count down. "We made cookies!"

Rory smiles, a bright and genuine grin. "I do love me some cookies. Don't remember the last time I had homemade chocolate chip cookies."

"They're gonna be delicious!" Riley announces. "And they're done in…" she counts down with the timer. "Five…four…three…two…one!"

I join her at the oven and pull them out, check them. "Yeah, they're done." I set the tray on the counter and slide a spatula under the cookies to loosen them off the parchment paper lining the baking sheet, then slide a few onto a separate plate to cool.

"Where'd you learn to bake?" Rory asks.

"When I was little, my mom loved to bake. It was one of the few things I liked doing inside. Mostly, I was a bit of a tomboy, hunting, hiking, fishing, riding, and roping with Eddy and Dad. But every Saturday, Mom would wake up early and turn on cartoons and brew some coffee and bake. I'd get up with her, and we'd bake. So that's where it started for me."

Rory watches me closely. "There's something else, there, though, huh? I can tell. You don't have to talk about it, if you don't want to."

I shrug. "My family just went through a hard time. My grandma passed away, and that was really hard for Mom. They were super close. So when Grandma Emmaline—who I'm named after—died, Mom just never quite recovered. She wasn't ever the same. And at the same time, Mom was pregnant. Just enough to start showing. It was an unexpected pregnancy since I was already seven and Eddy was ten. But she was excited." I sigh. "She miscarried a month after Grandma Emmaline died, and that just…it was one thing too many for Mom, I think. She just sort of shut down. Stopped baking. Quit the PTO, 4H, all that stuff she was doing. She's a little better now, but she's not who she was when I was little."

"Wow," Rory breathes. "I'm sorry."

I pick up a cookie and put it back down. "Still too hot." A bob of my head. "I mean, it's okay. I kept baking. I'd get up and turn on cartoons and bake. As I got older and moved out, I kept doing it. I don't bake on Saturdays as much these days, but it's still something I love to do. It's therapeutic, fun, and you get a delicious treat at the end."

"So when you go to Colorado for Thanksgiving, will you bake with her?"

I wince. "Not sure. Mom was the glue that kept the family together, emotionally. After everything happened and Mom sort of…retreated into herself, our cohesion as a family suffered. Dad and Eddy spent more and more time together, leaving me out. I'd resent them. I'd try to horn back in with them, and it'd be better for a while. But it wasn't ever like it was when I was little. Tagging along with Dad and Eddy on the farm, finish our chores and go back inside to Mom making something in the kitchen." I sigh, trying to shake off the sadness. "After a while, Dad started to pull inward, too. I think Mom pulled away from him as much as she did the rest of us, and it affected him. He wasn't as nice, or fun, or patient. Chores stopped being something fun to do with Dad and Eddy and started to be something he'd push onto Eddy and me so he could go tinker in the barn by himself. So now, things aren't…we're not estranged. No one's not talking to anyone. It's just…strained. Hard to be around everyone, because we're all aware that there's this big cold space no one ever directly addresses."

"That's rough."

I nod. "Yeah, it's not the greatest."

There's a lot I'm not mentioning, mainly because Riley is listening. Dad had multiple affairs, fairly openly, but Mom didn't care. They stayed together, out of habit more than anything. Mom had her own way of coping, in the form of prescription pills, to which we nearly lost her. She managed to crawl out of that particular hole via therapy and rehab, but it broke what remained of their marriage, and my relationship with her. Eddy never left the farm and resents me for leaving him to take care of the farm and deal with Mom and Dad.

It's a lot. And I don't like to think about it, much less talk about it. There's not much I can do. It's just one of those dysfunctional things, and I've got my own trauma to work through. Going back always leaves me off-kilter and upset and sad for days, so I'm not looking forward to it.

At least this time, I have Rory and Riley to come back to.

"When I come back," I tell Riley, "I'll teach you how to make apple pie."

She grins and nods. "I love apple pie." She glances at Dad. "But Daddy's favorite is key lime pie. Can we make that?"

I wink at her. "That happens to be my favorite, too, so you bet I make a heck of a key lime pie. Maybe we'll make that instead."

There's a lot Rory isn't saying, but they have to go. I put the cookies on a plate and give them each one to go, and there are too-quick, abrupt goodbyes as we leave at the same time.

It's starting to feel weird and unnatural, being apart

from them. Leaving them. The vision of us as a family I had the first time I went over is solidifying.

So, what's holding me back from jumping into that headfirst?

Something is. I'm just not sure what.

The last few days before Thanksgiving break are hectic. There are classroom parties, school celebrations and events, a skit put on by the fourth and fifth graders. I barely have time to see Riley and Rory, and Rory and I only text a few times about surface-y stuff. He's distracted—has been since the visitation. Which worries me.

My phone rings, Wednesday morning—Eddy.

"Hi, Eddy," I say by way of greeting.

"Hey." His voice is gravelly from his pack-a-day habit. "When will you be here?"

"My flight is at noon, out of LaGuardia, landing in Denver at…two thirty your time—I think? You're picking me up?"

He hesitates. "I think so…I'm planning on it."

I laugh. "Ed, what do you mean, you're planning on it? I didn't rent a car. Am I supposed to take a one-hour taxi ride? Who's gonna pay for that? You?"

He huffs. "No, no. Someone will be there to pick you up, I swear."

"What's going on that you can't?"

"I just need to be home. I've got Mom and Dad and Lacey and the kids, and there's a lot going on getting things ready. John, Lucy, Kyle, and Katie are all coming with their kids, plus Uncle Will and Aunt Nan. Nicky, Doug. They're all coming. And I'm the host. It's just gonna be tricky to get away for two hours."

Lacey is his wife of three years—she's twenty-three to his thirty-three. They met when she was just out of high school and only just barely legal, and married the week after her twentieth birthday. No one approved when they started dating, but he didn't care. And honestly, she's good for him, despite the age difference. She grew up on a farm and is content with the life. She had a pair of twins last year, which really makes things crazy in his life, but he seems happier now with her and the twins in his life than he was before.

I huff. "Just...don't send Dad. Last time I rode in the car with him, we almost died when he went the wrong way down a one-way street."

Eddy laughs. "He's only allowed to drive on the farm, these days."

"Is it his eyes? He's not that old."

"Age is more than a number," he says. "He may not be old in years, but...life has just been..." he trails off with a sigh. "Anyway. Someone capable of driving safely will be there to pick you up, I swear."

"If you send Nicky, I swear I'll never talk to you again," I say with a laugh.

Eddy chuckles. "Yeah, I'm gonna send Nicky...on his Hayabusa."

"His what?"

"He bought a crotch-rocket, like the fastest one on

the market. He's insane and going to kill himself on that thing, so no, I will not be sending Nicky. Just relax."

"Just relax," I say with a groan. "Yeah, okay. Now I'm totally chill, because you said that."

"You know what I mean." He hesitates. "I gotta go. Looking forward to seeing you, Em."

"Yeah, you too."

I hang up, and go back to finishing the pumpkin pie I'm making for Rory and Riley. I really wish I had more time to spend with them, today. I honestly wish I didn't have to go at all. I mean, I know I need to see my family. I love them, I do. Even Lacey is growing on me, kind of.

But I just want...

Ugh.

Something I can't even think about, right now. I have to finish this pie, take it to their house, and then head to the airport. Not going isn't an option.

Their front door is open, and I can see them through the storm door as I stand on the front porch, about to ring the doorbell. They're in the kitchen, and it appears they're working on mashed potatoes.

I knock on the storm door instead of ringing the bell, and Rory just looks up and waves me in. I kick off my boots—knee-high red rubber Hunter boots with thick wool boot socks, because you don't wear cute leather ankle booties to a working farm.

There's a fire going in the fireplace, *Brave* playing on the TV. There are mugs of tea on the counter, half drank and forgotten. A bag of potatoes on the floor, peels all over the sink. It looks like Rory got impatient with the mashing and smashed them a little too hard—he has mashed potato all over his shirt and hands, and Riley is clearly holding in laughter while Rory stubbornly continues trying to mash them with a regular fork.

I set the pie on the counter. "Rory, what...um. What are you doing?"

He looks me, hands over the stock pot, covered in clumps of potato. "Making mashed potatoes."

I bite my lip. "Why are you using a fork?"

He blinks at me. "What am I supposed to use?"

I saw a masher in the drawer on Saturday when I was looking for measuring spoons. I retrieve it from the drawer and hand it to him. "This."

He holds the utensil in his messy hand, staring at it. Blinks a few times. Then uses it to mash, working slowly.

"Goddammit," he mumbles under his breath. "This is way easier."

I can't keep a snort of laughter from escaping. "If you need to loosen a bolt, what are you going to use?"

He eyes me. "A ratchet or a wrench."

"Not a pair of needle-nose pliers?"

A frown. "Of course not."

"Why?"

He huffs, following the connection I'm making. "Because it's not the right tool," he intones, with a big dose of *yeah yeah I get it* attitude.

"Cooking is just like working on cars, Rory. You need the right tool for the job." I take the masher from him and nudge him away with a hip, pushing up the sleeves of my sweater. "Go wash up."

I continue the job of mashing the potatoes, which he did at least boil enough that they mash easily. He washes and changes his shirt while I finish the potatoes, referring to the recipe he has pulled up on his phone, which he has propped up on the cookbook stand, in front of a well-worn copy of *The Joy of Cooking*.

As I'm reading the recipe, a message dings, appearing as a banner across the top of his screen.

Mindy: *it was really nice seeing you last weekend. Maybe we could do it again this weekend? For drinks instead of coffee?*

Shit, shit, shit.

I was not meant to see that message.

My heart squeezes. Maybe she's just fishing. Maybe he'd shut it down. But...other ideas float through my head, too. What if she's changed and he has a shot at being a family with her? What if that's what he wants, deep down? What if I'm just a bit of fun while he figures out what's going on with Mindy? What if I'm just a placeholder?

He comes back with a clean T-shirt on, and sees that I've added the rest of the ingredients for his cheesy garlic mashed potatoes. "Thank you, Emma."

I nod. What do I do? Do I address it?

Riley is stirring the ingredients in, and I glance at her. "Keep stirring, kiddo. Make sure you scoop up from the bottom and mix it all down."

"Okay, I got it."

I hesitate, unsure where to go from here, what to do or say.

Rory frowns, reading me easily. "What is it?"

"Screw it," I grumble. "I was looking at your phone for the recipe. You got a message." I feel the fear, worry, and doubt bubbling up, and hope he's not about to break my heart. "I didn't mean to read it, but it just popped up and I couldn't exactly help it."

He makes a confused face. "Okay. A message? From who?" He grabs his phone even as he asks me the question and pulls up the message. His face tightens, and his eyes go to me. "Oh."

I swallow hard. "I'll be honest, I'm kind of freaking out a little."

He pulls me by the hand. "I want to talk to Emma for a second, okay, Ry? Be right back."

Riley just nods, tongue sticking out the corner of her mouth as she stirs the potatoes.

We go out on the front porch; it's cold, a sharp wind blowing, but Rory doesn't seem to notice. He takes my hands and holds them.

"Whatever worst-case scenario I'm sure you're justifiably imagining, Emma, don't. Okay? We met for coffee like I said. We talked about why she's back, why now. How I have reservations about her seeing Riley. Everything you and I talked about, I just put it all out there."

"And?"

A shrug. "She seems...the same as when she left. I dunno. Downeast old money. Surface. Shallow. Pretty, but…empty. I don't know. I had a hard time remembering what I ever saw in her, other than physical attraction."

"Is that still there?"

He drops his eyes. "She hasn't gotten ugly, if that's what you mean. But I'm not attracted to her."

"It's okay if you are, Rory. You and I aren't…together. Not yet, not really. I don't have a claim on you. I would just like to know the deal so I can adjust."

He shakes his head. "The fact is, she's better looking now than she was when I met her. She's aged well. She's still single from what I can tell. But…I guess a combination of how she treated me, how she just left me and Riley —and, well, honestly, and having you in my life… there's nothing there." He meets my eyes. "Maybe you and I aren't officially together, but you *do* have a claim on me, because I say you do. I put it there. And even if you weren't in the picture, there wouldn't be anything between Mindy and me. It's just not there. She hurt me, abandoned me without so much as a note or a goodbye. Worse, she abandoned her daughter. I can forgive that in the sense of not letting it keep me angry and bitter toward her in my day-to-day life, but I can't forgive it in the sense of letting her back into my life."

My heart swells a little. "The message just made it sound like…"

He nods. "I could sense when we met that she was probably sniffing around to see what's possible. She was…friendly. Flirty. Like nothing had happened, like we'd just amicably broke up and were meeting for coffee to reminisce." A shake of his head. "I promise you, there's nothing there. Is not, will not be. She's fishing, and I'm not biting, okay? I promise. I'm sorry you saw that message."

I breathe a sigh of relief. "You're telling me the truth? Not just what you think I want to hear because you don't want to hurt me?"

"No, it's the truth. I don't even want to see her again. I still don't know what her true motives are, but she did seem genuine about wanting to connect with Riley. She seemed remorseful about how she left, Riley most of all. We didn't talk about us, about her and I. I don't see a point in the conversation, honestly. I've moved on. Maybe she hasn't, maybe she regrets it and was hoping we'd rekindle things. But that's not going to happen."

I push it once more. "If that were to change, Rory, just…tell me. Okay?"

He huffs a laugh. "It won't. I want nothing to do with her. I honestly wish I didn't have to make Riley see her. I'm not convinced it's for the best for her—she doesn't know her and hasn't ever expressed a desire to. She barely even asks about her. We have our life, and it doesn't include her—which was her choice."

"Okay. I didn't mean to pry into your business, Rory."

He shakes his head. "It's your business too." He smiles. "I am grateful that you gave me a chance to explain, though, Em."

"Misunderstandings are cute in romantic comedies," I say, "but in real life, you act like an adult and communicate. You don't jump to conclusions and run off without giving the person a chance to explain. That's just not how life works. That's not how you adult."

"Well, I'm grateful you feel that way. Because I really, really care about you, and I want to keep exploring this thing between us, and I'm sure as hell not going to let Mindy get in the way."

"How she could blow her chance with a man like you is beyond me," I murmur, finally letting myself lean into him, smiling up at him. "What an idiot."

He kisses me, once, quickly, softly; we both glance inside—Riley has quit stirring and is watching *Brave*. "And if I were to blow this chance with you, I'd be an idiot. I really don't intend to let that happen."

"Thank you for explaining." My phone buzzes in my back pocket—a reminder that I have to get to the airport. "I have to go."

He sighs. "Sure you can't stay for a piece of pie?"

"I wish." I pat his chest as I step away from him—it's physically difficult to force myself away from his warmth, from his strong, firm, body. From his deep kind dark eyes. "I have to catch my flight."

"You're back when?"

"Friday afternoon."

"Come over?"

I nod. "I'd love to."

He grins. "And Saturday Riley has another visit. So we'll have an hour to ourselves."

I smirk. "I see where you're going with this, Mr. Kerr."

"Do you, now?"

"I do." I steal one more quick kiss. "And I have some ideas how we could spend that hour."

"So do I," he mutters, his voice husky.

"I'm gonna say goodbye to Riley." I can't go down that flirty path or I'll never leave. "I have to go, Riley," I say. "I have a flight to catch."

She turns to me. "Aww, you're not staying?"

I make a sad face. "I can't. I have to get to Colorado for my family's Thanksgiving."

"I wish you could spend it with us."

I hug her. "So do I, kiddo. But I'll be back Friday, and I'll come over and we can all hang out, okay? So think of some fun stuff for us to do while I'm gone."

She nods, hugs me once more, and then scampers to the couch to watch the queen try to catch a fish, and in so doing become, briefly, like a real bear.

Without looking away from the screen, she says, "I saw you guys kiss."

Rory leans over the back of the couch and looks at her upside down. "You did, huh? And what did you think about it?"

"You don't have to hide it from me. I'm not a little kid who thinks kissing is gross." She looks from Rory to me. "Plus, I want you guys to be together."

Rory taps her nose. "Sometimes, you're too grown up for your own good, you know that?"

He pivots to me, makes sure Riley is watching, and scoops me into his arms, twists me around in a dramatic swoop, dipping me like in a ballroom dance move, and kisses me soundly. Then, still holding in the dip, he glances at Riley. "So you're fine with that?"

She just rolls her eyes. "Don't be a dork, Daddy."

I cackle as he sets me on my feet. "Yeah, Rory. Don't be a dork." I lean close. "But you can totally sweep me off my feet any time."

He walks me to the door. "Oh, I'm working on it." He pinches my chin in his forefinger and thumb, kisses me yet again. "You better go. I'm getting carried away and liable to not let you go. Then you'll miss your flight and at that point you'll just *have* to stay."

I laugh. "And that would be a tragedy in your eyes, I'm sure." I stuff my feet into my boots and step out through the door as he holds it for me. I pause, duck back in and lift up, kiss him, once, quickly but deeply, with tongue. "For the road. Since she's fine with it."

He groans as I finally walk away. "Let me know when you get there safely, okay?"

"Will do."

I only look back at him a few times as I drive away. It's two days. I've gone way longer than that without seeing them. But this seems different, somehow. Especially since Riley saw us kiss and gave us her blessing.

I'm leaving Rory's hot kisses and deep conversation, and Riley's open affection and honest love…and I'm trading it, temporarily, for strained relationships with people I see a couple times a year.

14

THE FOUR-AND-A-HALF-HOUR FLIGHT IS BORING—which I suppose is good; you really don't want an eventful flight. I watch a rom-com, and part of another. The landing is smooth, and I exit the plane with the crowd.

Anxiety is surging through me. Going home always puts me on edge, but today, for some reason, it's worse.

Not knowing who's picking me up, maybe?

Something more.

Being away from Riley and Rory? I mean, we're not even in an official relationship yet, so while I miss them, I don't think that's the source of my anxiety either.

I just have one carry-on duffel bag, so I make my way through the concourse, crowded with holiday travelers. As I reach the domestic arrivals pick-up line, I text my brother; I'd messaged him from the plane when we were about an hour from landing to let him know we were on schedule.

I'm at the exit. You here?

His response is swift and curt: *red F-250 with a lift and diesel kit.*

Not his truck, then. His pride and joy is a 1955 Ford F-100 he restored himself, a frame-off restoration that took him two years of working on it nights and weekends. I don't know who drives a lifted F-250.

My anxiety is at an all-time high as I wait at the curb, scanning for a truck matching Eddy's description—my lungs won't open all the way, my stomach is in knots, and my thoughts are a scattered, chaotic mess.

I hear it before I see it—the low, rumbling snarl of a custom diesel exhaust on a powerful truck. There it is—a ten-year-old F-250 with at least a six-inch suspension lift, massive, knobby mud tires, an underbody exhaust pipe, chrome bull bar, and LED light bars on the roof and in the grille.

My first thought is whoever is driving this massive truck is compensating for something. But my mind then flags the thoughts as judgmental and not necessarily true.

The sunlight is reflecting off the windshield as he pulls up, so I can't see who's driving. But whoever it is clearly knows me, because he pulls right up beside me.

There's a step, but even with the step, I'm going to have to heave myself up and in. I catch a glimpse of a tan canvas coat and a flash of blond hair and a ball cap. But it's too quick to see who it is—he jumps down from the driver's seat as I open the rear passenger door and toss my bag onto the seat.

There's a duffel bag on the floor, black nylon. Open. A pair of well-worn gray camo NOBULL training shoes peek out from the open zipper. A white cutoff Denver Nuggets T-shirt, wadded up.

Something about these items is familiar. Twinges my memory.

It hits me as I hear the voice beside me. "Emma."

His voice hasn't changed—even and smooth and clear, not exactly deep but masculine, and almost musical.

"No." I shake my head and refuse to turn and look at him. "No way. Eddy did *not* send *you*."

"He didn't send me. I volunteered."

I reach back into the truck and grab my bag, turn to walk back into the airport. "No."

His hand catches my arm. "Em, wait. Please."

I close my eyes, inhale deeply, slowly, and turn to look at my ex-husband. "What are you doing here, Trace?"

"Picking you up from the airport."

I roll my eyes. "No shit, Sherlock. But *why*?"

"I stopped over to say hey to everyone. Eddy was talking about how he needed to go get you, but he had too much to do. And I've been wanting to see you for a while now, so I volunteered." He laughs. "I'm nervous as hell, you know that?"

He's more handsome than ever. Medium height, lean, trim. His blond hair is expensively cut and showcases his perfect features. Blue eyes, like lightning. Straight white even teeth as he grins, that adorable lopsided grin.

The imperfection of his scar only makes him more rugged—it jags across his forehead on the left side, into his eyebrow and up into his hairline. A reminder. A bucket of cold water on my immediate, visceral reaction to seeing him so unexpectedly.

I back away from him. "I'll take a cab. Or an Uber."

"It'll cost a damn fortune, for one thing." He gestures at the line of cars. "But also, you're not getting one. Not any time soon."

I huff. "Dammit, Eddy."

"Aw hell, don't blame him. He had the twins causing a ruckus, your dad is out in the barn as always, your mom is making a hell of a mess baking, Lacey has morning sickness that lasts all day, and all the rest of your family were all showing up as I got there. He couldn't have left."

I shake my head. "It sounds like you know more about what's going on with my family than I do."

He shrugs. "Mom got sick, so I moved back home. They sold off most of the land, so they only got about fifty acres now. Ain't much to do but throw some hay to the horses in the morning, and Eddy is fairly drowning, trying to keep your dad's old place running, so I been helping him out. We're good friends now, ol' Ed and me."

"When did you develop the good ol' boy twang?" I ask. "You live in Colorado."

"Well, I lived in Atlanta for a few years, till I moved back up here, so I came by it honestly."

"Atlanta, huh?"

His expression darkens. "Yeah, had some stuff there that didn't pan out."

I scan the pick-up line—we're holding up traffic, and it's clear he's not wrong about hiring a ride: that's not happening. "Fine," I huff. "But whatever it is you think we have to talk about, we don't."

He eyes me, his expression inscrutable. "Just get in. I'll behave."

I toss my bag back in and climb up—it's a *long* way up. I get the distinct impression that if he and I were together, he'd use every chance he got to "help" me up into the cab. Thankfully, he doesn't try that. He's up and in at the same time as me. The interior smells like air freshener and sweaty gym socks and old leather; there's a floppy, ancient baseball glove on the dash, with a baseball stuffed into the pocket.

He sees me eying the glove. "I play on a pickup team in Denver."

He always did love baseball. He was all-state varsity in high school, and got a partial athletic scholarship to CSU.

"Nice truck," I say. "I wouldn't have taken you for the jacked-up pickup type, though, I have to admit."

His fist tightens on the wheel. He doesn't look at me. "I don't remember what I drove when we were together."

I frown. How could he not remember? "You had a 2005 Mustang Cobra Saleen. Sometimes, I wondered if you were more in love with that car than you were me."

His eyes narrow. "I, um, have developed some… gaps in my memory. Weird, specific things. I guess with head injuries, you just never know what will happen. It started about two years ago. I was going to call my parents, but I'd gotten a new phone, and somehow, not all my numbers transferred. Their home phone number has been the same for fifty fuckin' years, and I shoulda been able to recite it backwards in my sleep. I couldn't remember it. I don't remember the Mustang. I don't remember the accident. I know your birthday, I know the anniversary of our first date, I know the anniversary of the day I proposed to you, our wedding anniversary. But I couldn't tell you the names of anyone on my high school baseball team."

"Those guys were your brothers. Your best friends. We spent more time with them than we did alone. Jase, Mickey, Tom, Robbie, Duffy, Mack, and Zack."

He sighs, a long, low hiss. "Yeah. Sucks."

"You developed memory issues that long after the accident?"

"Yeah."

"Strange."

Silence. A long, long stretch of awkward, tense silence. Ten minutes? Fifteen?

He's doing the thing that tells me he's chewing on what to say—that hasn't changed: he leans against the door, elbow on the armrest, chewing on his thumbnail with a vacant stare, driving with his right hand.

"Just say it, Trace."

He frowns at me. "Huh?"

"You're doing the thing."

"What thing?"

I gesture at him. "That thing. Whenever you're thinking hard about something you want to say to me, or…I guess probably to anyone—you do what you're doing. Chewing on your thumbnail, staring into space."

"I do that?"

"Always have, since the day you got your license."

"And you know this about me?"

I laugh. "Trace, I was your wife. We grew up together. I've known you literally since the day you were born. I know these things—assuming they didn't change."

"Like?"

"Again, assuming they didn't change since we divorced…you hate tomatoes but you never ask for no tomatoes on your burger because you don't want to be difficult, because your mom is the archetype for a Karen. You brush your teeth in the shower to save time. You always put your left sock on first, but your right shoe first. You drink your coffee black with three packets of Splenda." I gesture at his mitt. "That mitt was your dad's, which your grandfather got as a gift. It's signed by…god, I don't remember who. Someone, a baseball player from the fifties, not someone super famous. You know you should put in a display case, but you don't because every time you try to wear a different mitt, it just feels wrong and uncomfortable, and you're superstitious about it."

He's staring at me like I'm an alien. "Freaky."

I shake my head. "Why? Why is that freaky?"

"I feel like I barely know you. I mean, I know these intellectual things about you, those kinds of facts, but I can't remember the emotions I felt for you."

"So why are you here?"

He rolls a shoulder. "Hard to explain."

"Try."

"You won't like it."

"I don't like anything about this. I feel ambushed."

"I didn't mean to ambush you, Em."

"Doesn't change how I feel."

He sighs. "I guess I know stuff about you like that too. I know you always floss twice a day, but you're bad about remembering to brush your teeth at night, especially if you're tired. I know you like your coffee so black and so strong it could take the paint off the side of a barn from fifty feet. You don't like fictional TV shows. You prefer reality and documentaries, but you always watch the latest Disney movies so you can talk about them with your students, and I think you secretly like them yourself. You rarely wear matching bra and underwear, because I think you think it means something sexual, like if you wear a matching set, you're planning on something happening." A pause. "I remember the way you sound when you come."

"Trace!" I swivel away from him to the far corner of the cab. "Not okay. Not fucking okay *at all.*"

We're at a red light a few miles from the farm. I unlock the door and wrench it open. "I'll walk. I know the way from here."

He jams the shifter into park and grabs my hand. "Em, wait. I'm sorry. I'm sorry. It's cold and you're wearing a sweater. You'll freeze your ass off. And it's always farther than you think from here, right? We tried walking, once."

I sigh. He's right; I get back in, buckle, and he

continues driving as the light turns green. "You can't talk like that." I feel bitterness and anger bubbling up. "You gave that up, remember?"

He slams the steering wheel with his fist. "I didn't want to, Em! You think I wanted to get in that accident? You think I wanted to forget that I love you? You think… you think I *want* to forget my best friends and all this shit from my childhood? I wish I could forget you the rest of the way, but I can't!"

"Why did you come get me, Trace? I know you well enough to know it wasn't to be neighborly to Ed."

"I miss you." He says it quietly. "I may not remember the feeling of being in love with you the way it was before, but…in the years since the accident, I've missed you every day. I remember all this stuff about you and I miss you. But I know you're angry, and you have every right to be. I just…I wish I could explain it. I want to be in love with you again. And I think if I could spend time with you, I'd get there again."

I choke on something like a half laugh, half sob. "Goddamn you, Trace."

"What?"

"What do you mean, what? You know how badly I wished to hear you say those words for freaking *years*? I'd wake up in the middle of the night having dreamed you showed up at my door and said that to me."

"I'm saying it now."

"Too late, Trace."

"Why?"

"Because I'm in love with someone else." I shake my head, my breathing trembly. "Someone back home."

"Home?" He gestures at the dirt road leading to our farm, a stretch of dirt so familiar I could draw it in my sleep—if I could draw well, that is. "This is home."

"It's not, though. Not anymore." I'm realizing this as I say it. "This *was* home. Westport is home, now. Rory is home."

"Rory."

I nod. "The man I'm in love with."

"If you're in love with him, why isn't he here with you?"

"We're not at the stage of our relationship where I would bring him here. I may never bring him here. Hell, I'm not sure *I* even want to be here."

He winces. "That hurts a weird amount."

"It's not even really about *you*, Trace. Most of my memories of you here are good. It's about my family. We're all messed up and it just drags me down. I'm just now learning how to be happy. For the first time since your accident, I'm actually, really okay. More than okay, I'm *happy*." I laugh bitterly. "And then you show up."

"Why does that mess up your happiness?"

I don't want to say it. "Because…" I grit my teeth—it hurts to admit. "Because I don't think I've ever really gotten over you. I'm just now realizing I've never really healed. I just ignored the pain."

"Meaning…you still have feelings for me."

"I didn't realize it until I saw you back at the airport, but yes." I hold up my hand to forestall him. "But they're old, rotting feelings. I don't know how else to put it. Like a tree that looks healthy on the outside but is rotting on the inside. Seeing you, being in the car with you, talking about all this? I don't like it. I don't want it. I don't want to be here in Colorado, I don't want to be in this truck with you, I don't want to be talking to you, I don't want to think about us or the accident or anything. I want to be back in Westport, in the kitchen with Rory and Riley, baking pies and listening to music and watching football."

"You hate football."

"Yeah, it's stupid and ridiculous and it makes no sense. What I like is sitting on the couch with a man who makes me feel good about myself. Who I enjoy being around. Who appreciates me and wants to do things for me, just to make me happy."

He frowns. "The memories I have of us, we're happy."

"I know. I thought so too. But being with Rory makes me realize I just didn't know anything but you and how we were. You didn't put me first. Working out and school and baseball came first. You'd wash and vacuum your car on Saturday mornings instead of staying in bed with me. I just tagged along with you and your buddies all throughout high school, just like I spent my entire childhood following Dad and Eddy around. All I knew was following around some guy, so I followed you around." It's all coming out, the things that have been percolating in me, deep down, for years, and then coming to a boil the closer I've gotten with Rory. "You didn't *pleasure* me, Trace. If you want to talk about sex. It felt good being with you, because I loved you. But you didn't seek my pleasure for the sake of watching me feel good. You sought *your* pleasure in me. If I came, great. Nice. But if I didn't, I don't think you noticed. I'd make sounds because it *did* feel good with you, but that's not the same as reaching orgasm. Which I'm just now starting to realize, now that I'm with someone who desires my pleasure and knows how to give it."

"Damn, Em."

"I'm not done." I stare straight ahead as we turn onto the gravel driveway leading to my parents' home. "You didn't do things for me. You didn't make me feel safe. You were *familiar*. You were what I knew. We grew up together and our relationship just…*happened*. I didn't choose it and neither did you. It was just…the way it was. And I was too young and sheltered and naive and inexperienced to know any better." I hate the tear that leaks out. "Nonetheless, I loved you. I really truly did. I saw our lives unfolding. I saw us with a house and a yard and a golden retriever and a couple kids. I saw it all and I wanted it. Then the accident happened and I stuck by you and supported you and kept loving you and kept trying, even when it was clear something was off. That you weren't the same. I kept trying. But it wasn't enough."

I pause, sighing, thinking—we're in front of the house but I don't get out yet; I have more to say.

"I know you didn't do it on purpose, Trace. I know it was out of your control. You didn't betray me. But I'm still angry. You were taken away from me and that really fucked me up. I don't think I ever really realized *how* fucked up I am because of it until I met Rory and started developing feelings for him. I don't trust the feelings. I trust *him*, but I don't trust…I dont know. Life, I guess. I don't trust that if I let myself fall all the way for him and have a real emotional relationship with him that it won't be taken away like you were. Because I'm *fucked up*. I don't blame you, Trace. I really don't. There's nothing to apologize for or forgive, because you didn't do anything wrong. Our relationship not being right was simply because we were kids who didn't know any better. Loving someone is something you have to learn how to do. It doesn't come naturally. You learn by mistakes. By realizing you didn't do it right the last time around and so now you're gonna do better."

I go quiet again for a moment, and Trace says nothing.

"This time, I'm going to be clear about what I want. I'm going to speak up. I'm not going to just tag along. I'm going to be a priority. I've deprived myself of emotional and physical fulfillment for so long, out of fear. Not anymore. I know there's no guarantees in life. Something may happen. But I'd rather have happiness with Rory for as long as it lasts than be alone anymore. Because I *hate* being alone. He makes me feel good. He makes me want things—I'm not going to say what because it's none of your business." I look at him, now. "So, in a way, I guess I'm glad you're here, that you picked me up. Because seeing you like this brought a lot of stuff into clarity for me."

"Glad I could help?" This obviously had not gone at all the way he'd hoped it would.

I realize I don't have anything more to say. "I'm going in, now, Trace. Thank you for picking me up, I do actually appreciate it, unexpected though it was."

I slid down out of the cab, but his voice catches me before I close the door. "Em? Wait."

I wait, looking at him.

"I'm sorry."

I try to smile with something that resembles kindness. "There's nothing for you to be sorry for, Trace. I said that before, and I meant it. I'm not mad at you. I never was. My subconscious may have translated the pain of what happened into feeling like I was abandoned, but I recognize intellectually that you didn't. I'm just fucked up from what happened in there," I say, gesturing at the house I grew up in. "So you don't need to apologize. And I'm sorry if this causes you hurt, but I really am over you, for good. Whether I'm with Rory or anyone else or not—you and I are over, and I've moved on, and I'm realizing it's better this way, that there's no going back." I laugh. "You just have shitty timing, honestly. If you'd come to me with this six months ago, maybe even less, you may have had a different result."

He sighs. "Just my luck."

"I don't really know what else to say to you, Trace. Except goodbye, and good luck in your life. I really do hope you find your own happiness."

"And I hope you do, too. If you already have, then I hope it lasts."

"Thanks." I wave and turn away, close the door, retrieve my bag from the back seat.

He pulls around the circle drive and rumbles away, leaving me standing in the cold of a late November Colorado morning.

I know I have to go in.

I can't just turn around and go back home. I want to share with Rory the revelations I've just had, talking to Trace.

But I'm here.

My family is expecting me.

But my mind is not here. It's back in Westport. The house with the yard, the dog, the kids. It's there, in Connecticut, with Rory and Riley. I let my heart bloom open a little, let my hopes explore beyond the confines of old wounds.

What do I want? Whether it will happen, regardless of the risk, what do I really want?

Rory.

Riley, calling me Mom.

Coming home with Riley, making dinner. Rory coming in dirty and greasy and sweaty, kissing me as I pretend to be grossed out, when in reality the smell and sight of him like that drives me wild and makes me so horny I could jump him right there in the kitchen, if we're alone.

"Emma?" I hear my mom's voice from the front door.

The house hasn't changed: it's a two-story farmhouse in the style traditional to farmhouses built around the 40s and 50s, with a deep wraparound porch, and a root cellar entrance on the side. Detached carport on the right, with the big two-level gambrel barn a hundred yards behind the house. The barn's paint is faded until you almost wouldn't know what color it used to be. You can see daylight between the boards in places. The ramp to the upper level is on the right side, where Dad keeps whatever his latest car project is, and all his tools. Underneath, in the lower level, is the old tractor, a John Deere that was old when Dad was a kid. To the left of the gambrel barn is the newer pole barn, long and low and deep blue with a green metal roof, built when Eddy and I were little. Not sure what they use it for anymore. Between the gambrel and pole barns, set back a ways farther, is an old four-stall stable that predates even the gambrel barn and the house. Beyond the barns, the fields.

Keep walking from the house past the barns and over the fields, you'll come to Trace's family's spread. It'd take you almost ten minutes to drive to their house from ours because of the way the roads are laid out, but it's less than five minutes of walking, if you're quick on your feet. I can't see it from here, if it's even still there anymore, but right on the twenty-yard-wide strip of grass and shrubs that marks the property line is a giant old oak, easily two hundred years old if not more, with branches the size of a torso hanging low to the ground. Trace and I would meet in that tree and talk, escape our families and our chores. Later, we'd make out in it. Once, memorably, Trace brought a blanket and a plastic shopping bag full of bologna sandwiches and stolen beer, and we had a picnic under it. That was when we slept together for the first time, actually.

"Emma?"

I shake myself. "Mom, hi."

"You've been standing there staring off into space for almost ten minutes, dear. I said your name twice. Are you all right?" She's lost weight—decades of depression and inactivity and reclusiveness packed on the pounds, until I was becoming worried for her health.

Somehow, at some point since I last saw her, she's made some kind of changes for the better.

"Yeah, I'm okay. Just thinking." I head up the steps—they're soft and unstable. I embrace Mom. "Hey. How are you?"

She hugs me back—she's wearing a thick gray cardigan and fluffy red fleece pants. "Oh you know, I'm doing. Lotta people in there, you know how it is this time of year."

Her hair is steel gray and long and bound back in a neat ponytail—this too is a change; she's always had it in a messy, greasy bun, whereas now it's washed and brushed and neat.

"Loud, chaotic, hot, and awkward."

She snorts. "Exactly. Aren't you glad you came back?"

I don't know how to respond. Mom just huffs a laugh, and pats me on the back. "I know, kiddo. I know. Come on in, I'll pour you some of Uncle Will's hard cider."

"He's still making that stuff?" I ask, following Mom inside.

She cackles. "Still making it? He bought more'n a hundred acres of apple trees so he could make cider full-time. He's got a real-deal cider mill, now. He retired from the force and everything."

Uncle Will is a cop in Denver—or was, I suppose; he

joined the force the second he was old enough, and never looked back. Most of my life, he made small batches of hard cider in his barn, from a handful of trees in his five-acre backyard. It was famous in our family, and it was always a big deal if he gifted you some. But I'd never thought he'd retire from the force to make cider full-time.

"Wow. Uncle Will's a cider baron, huh?"

His big booming voice calls out from the kitchen. "Cider Baron! I like that." He comes out from the kitchen, carrying a clear growler of dark brown cider in one hand and a red solo cup in the other. "Emmy-boo! Missed the hell outta you, sweet thing. Been too damn long. When you movin' back, huh?"

That's Uncle Will in a nutshell—big, loud, sometimes a little tactless, but well-meaning and a good man. Couldn't be more different from his older brother, my dad—who's the opposite in every way except size. Dad is just as big and midwestern tough as Will, but where Will stands tall with his shoulders back and a grin on his face, Dad curls his shoulders in, as if hunched against a blow from the universe he's sure is coming any moment. He's taciturn, and sometimes just downright unpleasant.

Especially after Grandma died and Mom miscarried, I often wished Uncle Will was my dad. I felt guilty about it, but it crossed my mind on a regular basis.

Uncle Will catches me up in a bear hug, lifting me clear off the ground and shaking me like a rag doll. "Good to clap eyes on you, Emmy. How was your flight in?"

I stretch my ribs as he sets me down. "Oh, it was fine. The ride in was...interesting, though."

Mom and Will exchange glances.

"I told Eddy it wasn't a good idea," Mom said. "But you know how your brother is."

I huff. "Yeah, I do. I had a feeling he'd send someone else, but I wasn't expecting Trace."

Will lifts the growler. "I'd have come for you myself, but I've been into the cider since early."

I cackle. "Starting Thanksgiving off right, huh?"

"Yeah, well." He shrugs. "Quality control, my dear. Making sure I'm selling a good product."

I sniff. "Mom told me you're making cider full-time. What brought that on, cider baron?"

He shrugs. "Well, it was time." He sighs, sips cider. "I worked homicide in the city for thirty years. Took a toll on me. I tracked down a suspect and he took a pot-shot at me. Missed me by a whisker, and right there and then, I knew I was done. Too old to be getting shot at. I been making this cider for family and friends, and I enjoy doing it, so I figured, why not take a gamble. So I bought an orchard and a cider mill, and now I'm enjoying every second of life."

"How does Aunt Nan feel about it?" I ask.

The second the words are out of my mouth, I realize I've stepped in something smelly.

Uncle Will's eyes tighten. "Well, she ain't in a position to care. We got divorced just after Christmas."

I frown. "You guys were married longer than I've been alive. What happened?"

He waves, almost spilling cider. "Hard to explain, sweet thing. Was a long time brewing, I guess. Decades of little things that got swept under the rug, until it was a big ball of little things the size of a mountain. We just woke up one morning, looked at each other, and knew. Wasn't any fighting about it. Wasn't fun, and Nicky's still angry about it, but it wasn't some knockdown drag-out court brawl. She took the RV and a chunk of our savings and lives in Florida most of the year, and I got the house. Sold it, kept the truck, and bought the orchard and the mill. The orchard has a little shotgun shack that's perfect for just me. I spend most of my time here, though, putzing around with your dad and getting in your old mom's way." He bumps her with his hip.

That little gesture and the way he looks at her—it's quick, imperceptible. But it's a pebble in my shoe. Irks me, makes the back of my brain spin in sideways wobbles.

They're sleeping together. With this suspicion filtering my perception, I watch them as the day progresses.

Dad and Eddy are out in the back forty fixing fence and stay out most of the day—it's an all-day-every-day-for-a-week job, trolling the perimeter with the Gator, making sure the electric wire is intact all the way around and the posts are solid. We've even got some board-and-post sections along the road, for appearances purposes, and those have to be buttoned up and repainted.

Lacey is five months pregnant, and the twins, just under a year old, are starting to toddle around. Nicky avoids his dad, but we spend a few minutes on the back porch with cups of mulled hard cider, talking. He's not just angry about his parents splitting—he's irate. Confused. He's a grown man with a life of his own, but his parents splitting after thirty-five years has really messed him up.

I watch Mom and Uncle Will, closely but surreptitiously; they're never far from each other. There's nothing overt, so either I'm imagining things, or they're just careful. But now that I'm looking for it, I see signs of a relationship that's more than an in-law. It's emotional and physical. When Will tells a story, he looks to her first for a laugh or a reaction. When Mom brings chips and salsa out, she sets it closest to Will. If they're near each other, they touch, in some small way. A hand to the shoulder, briefly. A nudge of a hip. He leans behind her in the crowded kitchen to grab his cup from a counter, and his hand rests on the small of her back, intimate and familiar.

When they talk directly to each other, their eyes lock for just a little too long.

Mom is smiling.

She's bubbly.

She's...her old self.

This comes with very mixed feelings. It's good see Mom doing so much better, but the fact that I suspect it's because she's in a relationship with my uncle? Complicated.

I've been here for hours and I haven't seen Dad or Eddy, yet.

So I pour some mulled cider in Dad's favorite twenty-five-year-old green Stanley thermos, stuff my boots onto my feet, and don Mom's thick flannel-lined black Carhartt jacket with my hat and mittens.

I glance at Uncle Will as I pause at the back door. "There any horses I can ride out to see them?"

He nods. "Sure thing, sweet pea. Your mom's been riding a bit again, so we got her a nice dead broke mare. Name's Cupcake. I guess you know where all the tack is."

"Sure do." I laugh. "Cupcake, huh?"

He chuckles. "We didn't name her. She's a damn good horse. About ten or so, and she's got the best under-saddle manners of any horse I ever rode. I've shot rifles off her back and she don't spook."

"Thanks."

"They'll be on the east fence by now. Had some cattle escape yesterday, which is why they're doing this now."

"You usually help, don't you?"

He nods, holds up his right hand, flexes it. "Developed a pretty wicked case of arthritis. Part of why I retired. All the paperwork was hell on the old hands. I can barely hold a hammer for more than an hour, these days."

Also, I suspect, it's a good excuse to stay inside with Mom. But I don't say that.

I tromp out to the stable. Walking in is like stepping back in time. This, at least, hasn't changed—the smell of hay and manure is redolent and familiar and very nearly pleasant. It's warm from their breath and body heat. They whicker and stomp. I flick the light on, and the old fluorescents buzz, hum, blink a few times, and then stay on. The floor in here is dirt and covered in decades worth of layers of pine shavings. Four heads poke over the top of the stall doors, eying me with a variety of horsey sounds.

There's a bag of peppermint treats by the door, and I grab a handful, stopping at each stall to greet the occupant. I know three of the four horses: Moses, an old bay quarter horse gelding that's been around almost as long as I have; Mr. Dursley, a paint gelding belonging to Lacey; and TamTam, a seven-year-old Tennessee Walker who belongs to Eddy. Which means the one I don't know is Cupcake—she's a Rocky Mountain with beautiful lines and a glossy chocolate brown coat with a blond mane.

"Hi, Cupcake," I murmur, petting her velvety nose. "How are you, girl?"

She nuzzles me, smelling the peppermint treats. I give her one, and then fetch the rope halter. Not knowing how accurate Uncle Will's assessment is, I cross-tie her in the hallway to saddle her; if I knew her and trusted her, I'd leave her standing free, but being strangers to each other, it's safest to be cautious. She does indeed have wonderful manners, not moving a muscle other than keep her eye on me as I get her saddled and bridled. I walk her out of the stable, shut off the light and close the door. I spend a few more minutes standing with Cupcake, and then walk her around a little, testing her groundwork manners. She moves into a walk with a gentle tug and a word, and stops on a dime with a whoa as I stop. She turns both directions nicely, backs up, stands unmoving with the reins dangling.

I haven't ridden in a while, so I'm being extra careful. With the thermos and some sandwiches in a backpack on my back, I swing up into the saddle, and Cupcake holds her place, dancing a little as I find my balance. I turn her nose east, and click her into a walk, and then an easy trot. I reach the eastern fence line with a couple minutes and click my tongue to get her into a canter. She responds easily, and I find a moment of freedom in the cold air on my face and the horse under me.

I reach Dad and Eddy in a few more minutes of cantering along the fence. They're repairing a place where the fence is down completely, clearly the spot where the cows escaped. Or one of them. Cows are tricky, and like to find weak spots in the fence. Two major mistaken assumptions city folk have about cows: that they're slow and that they're stupid, when they are in fact neither.

Dad and Eddy hear me coming and pause their work. I pull Cupcake to a halt and swing down.

"Hi, hon," Dad says. His voice is rougher than ever, and where Mom has lost weight, he's gained it. "Came to find us, huh?"

I nod. "I'm only in town a couple times a year, and I'm not staying very long this time, so I figured I'd get a ride in and say hi."

Eddy is obviously nervous to see me. "Hey, Em."

I keep hold of the reins and stare him down. "Thanks for the surprise, asshole."

He sighs. "I'm sorry, Emma. He just…wanted to see you, and he was also the only one sober and able to come get you. Took Dad and Uncle Will and I the whole day yesterday to get the cattle back in, and by the time we did, it was dark, so we herded them to the western pasture till we found the break. And just, I just couldn't get away."

"You could have warned me. I'd have caught an Uber."

"And paid a fortune."

"I just don't appreciate being ambushed by my ex-husband, whom I haven't seen in close to four years."

He rubs the bridge of his nose. "I know, I know, I'm sorry."

"It was a dirty trick to pull, Ed."

He hisses. "I *said* I know, and I'm sorry." He eyes me. "Did you talk to him, at least?"

"And what, Ed? You think I'm gonna get back with him and move back here?"

He shrugs. "I mean, none of us would mind. Could use another hand out here. Uncle Will is…"

"Claims he's got arthritis," I say.

Dad harrumphs. "Yeah, I'll bet."

I glance at him. "What's that mean?"

He shrugs. "Nothin'. He does have arthritis. But that ain't why he's not out here."

I don't know how to address my suspicions. "Then what is?"

Dad shakes his head, goes back to the fence. "Nothin' you need to worry about."

"Dad."

He shakes his head again. "Forget it, Em."

I huff. "Fine, whatever."

Ed glances at me. "So to be clear, there's no chance of you and Trace…?"

"None." I tug my hat lower on my ears as an icy blast of wind skirls across the pasture, sharp as a knife. "I am honestly glad I talked to him, though. It was an unpleasant surprise and I'm mad at you for doing it, but in the end, I'm glad. It really put to rest in my mind any curiosity about how I feel. Everything that happened, it was unfortunate and painful, and I had to totally rebuild my life and honestly myself from the ground up. But I'm glad I did. I've got good things going on back home. I've met a man I…I love. He has a daughter, and things are good. Seeing Trace settled my mind and heart. I know he wishes he and I could get back together, but I'm happy, finally."

Ed nods. "Well, then, I did you a favor, huh?"

"You get no credit, Ed. You blindsided me, and it was a dick move."

He arches an eyebrow at me. "Whoa, a swear word from my goody-goody sister Emma. Times have changed."

I roll my eyes. Dad and Eddy swear like sailors, and for some reason it always irked me, so most of my teen years I went out of my way to avoid cursing, until it became somewhat of a habit—certainly not a religious belief.

"I'm heading back," I say. "Don't be out here all day tomorrow, too. I'm leaving first thing Friday morning."

Dad frowns. "Usually you stay the weekend."

"Well, not this time."

"All right." He gestures at the fence. "Once we're

done here, we should be mostly done. Just gotta follow this to the other end, but I think this is the last break."

I nod. "I can confirm it's all good between the stable and here."

"Great. Then we should be back in time for dinner."

I swing into the saddle and push Cupcake into a trot, not heading directly back to the stable. Instead, I ride to the old oak, sit on Cupcake and see if there's anything in my heart as I look at the scene of so much of my relationship with Trace.

Nostalgia, but that's about it.

I ride back, finally, thinking. It was awkward with Eddy—he's friends with Trace, now, and seemed as upset as Trace was that I've shut down any hope of a rekindling. Dad is a thousand miles away, emotionally. He barely looked at me, didn't hug me, and seemed to be just...barely present. And bitter.

There's definitely something going on with Mom and Will, and he knows.

I put Cupcake away, brush her down, put the tack away.

As I'm closing up the stable, my phone buzzes in my back pocket.

It's a text from Rory: *Guess who didn't show up for her Thanksgiving visitation?*

Me: *You're kidding! Did she at least call or text?*

Rory: *No to both. No call, no show. We sat in the parking lot for an hour and a half, waiting. On Thanksgiving.*

Rory: *Sorry for bothering you with this on a holiday when you're with your family.*

Me: *Don't apologize, please. I'm glad you told me. I'm sorry Mindy didn't show. How is Riley taking it?*

Rory: *Honestly, she's not super surprised or upset. I don't think she had very high expectations.*

A pause with the bouncing dots of him typing bloops into a new message.

Rory: *To be totally honest, I have a feeling Riley is glad Mindy didn't show up. I think she really just...prefers you. I don't think she wanted the pressure of trying to figure out how to feel about Mindy. And when it was obvious I wanted nothing to do with her, she gave up. Which is what I figured would happen. Not surprised, and I guess I share how Riley feels. We both just want you around.*

I swallow hard. It takes me a minute to come up with a reply. *I'd rather be there with you guys, trust me.*

Rory: *Selfishly, I miss you. But family is important.*

I don't bother trying to tell him via text how complicated and messy the situation is here. *I'll be back in Westport in a day or two at most. I can't wait to be with you and Riley.*

Rory: *Can't wait, either. Happy Thanksgiving, Emma.*
Me: *Happy Thanksgiving, Rory. Same to Riley.*

He sends a kissing/winking emoji; I send one back and pocket my phone as I trudge through the cold back to the house.

The afternoon is slow and kind of boring. Lots of awkward, stilted conversations with cousins and Lacey, half watching a ball game. We eat a lot of food, drink way too much cider. I'm tipsy by the time Dad and Eddy come back, and I notice there's a very carefully choreographed dance in the house.

Dad and Will can be in the same room, and Mom and Dad, but never the three at the same time. Mom and Dad behave like vaguely cordial strangers. They barely speak, never touch, never sit together or directly address each other.

Eddy is the balance between them. He shuttles from Mom to Dad to Will, acting as a buffer.

It's weird.

Being here was hard enough, with all the memories of my painful, lonely teenage years seething in the walls.

Trace was my only solace, then. The only bright spot. Eddy was constantly trying to placate Dad, to win his affection and attention despite the fact that Dad just wanted to be alone. Mom was a recluse, in her room more often than not.

Now, it's all just…a thick Gordian knot of complicated emotions, made further complicated by the weirdness between my parents and my uncle.

At some point, I find myself thinking *fuck it*, and I decide to just get toasted as the only way to get through the holiday with my sanity intact.

I just want to go home.

15

THURSDAY, THE HOLIDAY, IS FUCKING MISERY.

The house is stuffed to the gills with family and family friends. Trace shows up with his parents. It's hot in the house. There's nowhere to go that's not crowded and loud. It smells like sweat and cooking turkey.

I help Mom, whose new lease on life means she's back in the kitchen and cooking with a vengeance. She's making a billion dishes, with Lacey and her burgeoning belly. I've been replaced. Lacey and Mom have inside jokes, shorthand references, an ease with each other in the kitchen borne from working in here together frequently.

Eventually, I realize I'm unneeded and simply walk out, unnoticed.

All the men are crowded in the living room around

the TV, watching the football game and devouring corn chips and seven-layer dip and a veggie tray and drinking beer and Uncle Will's cider.

Oddly, Will himself is absent.

I find him on the porch, around the side of the house, smoking a cigarette and sipping cider straight from the growler.

I join him, glad for the fresh air and quiet.

"Come to escape the noise and the heat, eh?" he says, offering me the growler.

Well into tipsiness already, I accept. "You do make damn good cider," I comment.

He eyes me. "You don't usually drink your way through these things, Em."

"I know. Everything is different this year. Maybe it's me. I dunno. I just…I want to go back home."

"I wouldn't blame you. It's a weird time, around here."

I take a long swig, feeling the intoxication swirling in me, loosening my tongue. "Can I be a rude, nosey bitch for a second, Uncle Will?"

"Since you ain't ever been any of those things a day in your life, I guess you've earned a moment of it." He taps ash over the railing into the bushes. "What's up?"

"This isn't my question, but since when do you smoke?"

He eyes the glowing cherry contemplatively. "I'd always have one after I closed a case, or after a hard investigation. After I retired, I figured fuck it. I don't smoke as much as Eddy…it's a bad habit but one I admit I enjoy."

He sucks on the filter. "What's your question, sweet pea?"

"How long has it been going? With you and Mom."

He sighs out smoke. "You sussed that out, did you?"

"I suspected, but you just confirmed it."

"It's what you might call an open secret." He twiddles the end of the cigarette. "Been percolating for years. Then your dad went into town for a drink and was openly seen with Margie Conway, and your mom just kinda decided to quit pretending. They sleep in separate rooms, have for years. They're married in name and law only. They won't ever divorce, and we all know that."

"So when did you and Mom start...whatever?"

"It was more of a conversation thing for years, just talk, since Nan and I were...tense, and you know how your parents were. But after your dad went semipublic with his affair with Margie back in January, she and I decided to let it be...something else."

"She's back to her old self," I say.

He nods. "I won't take credit for it, necessarily. It's more that she's just happier. She was a mess for a long time, and your dad just sorta...quit trying to be there for her. Eventually, I stepped in. She needed a friend, and I was it. Now it's...well, we ain't gonna put a label on it. We don't go out in public together. But we make each other happy, and that's enough."

"Why won't they divorce?" I ask.

He shrugs. "She just said it ain't an option. Not my place to push it. I'm content with how things are, complicated and touchy though it is."

"If he's with Margie Conway and you guys are to-gether, why not just…go all the way with it?"

He shrugs again. "A question for your mom, not me."

"Eddy and I are grown. He's got his family. It's not like anyone would move away."

He swigs cider. "It's just better this way."

I huff. "It's dumb."

"It is what it is. Don't see why you got any skin in the game, Em." He eyes me.

It's as close to irritable as Uncle Will gets, and I know I'm pushing my luck.

"I don't, I guess. It's just…obvious. And awkward. And I don't know how to…*be*…around it."

He puts a hand on my shoulder. "You suffered more than anyone, with how things went on. You just…you don't fit here, and never have. I don't think anyone would blame you if you didn't come back as much."

"I'm only here for Thanksgiving and Christmas as it is."

Another shrug. "I'm just saying, we'd all understand if you have a life and a family of your own back East, and don't want to come out here, deal with our bullshit."

I sigh. "I'm not going to cut you guys off."

"Not saying you should."

"But I'm not happy here."

"I can tell. Like I said, do what's best for you. We've got an equilibrium, as weird as it is, and I understand that it might be hard for you."

I take another drink. I've probably had enough,

but…I feel like I'm regressing, being here, emotionally. I'm just…coping, the only way I really know how.

I stay on the porch with Uncle Will for a while longer, chatting about less serious things, until I start to get cold. I head back inside, just in time for the main event of Thanksgiving. Except for Lacey and Eddy's twins, there aren't any young children, so every year Mom and Dad bring in several folding tables and make a U-shape in the living room. The couch is slid against the wall, and the open-plan living room and kitchen become a giant dining room, with people sitting on both sides of the table; the opening of the U faces the kitchen and Mom and Lacey each sit at the top of the uprights nearest the kitchen so they can serve the food.

It's all delicious, and there's laughter and lots of wine and cider and an essentially endless amount of food. I've had enough to drink that I almost enjoy myself. Almost. Except for the fact that Trace ends up sitting next to me, with Eddy on the other, and they have a bafflingly involved conversation across me about something to do with an upgrade to Trace's exhaust system. I bump elbows with Trace several times, and once he elbows me in the boob—which causes a moment of tense awkwardness in which he doesn't quite apologize and I don't quite tell him it's fine; it's more of a stilted exchange of muttered inanities.

I don't drink much normally, so having been drinking all day yesterday and all day today, I'm starting to really feel it. As dinner winds down to dessert and then that finally tapers off to everyone scattering around the house to sit like bloated whales and trying to not fall asleep, I find myself no longer enjoying the buzz, too full and too lonely despite the crowded house, and at odd ends.

Will and Mom are out on the porch, chatting. Dad vanished at some point—probably to see Margie Conway, whom I remember as being one of those women who's always so hyper friendly that you're sure it's hiding a secret layer of viciousness which you can only hope you never see. Everyone else is huddled up in conversations of the type that have essentially been going on for years. Which leaves me by myself, with no one to talk to except Trace and his folks, which, no. I never liked his parents nor they me; we got along okay when I was their daughter-in-law, but it was never a familial relationship. His mom is too much of a Karen, high strung and judgmental and entitled, and his dad is an ultra-macho alpha male with more testosterone than personality and an overly developed sense of competitiveness.

I bundle up in my jacket and hat and boots and bring my phone out to the big gambrel barn. Dad has a hideout here, an easy chair, a space heater, and a humming, rattling, ancient fridge full of beer and Diet Coke. It smells like him, in here—engine oil, gasoline, diesel, hay, and cigarettes. It's familiar and honestly comforting. I curl up in his chair and call Rory.

It rings three times, and then he answers. "Hey, you."

"Hi."

"How's it going, there? Having a good Thanksgiving with your family?"

I sigh. "Honestly, no. Everything is weird, my parents

are separated and seeing other people but still married and living under the same roof, and the person my mother is seeing on the side is my uncle, who was always like a second father to me. I'm drunk and starting to regret it. I'm lonely because I've got nothing in common with anyone here except being born into this family. To make matters worse, instead of picking me up himself from the airport, my stupid asshole brother sent… guess who? My ex-husband."

A silence. "You're kidding."

"I wish I was."

"Um. How was that? Hard?"

"Are you jealous?"

He hesitates. "Should I be?"

"Are you?"

He laughs. "You *are* drunk, aren't you."

"Yes, very. My uncle quit his job as a homicide detective to make hard cider full-time. He brought, like, a whole barrel of it, and I've basically been drinking it since I got here, because it's the only way I can function in this fucked-up dysfunctional family." I huff. "I'm sorry."

"No reason to be sorry. I'm not jealous, Emma. If you were to tell me you're staying there and getting back together with your ex-husband, I'd be so shocked you could knock me over with a feather, and I'd be…honestly, pretty brokenhearted. But jealous? No. You don't sound like it was a pleasant or welcome surprise, and I don't think I have any reason to be jealous."

A pause, and then he continues.

"Also, are we in a place with our relationship where

it's...I dunno, within my rights to be jealous of who you spend time with?" His voice drops lower, goes rougher. This is a direct question the answer to which he's deeply invested.

"Yes," I say. "We are in that place."

"We are?" He sounds a little surprised.

"Yes." I close my eyes and pull the smooth wood lever to lean the easy chair back and put the footrest up. There's even a knitted wool throw blanket across the back, which I drape over my legs. "I want to be, at least, if you do."

"Yeah, of course I do."

"Seeing Trace was...I don't want to say good. But necessary, to a degree that I don't think I was aware of. Full disclosure, he wants me back. He doesn't remember some things, and hasn't, like, gotten back whatever it was he lost regarding our relationship. But he remembers me and us and our relationship. He moved back here, I guess, and wanted to...I don't know. Rekindle things. My brother wanted that to happen, too, since he and Trace are BFFs now. Which is super awkward, because they're here, Trace and his parents I mean. And in the whole hour-long drive in from the airport, talking to him, I just realized that I don't want to be here. I don't want to see him."

"You don't, huh?" It's a guiding phrase, meant to nudge me to keep talking. It works.

"No. I don't. At all. See, for years and years, I was all broken up about him. About losing our relationship. About losing the future I'd had planned out for him and me. And I was looking at our relationship through… whaddya call it? Rose-tinted lenses. I'd been looking back and seeing how we were so happy, so in love, seeing how it was so unfairly ripped away from me. I was a disaster, Rory. Stuck in the past and unable to really move forward."

He blows out a whistling sigh. "Oof, that sounds familiar."

"Yeah?"

"Ohhh yeah. You just described me."

"Well, in talking to Trace and honestly just being around him again after like four years of space, I realized something I'd been missing this whole time."

"And what's that?"

"My relationship with Trace honestly wasn't all that great. It was just the only thing I knew."

"Well goddamn, Emma. You're just pinging all my sore spots, ain'tcha?" he says with a teasing tone of voice, but I can tell I've really hit a nerve.

"Rory, I'm only trying to be honest about myself. I'm not trying to, like, assign any of this to you, or psychoanalyze you or your relationship."

His voice is soft and kind. "You're not, honey. It's just…in telling me the things you're realizing about yourself, you're explaining myself to me. Does that make any sense?"

"Yeah, I get what you mean."

"So, what did you realize wasn't great? About you and Trace, I mean."

"Well, everything. He had his friends and his

life—baseball and the gym, basically. And I just...tagged along. When we hung out, it was with his friend group. My girlfriends were his buddies' girlfriends. I didn't have a life or personality outside of him. We went to Rockies games because he loves baseball. I went to the gym with him at five thirty in the morning because that's when he went, and he got off on teaching me how to lift. We'd meet his team and their girls for breakfast, and if there was a girls' night out, it was with them. It never crossed my mind to wonder if I even *liked* those girls."

I close my eyes and let the past wash over me, let the flow of understanding melt into me, let my desires for the future rise up from deep within.

"That's part of it—our life together was centered around him. Now, to be fair, I didn't really understand this until recently. It was the life I knew and I'd thought I was happy. I never once questioned any of that, when I was in it. But it goes deeper. He did care for me, I can't deny that or try to take that away from him." I pause. "This is...pretty personal and intimate, but I need to get it out, and I'm sorry if it makes you uncomfortable."

"Tell me everything and anything, Em. There's nothing I don't want to know, nothing that's gonna be too much."

I hesitate another moment, even still.

"Our sex life wasn't very good." I laugh. "And again, I didn't realize it, like, as such, until you."

He lets out a little chuckle. "So, that reflects well on me, then, right?"

"Yes, Rory, it does." I fake a stern voice. "But I'm not

talking about you and me right now, so stop fishing for compliments, buster."

"Oh, I see. Very well."

I love that I can tease him and not have to explain it or worry he's not getting it or that I'm going to accidentally offend him. He just gets it. Gets *me*.

"See, I'd thought, for years, after Trace and I divorced, that there was something wrong with me. That my sexuality was broken. I told myself that I'm just picky. That it's difficult for me to connect. That I have to have all these factors in place before I could allow anyone close enough to me to feel comfortable getting naked and having sex and all that. I needed the *emotions*, I needed the *connection*."

"Well, hold on. I thought we had those things."

"We do, but that's not the point."

"Then I'm confused."

I huff. "I'm not explaining myself very well." I pause and rally my thoughts through the swirling cloud of inebriation. "Okay, so it's like this. The only reason I had a connection with Trace was because we grew up together. He was my escape from my family, from my confusion and hurt about Mom and Dad, and about Eddy being more concerned with getting Dad's approval than caring about me. A whole bunch of stuff, really, but basically, just my childhood and teenage years were complicated and painful and Trace was the constant, the one thing that I felt I had for myself that brought me anything like happiness. And he did, genuinely. He was proud that I was *his*. He liked to make sure I dressed up, looked hot and would take me out with his friends. He'd be handsy and turn me on. I felt desired. I felt sexy. I liked that feeling of belonging and being desired. But then the reality of sex with Trace was, looking back, pretty disappointing for me. He was very selfish, as a lover. He'd turn me on so I wanted it, which honestly wasn't hard, but then once he got off, it was pretty much over. Sometimes, he'd do stuff for me. Usually as foreplay, to get me more receptive to what he wanted. Which was, just saying, pretty vanilla. He didn't excite me. I never felt…desperate for him. I never woke up in the middle of the night thinking about him, wanting him. I could go days without needing him or wanting him. He couldn't, but that's different. My pleasure was not his concern. If I felt pleasure from sex with him, it was like oh, nice for me, but that's not really the point."

Rory is quiet. "That's…shitty."

"Yeah, so I'm realizing."

"You deserve better." A huff. "Women deserve better, but I feel like that's honestly a pretty common theme, what you're saying."

"Yeah, I think it is."

"And you know, I think I was guilty of that, to some degree, with Mindy. Since we're sharing super intimately personal stuff. I don't think I was a very good partner to her, sexually. I took what I wanted and I didn't always stop to make sure she was enjoying it as much as I was." A pause, I let it stand, let him decide when to break it. "I think what made the difference was she was pretty outspoken. She didn't let it slide if I was being selfish. This is early on, I should point out. As she became more and more unhappy with our life, we stopped having sex regularly, until the months leading up to her leaving, we never did at all." Another brief pause. "And I really did a lot of thinking, in those months. About us, her and I, about sex, about what I'd do differently if she were to suddenly want me again. It really made me realize, that period when we were still together technically but not actually *together*, what I'd had, and lost. And I vowed, after she left, that if I ever met someone who could..."

He stops. Swallows.

"Don't hedge for me, Rory. Say whatever it is."

"My thinking was, if I ever met someone who could make me forget about Mindy, who could replace her in my heart, that I'd do better next time than I had with Mindy. I'd be a better lover. I'd put her pleasure ahead of my own, because I realized at some point that if I put *her*, meaning my partner, not a specific person but just the *her* that I would be with, hypothetically—if I put her first, her pleasure and enjoyment, I would enjoy the experience more. She'd be more likely to want to make me feel good, because she felt good. She felt wanted. She felt sexy. She felt like she was the priority. By putting her first, I'd ensure my own needs were met. That was my thinking." A laugh. "Of course, the reality was, I was too scared of being hurt again to be willing to risk letting anyone close."

"Which, if you're anything like me," I say, "might make you kind of wonder what it is about me, about us, that was so different? Because I know for me, my physical attraction to you almost outpaced my emotional connection. Which for me is very, very confusing."

Rory clears his throat. "Honest truth?"

"Always."

"It was a conflict, for me. I was more attracted to you physically than anything, at first. Mainly because I was refusing to let myself look at you as someone I could have an emotional connection with. I was too scared of that to let it happen. And honestly, that never changed. It just happened anyway. So being attracted to you, that was something I couldn't deny and honestly didn't try to. I just…I didn't know what to do with it. Because I'm not the kind of guy to casually hook up, and I could tell you were either not that type of girl or not in that place. But I wanted you. But I didn't know what to do with it."

I laugh. "Thank god you said that, because same. Which was even weirder for me than anything else. I've never had that. I had the lifelong friendship with Trace that sort of naturally and almost inevitably turned into a romantic relationship, and the sexual nature of it was just an extension of the romance, of discovering all that together." I think back. "I've been attracted to other men, since Trace. But I was never able to get past my emotional hang-ups long enough to do anything about it. And then I met you. And I thought at first it was just a crush, just, oh he's a hot dad in the school, but nothing will come of it. And then Riley and I became friends and you and I started seeing each other more frequently and the more frequently I saw you and was around you, the clearer it became that I wasn't just attracted to you, that

I *wanted* you. And I wanted you in a way and to a degree that it was, like, short-circuiting my own supposed emotional hang-ups.

"Which made me feel weird. Like, I don't know how to have a physical relationship without the emotions. Or do I? Do I even know how to have an emotional relationship? Do I know anything about myself? About sex? About…relationships? I don't think I do. What I had with Trace is all I knew, and it was messed up. I don't want that, what he and I had. I don't want him back. I don't want our relationship back. Even if you weren't in the picture, I wouldn't. But there is you, and I know we have an emotional connection. I care about you. I care about Riley. I can see us having a real, lasting, meaningful relationship. It's building, between us and I want it. I want it all."

A silence, full of a thousand thoughts and half-expressed ideas and partially explored thoughts. This conversation has been so disjointed and intense and wandering and personal, but I think the only way I could have expressed any of this is over the phone, without his physical presence to distract me, in juxtaposition with how uncomfortable and unhappy I am around Trace and my family.

"But in a way, my physical desire for you is the thing that's most…I don't want to say important. But it's at the forefront. I don't know how to express what I'm feeling, Rory. Wanting you is so intense and so all-consuming, and that's so unexpected and so unfamiliar and it's kind of…intoxicating. Addicting. I want to just…be crazy. I want to have this wild and intense sexual relationship with you, and maybe just hope that our emotions catch up. Does that make any sense? Because you make me feel…desperate. And I love that."

I sigh.

"I'm all over the place, and I'm sorry."

"No, don't be sorry." He laughs. "Weirdly, I'm actually kind of following you. We've both had hard, unusual experiences, romantically and relationally. We both have scars and fears and hang-ups. And I think for most people, or a lot of people, sex is easy, right? It's all too easy to base a relationship on sex and never really get around to the emotional aspect. But you and I are different, aren't we?"

"Yeah, we are."

"I know I can fall in love with you, Emma. And hard. I dunno, maybe I already have, and I'm just learning to accept it. But I know that falling in love with you is… there's a finality to it. There's no going back from it. And I'm scared if I let myself fall for you all the way, that you won't feel the same way. It's scary admitting that, Em. But I want it. I want you, all of you, body and heart and mind and soul, badly enough that I'm willing to admit that I'm scared and that I'm falling in love with you, hoping that I'm not misreading you. Because I think you are too. And maybe—maybe if I have enough courage to admit that I'm falling for you, it'll reassure you. It'll help you feel safe enough that you'll let yourself fall for me."

I swallow hard, but the thick lump in my throat won't be swallowed.

My voice won't work.

"Em? Say something. Please?" His voice is rough and low.

"I can't," I whisper, my voice breaking. "I'm trying not to cry."

"What kind of cry?"

I clear my throat. "The good kind." I breathe slowly, deeply. "Rory, there's no falling. I'm already there. I already love you. I've been denying it and fighting it for weeks. But I can't. That's what I realized, that's why I'm calling you." I feel tears sliding down my cheeks, and let them slide. "I didn't want to leave, Wednesday. Honestly, I never want to leave. I want to wake up in bed with you, and make breakfast for you. I want to fall asleep with you. I want everything with you. It's scary, because it feels so… big, so intense. So much *more* than what I had before."

He sniffs hard, a gruff, masculine sound. When he speaks, his voice is thick. "I'm not crying, you're crying."

"Well, I am," I say with a soft laugh. "And I love that you are. That I mean that much to you."

"It's just weird and disorienting. Feeling this strongly. I feel like I've known you forever." Another of those rough, impatient sniffs. "I wish you were here. I'd kiss you so hard you wouldn't know which way is up."

"Joke's on you, I never know which way is up when you kiss me."

He rumbles a laugh. "That's a good thing, I hope."

"A very good thing. You kiss me, and I just lose all sense. I don't know which way is up, and I don't want to stop kissing you, and my clothes just seem to fall off spontaneously, and I get this craving to touch you and the more I kiss you the more desperate I get to be naked with you and make you come."

"Aww Jesus, Em…you're gonna make me hard just talking like that."

A decision hits me. "Rory?"

"Hmmm?"

"I don't want to be here anymore."

"Your flight's in the morning, right?"

"Yeah, but…what if I got one sooner?"

"Like a red-eye?"

"Anything."

"You said you've been drinking."

"I'd get a ride to the airport and I'd have four and a half or five hours—maybe even more if I can't find a direct flight—during which to sober up for the drive home to you from the airport."

"Home to me," he repeats.

"I said what I said."

"I like it." He sighs. "Just…be safe. Don't take any risks. I'll be here. I'm not going anywhere."

I laugh. "I know that, the problem is that I'm *here* and I want to be *there*."

"I'll leave my door unlocked for you." His voice is thick.

"Are you a heavy sleeper?"

"No, not really."

"So if I were to climb in bed with you…"

"I'll have you biting down on a scream so fast you won't know what hit you."

"I really, really like the sound of that."

"I'll see you soon, then?"

"Not soon enough."

He huffs a laugh. "I've really missed you, Em. Thank you for calling me."

"I just have one question for you."

"Okay?"

"What are you and Riley doing for Christmas? Because I think my plans have changed."

"What are Riley and I doing for Christmas?" He muses. "Well, usually it's a lot like Thanksgiving." He sighs. "I think this year will be the best year ever."

"Oh?"

"Yeah. Because you're in it."

"You know what I'm thinking?" I don't wait for him to guess. "I'm thinking we go cut down a real tree together, the three of us. I'm thinking…we go ice skating. We pick out some ornaments together. I'm thinking… Riley and I will have a girls' day to go shopping for you. And I'll get a sub and you and I can go shopping for her." I lower my voice. "And since I'll have the day off anyway, once we're done shopping, we go home and get naked and do every delightfully dirty thing to each other we can think of."

"I'm thinking you, me, and Riley, Christmas morning. Coffee, pajamas, and presents. I'll make pancakes."

"Spend all day Christmas Eve baking cookies and pies, and then we go to Christmas Eve church service."

He sighs. "Christmas with you. It sounds like heaven."

"Christmas in Connecticut, with you and Riley. Yeah, that does sound pretty perfect."

"I'm feeling so festive I might start putting the lights up right now."

"You put lights up?"

"Yeah, it was Riley's idea. She was…four? Christmas before last. We went for a drive the week before Christmas just to look at the houses with all the lights. And she started begging me to do that to our house. So, while she was at school, I went and bought several thousand linear feet of white lights and extension cords." He laughs. "It looked like shit, that year, because I had no idea what I was doing. But she loved it. She was over the moon. Last year, I watched a bunch of how-to videos and it looked a lot better."

I can't help a giddy laugh. "Ohmygod, Rory, I always wanted my dad to do that to our house. He always just laughed at me and went back into the barn. Which is where I am right now, actually, where Dad always went to hide from the rest of us. It's kind of cozy in here, actually."

"So if my house was decorated for Christmas when you came back…"

"I'd be so happy I don't think I'd know how to handle it." I laugh. "But just the outside. I want to help decorate the inside."

He chuckles. "That's easy enough. I have precisely one strand of garland that goes over the fireplace."

"Lucky for you, my entire basement is stuffed full of bins of Christmas decorations."

"You must really go all out."

"It's actually a funny story. Yes, I do love to decorate for Christmas. Every room has to have something festive. But actually, right when I first moved to Westport, I only had one sad little cardboard box of decorations, like, some garland and a little snowman-penguin thing, and a few cheap knickknacks like that. Then, I was running through my neighborhood right after New Year and someone had put literally a mountain of old decorations out on the street. Like, stacks of bins as tall as me. It was expensive stuff, too. Pottery Barn and Pier One and Nordstrom, all in perfect condition. So I knocked on their door and asked if I could take it all. The guy that answered the door was drunk and told me to burn them for all he cared. So I went and rented a U-Haul and took them all home. And now I have enough decorations for three houses."

"The thought of you and me and Riley all together, putting up the tree and decorations and listening to Christmas music and drinking hot chocolate?"

I sigh. "Yeah, exactly."

"Can't wait for you to come home, Emma."

"I could stay on the phone with you forever," I say. "So how about we hang up and I see about getting my ass home to you as fast as possible."

"Just be safe, okay?"

"Promise."

"See you soon, then."

"Bye." I hang up, and just hold on to the phone,

daydreaming of a Connecticut Christmas with Rory and Riley.

A voice startles me out of my delightful reverie. "Here you are." Eddy. "Pulling a Dad move, hiding out here."

I close the footrest, stand up, fold the blanket over the back of the chair, and stuff my phone into my back pocket. "I can see why he liked it out here," I say. "It's cozy and quiet."

"We all looked up and you were gone."

I laugh. "After what, an hour?"

"C'mon, Em."

I sigh and shake my head. "I'm going home."

"What? Like, back to Westport?"

I nod. "Yeah."

"Your flight is tomorrow."

"I'll change it. I may have to do a layover or something, but I just…" I shrug. "I'm not…I dunno, Ed. This isn't home anymore. It hasn't been for a long time. And for the first time in years, I have someone in my life who loves me the way…" I swallow hard. "The way I deserve to be loved. You, Mom, Dad, Uncle Will, you're my family. You always will be. But I just…I've been half alive for years, since Trace's accident. Rory makes me alive, all the way, in a way I've never felt."

Eddy nods, scratches at his head. Lights a cigarette. "Yeah, I get that," he says, exhaling smoke. "I guess I can't argue with that." A glance at me, through a screen of acrid smoke. "You're coming back for Christmas, though, right?"

I smile at him, somewhat sadly. "Actually, no. This year, I'm staying home. I'll call, though, and say hi to everyone."

He nods again. "We'll miss you."

An awkward silence. "Can I get a ride to the airport?"

He winces. "We're all pretty tipsy, Em." A frown. "So are you, for that matter."

"I don't have to drive till I get back to LaGuardia, though." I wave. "I'll get an Uber."

"It'll cost a fortune," he says.

"What about Dad? Where'd he get off to?" I ask.

He shakes his head. "He's not an option for a ride to the airport."

"Eddy. I know. About him and Margie."

A gesture with the cigarette. "They hole up at McGee's and then go to Margie's place down the road, since she lives within walking distance."

"Since when?"

"Since Boyd Conway left her for a twenty-six-year-old ski instructor from Vail named Candi with an I." He harrumphs, sounding exactly like Dad. "She's actually good for him, and Will is good for Mom."

"Except none of them will make it official."

A shrug. "Their business. They're all happy with things the way it is. I don't get it either."

He stubs his butt out on the sole of his shoe in a waterfall of orange sparks. "Trace could probably drive you. He's sober."

I shake my head. "Once was enough."

"Well, you'll be paying someone from Boulder to come here and bring you to DIA."

I nod. "Worth it."

"Ouch."

I frown. "It's not anything against you all."

"It kind of is."

I laugh. "Okay, well, believe that if you want."

I bring up the Uber app, put in the request—a driver in Boulder accepts the fare. It's going to cost a bazillion dollars, and changing my flight probably will, too. But, I've always been conservative with my money, and I have a lot saved up. This is a splurge that will be well worth it.

I head back inside and pack my things, say my good-byes to my family. No one except Uncle Will gets it, Mom least of all. She actually cries, which makes me feel bad, but I explain to her that I have someone back in Westport who makes me feel alive the way Uncle Will does for her. She just stares at me for a long time, processing that I know about their relationship and how it makes her feel, and then she just nods and hugs me.

I don't even see Dad again, which…figures, I suppose.

While I'm waiting for my ride to arrive, I drink a cup of coffee and probably way too much water. I know the only real way to sober up is time, but flushing out my system can't hurt.

By the time I get to the airport and arrange for a flight, I'm feeling excited to get home, and that helps sober me up.

My flight out of DIA is a six-p.m. flight that stops in

Detroit by way of Minneapolis, but gets me to LaGuardia by two a.m., East Coast time.

While I was waiting for my flight, I bought several gobsmackingly overpriced bottles of Fiji Water, and a large coffee; during the first leg of the flight, I drink all of it...which means I spend most of the flight going between my seat and the bathroom. The hour layover in Minneapolis I spend power-walking around the airport, and drinking more water.

The layover in Detroit is short, and I'm finally starting to feel sober and awake. I buy a paperback romance novel and read most of it on the flight from Detroit to New York.

It's bitterly cold in New York, and the long walk from the terminal to my car at the farthest end of the long-term parking lot wakes me up. I'm nursing a paper cup of green tea—hot and something to sip on while I drive, but not so caffeinated I'll never sleep tonight. I put on a high-energy playlist and crank it up, dance in my seat as I begin the drive from LaGuardia back to Westport.

At first, I'm merely eager to get home.

Then, I'm anxious to see Rory.

By the time I'm in the familiar stretch of I-95 past Stamford, I'm feeling wired, half crazed with missing Rory and ravenous for his touch, for his hard body under my hands. I'm driving on autopilot, daydreaming of how I'll wake him up, trying to decide what I want to do to him first—kiss him awake, fondle his manhood to full arousal, or maybe just skip the middleman and wake him up with my mouth.

I've never wanted anything so badly in my life, as I reach his neighborhood, as I want to be naked in bed with Rory right now.

My thighs clench together.

Heat pulsates in my core, soaking me with desire. You read in steamy romance novels where the heroine is so turned on that "her panties are soaked with desire." But I've never experienced it myself, firsthand. Until now.

They're very literally damp with the leaking of my need and my arousal.

God, I want him.

I have to force myself to drive the speed limit as I near his house. I have to go back to turn my Jeep off, and then I forget my bag in the backseat.

Finally, I'm at the side door.

I pause, realizing through the fever of desire that Rory has followed through on his promise: the house is lit up with strings of big multicolored Christmas lights running around the eaves, down the corners, and framing the porch. There's a huge wreath on the front door, made of real pine and holly, with a giant red velvet bow. A little light-up snowman stands sentry beside the front door.

My heart—already swollen with eagerness and boiling over with the realization of how deeply I'm falling for this man—swells even farther, boils over even more. It's so beautiful, and it's such a small thing, but it means so much to me, that he did this for me.

I'm shaking all over, knees quaking with the fierce intensity of my desire. I'm going to ravage the man.

Tiptoe through the door, close it behind me, lock it.

The house is dark, except for the light in the hood over the range, which leaves just enough illumination for me to navigate through the kitchen.

There's a small square LED nightlight in the outlet of the hallway leading to Rory's room.

Our room, maybe, someday soon?

My breath is hot in my throat. I'm hot all over. I pause in the kitchen to pull my boots off so they don't clomp on the hardwood floor. Carry them in one hand, purse on my shoulder, carry-on in the other hand. Tiptoe, tiptoe. Past Riley's door, which is closed but not latched, open a crack. I nudge it open a smidgen so I can peek in on her—she's starfished on the bed, arms thrown out wide, legs dangling on either side of the mattress, her blankets rucked up around her middle. I smile, because she's so cute and peaceful, and I wish I could go in there and tuck her in and give her a kiss, I don't dare risk waking her up; I know what Rory said about how a tornado wouldn't wake her up, but I'm not taking any chances. Not with the things I have planned.

I latch her door and continue down the hall.

Rory's bedroom door is closed and latched, and I open it slowly, carefully, silently. I can hear him snuffling in his sleep, sounding for all the world like a bear. It makes my heart squeeze and leap, even as it also ratchets my desires even hotter. But at this point, I'm not sure it's possible for a human body to experience sexual arousal any more intensely. I'm vibrating with it.

That could be the coffee, but a caffeine high isn't usually accompanied by this ferocious pounding sun-hot need between my thighs, this ache in my nipples that has them diamond-hard and begging for his mouth, this pebbling of my skin all over, this throb in my engorged, hypersensitive clitoris. One touch, and I'd explode, I think.

I close and lock the bedroom door behind me, set my purse, boots, and bag on the floor. He's on his back, like his daughter. One arm is flopped out wide, the other resting on his stomach. He's kicked the blanket down over his feet, leaving just the flat sheet cover him up to the waist.

Which leaves it very, very obvious that he's sleeping nude.

My smile grows until my cheeks hurt.

Finally.

16

I PEEL OFF MY BOOT SOCKS FIRST. COAT SECOND. JEANS next, for once not bothering to pull them off by the cuffs but simply yanking my feet out so they come off inside out, which normally irritates the crap out of me. I simply don't care, in this moment. T-shirt joins the pile of clothing. My eyesight has adjusted to the moon-lit silverine glow, and I soak up the beauty of his body as I strip out of my bra and panties—he's so big, so hard with muscle. The body hair makes him masculine and rough. His hair is wild and too long, and I've decided I like it that way. His beard is long and thick, and I long to bury my fingers in it, my nose. His abs aren't razor-sharply defined, but rather hard blocks of solid muscle. The sheet is molded to his massive thighs, and tented over his manhood.

So beautiful.

And all mine.

Naked, I tiptoe across the room, climb stealthily onto the bed. He shifts a little, and I freeze, wanting to enjoy the game of waking him up. He just wiggles a little, burrowing his head deeper into the pillow, turning it to the side, both hands on his chest, now.

I lick my lips, hungry for the taste of his arousal. Needing his erection in my hands, my mouth. Inside me. His skin, his muscles, his breath, his hands all over me.

I gingerly drag the flat sheet down to expose his sex. It's at rest, curled to the left, pointing across his hipbone. Even like this, it's an impressive piece of equipment. He sniffs sleepily, grunts, shifts. I think he senses me.

I lie on the bed on my side next to him, and take his limp cock into my mouth, lifting it away from his body with my lips. He moans, a small quiet sound in the back of his throat. I feel him responding, feel his sex hardening in my mouth. I move slowly, keeping him in my mouth and licking the tip, moving back and forth. He huffs, and stirs.

I let him fall out of my mouth, and he glistens with my saliva in the moonlight. He breathes in deeply, makes another little sound in his throat, and his hips give a little upward tilt. He wants more. Maybe he's dreaming of me, now. Dreaming of me doing this. And he'll wake up, and it'll be real.

Oh god, he's getting big. His cock thickens as I watch, and I cup his heavy balls in my palm, wrap my fingers around his hardening, lengthening manhood, bring my lips to the broad, plump head. He moans again, louder this time. His hips lift, push.

He's fully engorged now, and his breathing is fast.

He thrusts.

He murmurs something I can't quite make out. A grunt. A thrust, plunging between my lips. Yes, yes, I love his responsiveness, even asleep, the way he huffs and gasps, groans and grunts. The way his hips pivot gently, inviting me to take more of him. I accept his invitation, taking him until I can't take any more, and swallow around him.

"Ahhhhhh…god," he grunts, his words slurred with sleep. "Em."

I watch him as I twist my fist around his base and caress his heavy sac, as I slide my lips around his thick member, pausing at the top to swirl him with my tongue.

"Em, ohhhh god, Em." He's not quite awake yet. Still thinks it's a dream. "Feels…so good. Don't…stop."

I keep it slow, taking my time. I could spend hours like this, making him feel good, bringing him closer and closer to release. All night. Just this.

Not really. I want his mouth on me.

I want this thick hard beautiful cock inside me, I want to come with him.

But first, I want this.

All of him, like this. Until he wakes up.

I use my hands and mouth and tongue together, use every trick I know. He huffs and grunts, writhes, twists, thrusts. After several minutes, he begins to thrust rhythmically, accompanying the thrusts with soft, low grunts.

"Emma," he growls. Glance at him—eyes are still closed. His hands tighten on his belly, fisting against his clenched taut abs.

I move his hands to my hair—use one hand to rip the elastic off the end of my braid and shake the woven strands loose, and then I help him bury his hands in my hair. He does so automatically, instinctually. Even now, governed purely by base instinct, he only gently encourages my movements, doesn't try to force me to take more of him than I want.

His thrusts increase, speed up. His grunts become… strained. "Emma…" He swallows hard, growls as I swirl my tongue around him and then plunge my mouth down around him. "God, Em. Em. Em."

I can't help responding, finally. "Mmm-hmmm?"

I feel him reaching the edge. His movements grow slow and shaky, stuttering with intensity. Shaking. His thighs bunch and harden as he lifts up, pushes himself into my mouth. His hands tighten around my scalp, and I feel him throb between my lips, in my hands.

He thrusts once more, and then his belly goes concave and his hips lift and there's no warning, just a flood of his cum and he's snarling between clenched teeth.

I steal a quick glance up at him as I swallow frantically—just in time to see his eyes fly open.

"Emma?" His voice is ragged, hoarse, destroyed. "Ohhh fuck, fuck. Fuck!"

I hold his gaze as I move my lips down his shaft, and fist pulsing in swift shallow strokes at his root, and I watch his eyes go wide even as his brows lower, his mouth dropping open, hips locked in upward as I wrench his orgasm out of him and milk it for all it's worth. Taste him on my tongue, feel him coating my throat, a thick salty musk, slightly sweet.

He coughs a grunt, which turns into a long, low groan as his head lolls back to the pillow even as another spurt leaves him. Then it's little dribbles, and I keep going around his still-hard but fading cock, licking and stroking with my fist and plunging my mouth around him until he's gasping raggedly and utterly limp, head to toe...except the part of him still in my mouth.

I don't stop until he's totally limp once more.

"Emma...holy shit."

I crawl up his body, scraping my sex over his hard thick thigh, then wedging my thighs around his waist, draping my breasts against his face. "Hi."

His hands close over my hips, then grasp my buttocks. "Emma, my god. I'm ruined."

I just laugh, grinning, pleased, and now so aroused I'm restless and wild. "Good."

"I was dreaming. Of you. I was dreaming you were giving me a blowjob, and it was the...the best dream I've ever had. Usually, those dreams fade before I come, and then I have to wake up and finish the job myself, thinking about you and your sexy body and your amazing mouth." His hands scratch up my back, into my hair, over my shoulders. His lips pause speaking and close over my nipples. "This time, the dream didn't stop. You kept sucking, and doing the most incredible things to me. And then I actually came." A disbelieving bark of laughter. "I woke up, and you were there, you were real, it wasn't a dream."

"Nope, I'm real, and it wasn't a dream." I gasp as he licks a nipple. "I can still taste you."

He groans, delighting in the heft and silk of my breasts in his hands, my nipples in his mouth. "So fucking incredible, Emma."

"I was fantasizing about waking you up like that all the way here from the airport."

"I fell asleep fantasizing about you…" he whispers, and his hands grip my hips.

"What did we do in your fantasy?" I ask, writhing on him, grinding my sex against him.

He grabs my wrists and guides my hands to the top of the headboard, slides between my thighs until I'm hovering over his face. "I had a fantasy I made you come so many times and so hard that you had to beg me to stop."

"The last time you ate me out, I think that was exactly the case." I gasp as he flicks me with his tongue. "Make me come, Rory. No mercy. Not even when I beg you to stop."

He begins slowly and gently, tongue flicking my folds, lapping at my clit. His hands are busy, caressing and kneading my ass, reaching up to cup my breasts, fondling my nipples until I lose my breath—it feels like my nipples are connected to my sex by a live wire, a white-hot cord of electric energy, and every time he tweaks, twists, pinches, and twiddles them, the wire brightens, heats, and my core sizzles, sears. His tongue circles my clit, and he toys with my nipples until I'm panting—I'm so close already and he's so skilled that I'm toppling over the edge for the first time within a single minute. He doesn't stop. If anything, he heightens his attentions. One hand remains at my tits while the other steals between my thighs, and he slides two fingers into me. Fucks me with them while his mouth devours me with eager voracity.

My hands tighten on the headboard as I creep up the mountain toward another climax, but this time he slows as I reach it, teasing me away from the edge and back to it, fingering my slick seam and barely touching my clit with his tongue tip, until I'm aching with the denied orgasm.

"Give it to me, Rory," I gasp. "Please."

He complies instantly, slithering his tongue into my sex and driving his fingers into me and pinching my nipple until I have to bite down on a scream—it comes out through gritted teeth, and I lose myself to his ministrations. My grip on the headboard tightens until my knuckles hurt, and I writhe on him, grinding my sex against his mouth. He growls, the sound of a ravening beast feasting on flesh, delighting and devouring. His hands grip my ass, spread me apart and guide me to ride him, telling me to let go, let loose, to take my pleasure upon him.

I take it all.

I throw my head back and gasp breathlessly, wild with thrilling ecstasy. His fingers plunge and spear, his tongue darts and flicks, laps and licks, and his beard is the perfect mixture of soft yet rough against the tender skin of my inner thighs and sex.

My panting gasps ratchet into near hyperventilation

as he drives me to insanity, to the sheer edge of a climax unlike any other. And now, he throws me over that edge.

This one is...combustive.

It makes jelly of me.

My hands clench, and a scream bubbles in my throat as the orgasm spreads through me like wildfire, shaking me like an earthquake. I grab a pillow and press my face into it, let the scream cut loose. I'm frozen, sitting upright now, spine arched into a bow, pillow pressed to my face to muffle my scream as Rory's mouth and fingers fling me into a beautiful oblivion of rapturous orgasm.

It lasts forever.

And not long enough.

The world tilts, and I'm so dizzy and disoriented from the crushing delirium of the climax that I'm not sure what's happening, right away. But then I find myself on my back on the bed, and Rory's dark bulk is above me, eyes glittering in the moonlight, teeth showing his grin.

He nuzzles my breasts, one and the other, nosing them and licking. "You done, Emma?"

I shake my head floppily. "Nope."

He rumbles a dirty laugh. "You want more?"

"Uh-huh."

"Can you move?"

"Nope!"

Another laugh. "God you're fucking adorable, you know that?"

"Yup!"

He kisses my breastbone, my stomach, and a thought occurs to me. "Rory!"

He lifts his head. "Yeah?"

"You have condoms? Tell me, please god, tell me you have some."

"I have some. I bought a box while you were gone."

"Good man." I fondle his hair. "I was legitimately gonna send you to Walgreens if you didn't have any."

"I actually ordered a thirty-count multipack online." His voice is a smile, a devious, playful smirk; his fingers tease my sex as he speaks. "We've got original, studded, and extra lube."

"Oh my, such a wealth of choices." I cackle a laugh. "Too bad I have no idea what the difference would be."

"We'll just have to try them all, in that case, so you can decide which kind is your favorite."

"I like this plan," I say. "But Rory?" I clutch his head and push him downward. "Enough talk. Do the thing with your fingers while you suck on my clit. I really enjoy that."

With a laugh, he traces my seam with a fingertip, slowly plying inward. One finger, delving into me. Then a second joins it. And then, wonderfully, a third. Driving into me, and then curling against my inner wall as they withdraw. While his fingers find their rhythm within me, his lips suckle around the aching bud of my clit, already begging for his tongue. I tangle my hands in his hair, knotting and tugging gently as he slowly begins taking me to a third climax.

This one is slow and dull, at first. Slow to build. A dull ache behind my belly button, gradually building to a hot pressure in my sex. And then, as he intensifies his efforts, the sensation becomes almost unbearable, the aching weight of needing to come now titanic. He doesn't hurry.

"Oh, god, Rory," I breathe. "What are you doing to me?"

"Showing you how much I missed you."

"Don't stop, Rory. It feels so good. Too good. I love what you do with your mouth."

Rising, rising. I bring my knees up, rest my feet on his back and shoulders. Claw at his hair and try to keep my gasps and pants and whimpers and moans quiet.

I'm going to need that pillow in a second.

Slowly, slowly, it builds from a titanic and unbearable pressure into something else, something I don't have words for, something my mind can't even comprehend. I writhe helplessly as he works me into a frenzy.

It feels like I'm coming apart at the seams.

It feels like I'm finally, truly having a *real* orgasm, for the first time. As if all the others that have come before have been merely practice.

This is the real thing.

Lights explode behind my eyes.

My body convulses, and there's the pillow over my face as I scream into it like a banshee, and I feel tears leak out of my eyes.

No mercy.

He pauses for breath, and then dives back in, just when I'd started to descend from the peak of climax—he sends me right back over.

Keeps me there.

Suckling and licking and tonguing and flicking,

fingers fucking me hard and fast. I come and I come, and I don't know where one ends and the next begins, and he's utterly without mercy, giving me a moment to think I've had enough, and then crashing me right back into paralyzing paroxysm of pleasure without end.

Until I'm wrought, wrung into jelly.

I catch at him. "Rory," I breathe. "Enough. Please, enough."

He releases me. Slithers up my body to lie almost but not quite on me. His beard tickles my jaw as he nuzzles my chin. "You're so incredibly gorgeous when you come, Emma." I smell myself on his beard, on his breath; not only do I not care, perhaps bizarrely, it turns me on. "You're gorgeous all the time, but when you're coming? So fucking sexy I can't stand it."

I grip his beard and bring his mouth to mine. "I'm never leaving this bed."

He growls. "I'm okay with that."

"I'm just going to stay here and make you eat me out. All day and all night. Maybe we'll switch once in a while."

He laughs. "Once again, I'm totally fine with that."

I breathe a laugh with him, and turn into him, reach between our bodies. "You are?"

"Uh-huh." He kisses me back, a series of quick pecks between words. "I don't know if you've noticed, but I happen to really, really love eating you out. I could start every day with a nice little round of make Emma scream. End the day that way, too."

"Well, you'll hear no complaints from me if we start and end each day together, with you eating me out like you just did." I clutch his member, which is beginning to show signs of life; now that I'm touching him, the process of rejuvenation quickens. "You'd get a lot of blow-jobs, that way, I can assure you."

"Am I supposed to stop you?" He breathes a deep sigh as I slowly, lovingly caress him to hardness. "I wouldn't stop you. Does that make me an asshole?"

I laugh. "Not to me. If I choose to go down on you, it's because I want to. And if I choose to go down on you, I'll choose how far I want to go. If I want to make you come, that'll be my choice. If I choose to suck on you a little as foreplay? That's my choice." I play with his balls, which makes him shiver and gasp. "If I start something, and you have other ideas, we can communicate. But no, Rory. If I put your cock in my mouth, it's because I want it there. So trying to stop me out of some kind of false sense of chivalry? No thanks."

He groans as I give him a twist on the way down, a squeeze at the top. "So if you're doing that, I should just let you do your thing?"

"Mmm-hmmm." Both hands, then, caressing, fondling. Loving his cock with my hands—affection, enjoyment of his body, arousing him for what comes next. "Because trust me, Rory, if you're going down on me? I am *not* stopping you."

His laugh is deep, rough. "Nor should you. It would be depriving me of the deliciousness that is your sweet, sweet pussy."

I laugh, wriggling. "I don't like that word."

"So what do you call it?"

I pause, thinking. "You know, I don't really call it any-thing. I don't refer to it very often."

"What do you want *me* to call it?"

I roll into him, straddle him. "Don't call it anything. Just…make love to me, Rory."

He stretches out to the side, tugs open the drawer of his nightstand, comes back with an unopened box of condoms, very nice, very expensive ones. I take the box from him, open it, pull a string free and rip one off. He returns the box to the drawer while I open the foil wrapper. Sitting on his thighs, I roll it onto him, seating it firmly around the base, tugging the tip away a little.

I lift up. Brace one hand on his stomach, reach be-tween us and grasp his cock. Lean forward, nuzzle him against my opening, fit him just inside me. His eyes are wide and dark on mine. His hands rest on my ass, pos-sessive. He's in more of a hurry than I am—we're savor-ing this, every moment of it.

"Emma?" His voice is low, hoarse.

I circle my hips, moving the head of him inside me. "Mmm?" This feels too good to say anything else.

"I want to tell you, now, so you understand without a doubt that it's not just the heat of the moment." His eyes bore into mine, serious and open, vulnerable and intense. "I love you."

I sink down on him, impaling myself on his massive erection. Fill myself with him. It's a slow slide, by inches rather than all at once.

"Ohhh *fuck*," I breathe, as he stretches me to beau-tiful aching fullness.

When he's full inside me, and I'm aching with him and need a moment to let my body adjust, I lean forward and touch my forehead to his. My lips move against his. "I love you," I whisper back. "I honestly wasn't sure I'd ever say those words again."

"Me neither." His grip on my hip creases is hard, rough fingers indenting my flesh. "My god, Em, you feel...*so* fucking incredible."

My mouth touches his, tasting his words as much as hearing them. "Fuck me, Rory," I gasp. "Make love to me."

He groans, and drives up into me. I whimper at the feel of him going from deep to deeper, and I have to lift up, have to give him space...to thrust back into me, slowly, gently. It's just like that, for a while. Slow, intermittent thrusts. I lift up, and he pulls his hips down. I sink down, and he meets me with a thrust. It doesn't speed up, not for a long time. We're content to explore each other like this, to absorb and memorize the feel of our union, the merging of our bodies and souls. There's only the sound of our breathing, our gasps, his groans and my whimpers, only the sound of our joining.

"Touch yourself," he grates out. "I want you to come first."

I sit upright, balance on him. He holds my hips and guides my rising and falling. I reach between my thighs, frame my clit with a V of my fingers, feeling his shaft sliding past my fingertips. Touch myself, then, with the just-right touch of my own fingers circling my tender, aching bud. I gasp, then, and groan, and my rolling, driving hips find more speed. My voice grows louder. The flame in my belly becomes an inferno.

He holds me in place, balances me, helps me rise and tugs me down onto him. Fingers fly, hips gyrate—I feel the detonation impending, an imminent implosion gathering in my core. I fall forward and catch myself with one hand on the headboard, the other at my center, circling as fast as my hand will move. Rory, beneath me, drives up into me, hard and fast, his hands on my ass cheeks, clutching and pulling them apart so he can drive even deeper.

I combust all at once, with a loud scream I cannot quite muffle—I clamp my jaw on it, screaming through gritted molars as I come, once again so hard I see stars bursting behind my tight-shut eyes. His hard, upward driving thrusts hit me just right, striking deep, his thick shaft sliding against me in a way that has me shuddering and coming all the harder, every muscle within me constricting, leaving me shaking and trembling and breathless.

I slam down onto him, growling like a caged lion through my teeth, throwing my head back and rocking on him, grinding and circling as I come and come and come.

I'm left dizzy and panting as the orgasm relinquishes its grip on me.

Rory's hands slide up my thighs. He grasps the crease of my hips, then scrapes his palms over my ribcage to cup my swaying breasts. "So fucking beautiful when you come."

"Did you?" I gasp, blinking my eyes open and trying to catch my breath.

He shakes his head. "Not yet."

"I want you to."

He rumbles a laugh. "Oh, I will. I just had to make sure you did first."

He sits up, and my legs go around his waist. We're clenched in an embrace, bodies sweat-slick and tongues tangling as we kiss, as I writhe on him, moving him within me. He moves with me, but it's slow and lazy, his cock buried deep, so deep he can't go any deeper. I'm glutted on him, full of him, aching around him, still panting, sex still pulsating around him. We move like this, kissing and rolling our hips together, for a minute or two.

Then Rory grows impatient. He leans forward so I topple backward. I think he's going to lever over me and take me missionary, but he doesn't.

He grabs my hips and rolls me to my stomach, presses me flat with a gentle but insistent hand. I turn my head to the side and watch him out of the corner of my eye. He bends over me, and his lips find the back of my thigh. My left buttock. The small of my back. Right side. Down to the other thigh, and back up. I shiver at the soft, warm, damp touch of his lips to my buttocks, then upward along my spine. I writhe under him, wanting him back inside me, wanting—needing—to feel him come, to feel him lose control and take me and fill me and find his release within me. I can see his cock swaying between his thighs, pointing upward, tip bobbing at his belly button. I want it. Need it.

"Rory," I breathe. "I need you."

"Patience, love," he murmurs. "There's parts of you I haven't kissed yet." His lips touch my shoulder blades, one and then the other. "Here, and here, for example," he says, as his lips touch me. "And here…and here." My shoulder, the nape of my neck. "And pretty much all along here," he whispers, kissing along my back, down the left side and then up the right side.

He lowers himself onto me, bracing one hand in the bed beside my face, grips himself, and I feel one finger search my seam, find my opening, and then I feel him nudging his erection into me. I gasp as he slowly fills me, one thick, hot inch at a time.

"Oh *god*, Rory," I gasp. "Oh god, you feel so good inside me."

Once he's fully inside me, he shifts so he's up on his knees, sitting on my outstretched legs. "Fuck, Emma. You're so…*tight*. My god." He thrusts once, slowly, gently. "Fuck, won't last long like this."

"Good," I whisper to him. "I don't want you to. I want your cum. I want you to come so hard you can't see straight." I catch his eye over my shoulder. "Like you made me come."

He just growls as he slowly finds a rhythm, each thrust taking him deep, his hands braced on my buttocks. He caresses, pets, squeezes, and kneads my ass as he moves, as if my ass is the greatest thing he's ever put his hands on. I'm certainly not going to argue, if that's how he feels. I've never in my life felt sexier, more powerful, more potent—more needed and wanted. More beautiful. More…perfectly possessed—and I want nothing more than to belong to him.

He starts thrusting harder. His hands tighten on my ass.

A crazy thought bolts through my mind—something I suddenly want. It's never crossed my mind before, I've never understood it, much less wanted it. But now, suddenly, now that I'm thinking about it, I can't get it out of my head.

"Spank me," I breathe. "Rory, spank me."

He groans, a wild grunt of disbelief and incredulity. He smacks my buttock, but it's barely a tap.

"Harder."

He thrusts into me, and as he does so, he spanks my ass cheek—hard enough that I squeal and rock away… only to shove back against him.

"Yes!" I cry. "Again!"

He grips one hip and spanks me with the other, again and again, until the sting is almost unbearable. And then, as if he knows without being told, he switches to the other side. His thrusts grow faster. More reckless. Harder. His smacks echo loudly, and my arousal builds. I feel him inside me, and I'm so tight around him that I can feel every ridge, every vein sliding against my walls.

Then, as I feel him beginning to rise into climax, he pauses. Sinks back to sit on his heels and hooks his arm under my belly. Lifts me to my knees—I know what he wants, and I give it to him. I press my upper torso into the bed and lift my ass high, and he sits up on his knees and grips my hips and drives into me, all once and all the way.

"Come with me," he snarls. "Touch yourself, Em. Finger your sweet pussy. Come with me."

"I lied," I breathe. "I do like that word."

"Yeah?" he mutters. "You like it, now?"

"I like it when you order me to do things."

"Then do it, Emma. Finger your pussy. Come with me."

I huff, gasping as I press two fingertips to my clit, and then, just like that, within seconds, I feel my body responding. "I'm gonna come fast, Rory," I warn. "I'm already almost there."

"I love that," he murmurs. "I love how fast you can come."

I'm shaking already, and he's thrusting into me, now. Slowly at first, the way he always starts. Gently, lovingly. Faster, then.

I glory in each thrust, feeling him sink deep, loving the soft smack of his hips against my ass, the wet squelch of our bodies joining. I love every part of this.

But most of all, I love that I feel *him*, that I feel our souls and hearts connecting and merging through this. He's not just inside my body—he's braiding himself into my soul.

"I'm gonna come, Rory," I whimper. "I'm so close."

"Not without me," he grunts. "Wait for me, love. Come with me."

"Hurry!" I cry, throat thick and voice catching as I feel my orgasm rising out of my control, feeling my heart preparing for whatever the emotional version of an orgasm is. "I can't stop it, Rory. Come with me. Come right now, Rory!"

He's rough and frantic, now, slamming into me, hard, and I cry out with each slapping thrust, and I want to reassure him that I love it like this, that I want him to fuck me like this, hard and wild and without control. I can't manage words, though, too fraught with the intensity of what's building inside me. I can only rock back to meet him, my movements primal and ragged with my own need, my own chaotic frenzy of raging climactic bliss.

"Oh fuck, Em," he snarls. "I'm—oh god...*fuck.*"

"Yes!" I cry. "Now!"

I let go, releasing the last of my hold over the orgasm—it explodes through me, ripping me to pieces, tearing away my breath and making me drive back into him as hard as I can. I feel him buried deep, and his hands grip my hip creases with bruising strength as he jerks me back into his frantic thrusts. Our bodies meet with loud slaps, and I feel him pulsing inside me. He's so thick and so big and so long that I feel it all along his length, and I'm so tight around him that it's all I feel, in my physical body...all else is orgasmic wave after wave, liquid heat and lightning energy searing me head to toe, each spasm shaking me, wringing me like a wet cloth. I can't breathe to scream, and I come so hard tears squeeze out of my eyes.

At exactly the moment that I reach the trembling, gasping, screaming pinnacle of my orgasm, Rory unleashes inside me with a shout, his jaws clicking to bite

down on the roar. He's grating my name in a chant—
"*Emma, Em, Em, Em!*"

He comes for an age, driving into me in staggering,
shaky thrusts.

Finally, our climaxes fade, releasing us.

He collapses onto me, and I collapse beneath him
to the bed. He's crushing me, and I can barely breathe.

"Lift up, just a little," I manage.

He does a half push-up, and I roll to my back,
shimmy up to the pillow. Thus positioned, I reach up
and pull him down. I cradle his head to my breasts, and
his weight, while still considerable, isn't crushing me.

There's a moment of intense silence.

"Holy fuck, I love you," he whispers.

More tears leak out. "I—I…I love you too, Rory.
Good lord, do I love you."

"I feel like I just went from 'I think I'm in love' to
'I'm so in love with you I can't stand it and I want the
whole world to know' all at once, just now." He rests on
me, and I can feel his heart beating like a tympani in his
chest, against my belly.

"I know," I whisper. "Me too."

"I'm liable to fall asleep like this," he mumbles.
"I've…I've never been held this way before."

"I love it," I say. "I love holding you like this."

"I love it so much it makes my insides feel all…melty."

I huff a laugh. "Let yourself fall asleep, Rory. I've
got you."

He's already halfway there. I'm exhausted, but the
amount of coffee I had has me unable to quite fall into

sleep. So I just hold him and count his heartbeats and drift, deliriously happy.

Not just happy. Joyful.

"Em?" His voice is low, rough, more than half asleep. It actually startles me—I'd thought he was asleep.

"Hmmm?"

"Stay with me."

"I'm not going anywhere."

"No, like…always." He grunts, sounding frustrated that he can't find the words—he's too much asleep. "Move in."

"Yes."

"Yeah?" He sounds happy—I hear the smile in his voice—feel it curving his lips against my breasts.

"Yeah."

"Riley…g'na love it…" a soft snurk.

"So am I."

He sighs, sleepy and happy. "You're my girlfriend."

I laugh. "Yeah, Rory." I didn't know it was possible to be this happy. "I'm a lot more than that."

He twitches a little. "Gonna marry you…in the backyard."

"Promise?"

"Mmm. Promise."

I toy with his hair. "Good."

I drift, slowly.

Eventually, his heat and his heartbeat, his presence and his protective weight lull me to sleep.

17

I WAKE UP AS GRADUALLY AS I FELL ASLEEP.

I'm naked, on my side, and being cradled from behind. Rory is a huge bulwark up against my back, his thick strong arm draped low over my hip. His nose is against my spine between my shoulder blades, breath hot. His erection is thick and full, and wedged firmly between my ass cheeks.

I just lie there, at first.

But then nature begins to call. And then, the more I ignore it, not wanting to open my eyes or get out of bed or leave Rory's warm embrace, the more I need to go.

I wiggle away from him reluctantly, toward the edge of the bed. Through his window, I see the dim gray of early morning. Thank god I have today off, and I don't have to leave. I can pee, get back in bed, and hopefully find the same position I was in before.

His hand tightens on my hip, and he grunts. "Don't go."

I giggle. "I just have to pee."

"Come back quick."

"I will."

"I woke up and for a split second I thought last night was a dream. But then you were still right here, in my bed, naked and sexy."

"Naked, sexy, and about to have an accident."

He pushes me. "Go, then."

I pee for what feels like half the morning, clean up, wash my hands. I catch a glimpse of myself in the mirror: my long brown hair is wild and tangled and loose around my shoulders, my makeup is smudged since I never took it off the night before, but my skin is…glowing. Last night was…incredible. Even as I think about it, I get aroused, and my nipples pebble.

I rinse my mouth with mouthwash, because I want to kiss him, and I know my breath is probably awful.

He's rolled over to face the bathroom, eyes slitted open to watch me as I walk back to the bed. "Good lord, Emma."

I make a face. "What?"

"Just you. You're so freaking beautiful it hurts. Watching you walk toward me, naked? You're a goddess, Emma Cole. And I just can't believe that I am lucky enough to…to have you in my life at all. Let alone the incredible things we did last night."

My heart melts and twists all at once. "Last night was the best night of my life, hands down."

"Mine too."

I reach the bed, and he lifts the blankets for me. I crawl in under the covers and onto him, straddle him. He's there, ready, touching my entrance. Unwilling to lose this connection, the warmth of his body and the feel of him beneath me, I stretch across the wide bed without getting off of him, and reach into the drawer. Pull free a condom and return to straddling him. Put it on him, toss the wrapper aside, and grasp his hardness. Guide him to me, lift up, nestle the fat springy tip of him against me, hesitate, with his eyes on mine, gazes locked and trading a wealth of unspoken emotions. And then I take him into me, all at once, lower lip catching in my teeth to muffle my whimper.

He reaches up and pulls me down, drapes the blankets over us, covering us. I lie flush on top of him, lock my arms under his neck and kiss him.

He grunts and tries to dodge my kiss. "Bad breath."

"I do?"

He shakes his head. "Me."

I just laugh and cup his face in my hands, smash my breasts against his chest and kiss him anyway. "All I taste is your beautiful mouth. Just kiss me, Rory."

He growls, and one hand cradles my ass while the other delves into the wild mass of my hair to cup the back of my neck. His kiss is hungry and desperate, eager and thorough. We move in unison. In perfect sync. I gasp, and he grunts. We break to breathe, forehead to forehead, as he pushes into me and I arch to pull away, only to meet again.

My heart lifts. Expands.

"Do you remember the things you said before you fell asleep last night?" I ask.

"Yes," he huffs, "I remember every word."

There's a moment where we can't talk, then, as he shifts under me to find a better angle, gripping my ass with both hands now to guide me, to lift me and pull me down.

"I asked you to move in with me."

"And I said yes."

"I told you I was going to marry you in the backyard." He groans, and buries his face in my throat. "That wasn't a proposal. Just a statement of intent."

"Well, when you do ask me, you won't have to wonder what my answer will be, Rory. I'll say yes. I'd say yes right now."

"You would?"

I nod, hair in my face. I shake it away, blow at it, unwilling to move my hands from the column of his neck or the soft tangle of his hair, my handholds as I move above him, still lying flat against him, held by him, cradled against him as we join.

"We need to give Riley time to adjust, I think," he says. "Before we jump to that."

"I know. I agree."

He's moving faster, now, his thrusts harder, rougher. "Soon, Emma. Come with me."

I press against his torso to lift my hips a little, making space for my hand. I bury my nose in his neck and hold myself up with one hand on his chest. Touch myself.

Find the right pressure, the perfect rhythm, and his hard thick cock inside me is everything, driving and stretching, making me ache, making me shudder, shake.

I rise quickly, turn from shaking and shuddering to whole-body spasms as the climax rips through me, and I start taking over the pace, slamming down on him and grinding my sex against his, around his, needing him deeper and deeper as the pressure powers through me in a blasting release that leaves me gasping and crying, literal tears of intense ecstasy leaking out of me.

"Love me, Rory," I breathe. "Love me."

"I am, I am." He rolls and he's above me, and I don't need to touch myself anymore, the pleasure has taken me with it and his release is bringing me to a new high. His arms circle under my neck and his mouth slashes across mine, stutters there, and then our lips are touching but not kissing as he drives into me to his release. I lock my legs around him and cling hard, hands in his hair, gasping in his ear.

"Rory, Rory, yes, I love you, I love you—" Another climax washes over me, and this is like the one last night, as powerful emotionally as it is physically, an orgasm of our united souls, a climax of connection, bound up in the crushing waves of sexual release battering me to breathless shrill gasps.

"Em, Emma, you're mine, you're mine. Oh fuck, I love you..." His voice is ragged as he comes inside me.

"Yours," I echo. "Yours. I want to be. I am."

We come together...shaking and gasping, kisses staggering against mouths, skin flushed and damp with sweat, bellies heaving against each other. He's buried deep, and I leave him there as we collapse on our sides, facing each other, foreheads nuzzling.

"I should clean up," he mutters.

I hook a leg over his. "Not letting you go, yet."

He just laughs. "Not gonna argue with that." He tucks my hair behind my ear. "I really did wake up and panic, thinking it had all been a dream…you waking me up with your mouth. The earth-shattering sex. Falling asleep with you. For a split second, it was just a dream and I was…devastated."

I caress his jawline. "But when you actually woke up and realized it was all real and I was still here in your bed with you?"

"Our bed," he corrects. "That realization, that it was all real, that everything we did together was all real and not just a vivid wet dream? It was like…when you wake up before your alarm and realize you can go back to sleep for a few hours. Except, times a million."

"And just think—once I move in, this will be…life. Waking up like this every day. Going to sleep together every night."

"Every morning and every night, huh?" he says, smirking.

"I mean, except when you're too tired…"

He pinches my nipple, making me squeal. "I'll show you too tired." He kisses me breathless, and even though we just finished, I feel him stirring, feel myself responding. "I don't know that I could ever get enough of you."

"Challenge accepted," I whisper. "Because I can't get enough of you either."

We just kiss, then, for a while. But the kissing burns hot, soon. And then he's rolling away, removing the old condom and wrapping it in a handful of tissues, replacing it with a new one. And then he's back to me, facing me on our sides. I lift my leg high and hook it over his hip, and he's inside me, completing me.

Again…

It's beautiful. Endless.

Everything I've ever known is erased, until there's only him, and me, and this bed, and our bodies.

We doze, after that.

We're roused by knock on the door. "Daddy?" The knob rattles. "Why's your door locked, Daddy?"

He looks at me. "Ready?"

I laugh. "I mean, I'm naked."

He slips out of the bed. "One sec, honey." Tugs on his underwear—fortunately, he'd removed the condom after our last round, before he dozed off with me. He unlocks the door and opens it a crack—I pull the blanket up to my chin. "Hey, sweetie."

Riley's sweet little voice floats through. "I'm hungry. Can you make pancakes?" I can hear the puzzled frown in her voice. "Why was your door locked? You never lock your door."

"I, um." He huffs. "I just…needed a little privacy, that's all."

"You're being weird."

I see her little head duck through the door, under his arm. She sees me in her father's bed, blankets up to my chin, and her eyes widen, a huge grin spreading across her face. "Emma's here!"

She darts under her dad's arm, intending to jump into the bed to hug me. Rory catches her around the middle and swings her up to hug her to him. "Whoa there, little lady. Let's give Emma a chance to wake up before we hug-attack her."

She eyes him, and then me. "Were you guys having a sleepover?"

Rory looks at me for help, but this is territory *not* covered in elementary school. I just widen my eyes and shrug a little. "Um. Sort of."

"Is she gonna stay?"

"Yeah, I think she is."

She looks at me. "Are you gonna stay, Emma?"

I smile at her. "Yeah, I will."

She giggles and wriggles with joy. "Yay! For how long?"

Rory sits on the bed with her on his lap. "So, um, Riley. How would you feel if...if Emma stayed with us... like, always?"

Her eyes go so wide they're about to pop out. "Like live with us?"

Rory nods. "Yeah. Live with us. How would you feel about that?"

Riley is about to explode with excitement. "That would be the best thing ever!"

I laugh. "I think so too, Riley."

She eyes her dad. "Are you gonna get married?"

He grumbles a laugh. "I mean, yeah, probably, at some point. Not, like, tomorrow, but…yeah."

She looks at me. "Well, you should. Because then I can call her Mom instead of Emma, and that would be literally the best thing ever."

The lump in my throat is hot, and hard to swallow past. "I think it would be too, honey."

She hops off her dad's lap. "Okay. Well you just made my whole life." She claps her hands. "Pancakes!"

Rory does an elaborate, foppish, courtly bow, hand flipping in front of his face. "At once, m'lady."

She giggles and scampers off.

He glances at me. "Well, that went well."

"She's really awesome. Thanks to you."

He just shrugs uncomfortably. "Come on, let's get dressed and make our little monkey some pancakes."

Our little monkey.

The best day ever, including last night, gets even better, with that phrase echoing in my head.

Just when I thought I couldn't get any happier.

18

I T'S BEEN A FULL DAY, AND WE'RE ALL SORT OF DRAGGING a little, but happily so. It started early this morning with what has become our traditional family Saturday morning routine, since I moved in a few weeks ago: Riley, Rory, and I make pancakes and bacon together, listen to fun music, and spend an hour or two after cleanup lounging, watching whatever cartoons or TV Riley picks, and then we get dressed, do some more chores around the house, and then head out for Saturday adventure. Usually that means shopping, a movie, sometimes just lunch, other times a day trip somewhere within an hour or two of home.

Today, it was down to Manhattan for shopping on Fifth Avenue, ice skating at Rockefeller Plaza, lunch at a cute little uptown cafe, followed by a carriage ride through Central Park, bundled up against the cold with a blanket across our knees.

It's a perfect winter day, a few days before Christmas: clear and cold, but not bitterly so, just cold enough and still enough that the snowflakes float down from the darkening sky, fat and perfectly formed, creating a blanket of quiet broken only by the clip-clop of the horse's hooves. Rory's arm drapes over Riley's shoulders, his big hand resting on my back.

As the carriage crunches over the path through Central Park, I find myself wondering how this is my life. How after everything that happened with Trace, the years of isolation and loneliness, I could so suddenly and unexpectedly find Riley and Rory, how I could fall in love so quickly. It seems magical.

We actually had our first fight, last week. The funny part of it is, neither of us can remember what it was actually about—maybe because it wasn't really about anything in particular. He'd had a rough day: a boat engine he'd spent weeks rebuilding seized totally, because a well-meaning apprentice had tried to help and managed to do…something horrible. I'm not sure what, but it had essentially destroyed the engine, ruining weeks of work and costing the shop thousands of dollars. It had left him a truly, astoundingly foul mood. He'd come home snapping and snarling, and I'd told him maybe he should go putz in the garage for a while until he could calm down.

Wrong thing to say, clearly.

I'd meant well, but we'd had a teacher in-service all day, which had been long and boring and had left me in a funky mood of my own, with a headache that wasn't going away.

He blew up, I blew up back.

I don't handle conflict like that well, it seems—Mom and Dad never fought like that, mainly because they spent most of my life ignoring each other almost completely. So I just...don't know how to fight, I guess. I rarely argued with Trace, mainly because I worshipped the ground he walked on and didn't dare offend him. Something I'm only realizing now—that there were a lot of things he did that I hated, that offended me, upset me, confused me, but I just didn't know how to verbalize it, how to stand up for myself.

So this fight with Rory, it's really the first real, adult argument I've ever had.

It ended when Rory made some kind of snarky, snide comment to me in response to something I'd said to him...and I started bawling.

Like, ugly sobbing.

Snot, tears, hysterics.

That ended it immediately, by virtue of Rory deflating like a popped balloon, gathering me in his arms, and apologizing repeatedly until I had to ask him to stop.

Thankfully, Riley had been at a friend's house for a playdate, so she hadn't had to witness it.

Nor the makeup that followed. Which began in the living room where we'd been arguing, continued into the kitchen, where he apologized yet again, with his mouth but nonverbally, if you know what I mean. It had then moved into the bedroom, where'd I'd made my own apologies, and then we'd loudly and repeatedly assured each other of our renewed love. Like, three times in an hour. But who's counting?

After, laying in his arms, shaking with the afterquakes still, we'd talked about conflict, how neither of us had much experience with it, and we'd discussed ways to make sure they didn't turn ugly like that again.

I won't say I liked the fight, but I certainly liked the makeup sex, and with the strategies we'd discussed to resolve conflict in place, I'm confident the next time tempers flare, we'll handle it better.

It honestly makes the relationship feel even more real.

What I'm really looking forward to is Christmas morning.

Tomorrow is Christmas Eve. I can't wait.

The kitchen smells like cookies—Riley and I have spent the day baking. Rory tried to help, but really just managed to get in the way more than anything; I eventually told him the cookies would be done faster if he just went and watched football. Which, somehow, leads to three of his work buddies coming over, which honestly makes me super happy.

He's come alive since I first met him—he was quiet, almost reclusive, going from work to home and rarely anywhere else, and seemed to find humor and even smiling exhausting, except where Riley was concerned. Now? He's loud and laughing with his friends, sharing beers and telling jokes, cheering as their team makes a good run, groaning when they get sacked or whatever.

His friends are a lot like him—salt-of-the-earth men, a little rough around the edges but genuinely kind to those they care about, big, bluff men with hard hands and loud voices and a tendency to forget Riley's in the room and start cursing every other word before they remember and turn "fuck" into "fudge" and "shit" into "shoot"... for ten minutes or so.

Toward the end of halftime, one of them—Rob? I think his name is Rob, the introductions were brief and interrupted by a lot of manly roughhousing, as if they don't see each other every day—receives a call from his wife.

Which leads to me inviting her over. I'm not sure what's come over me—I haven't had a circle of girlfriends since I divorced Trace and thus his group of friends, none of whom tried to keep in contact with me after the dust settled.

I glance at Rory as I invite Rob's wife over, and he just shrugs and grins. "The more the merrier," he says.

So then, an hour later, the four men—Rob, Charlie, Zeke, and Rory—are watching football and the kitchen is crowded with their wives—Amy, Rebecca, and Allie; Westport natives all. They immediately make it clear I'm being hauled into their little clique of Westport Marine Repair women. They each brought a dish to pass, and how they whipped this stuff up so fast I'm not sure; there's a giant Caesar salad, a casserole dish of homemade mac 'n' cheese, a stock pot of tomato bisque being rewarmed on the stove, and a basket of biscuits.

Riley is sitting at the island, chiming into the conversation now and then, which wanders from the adorable and annoying foibles of their husbands to favorite places to shop for purses and shoes, to local gossip. They all include Riley, listening when she speaks and asking her opinion on things—which has Riley preening and glowing, over the moon to be part of an adult conversation.

The din of the football game and the men provides a background to our conversation, and the house lights are all off, except for the ones over the island, the eight-foot Christmas tree with its twinkling white lights providing all the illumination. We spent the whole Sunday after I got back, the three of us, decorating the inside of the house together. We took Rory's truck to my house, sorted through the bins and brought the best stuff to the bed of the truck, and took it home. Now, the house is exploding with festive decorations. Garland drapes the mantle, with a string of white lights to match the tree. There's a mini tree on the counter in the kitchen. Snowmen salt and pepper shakers, Christmas-themed throw pillows, candles and candlesticks, knickknacks of a thousand varieties. It's kind of an eclectic hodgepodge, but it makes it feel…like ours. Homey. We chose what to put out and what not to, and even went out later and bought a few items of our own.

Now, with the house full of new friends, noise and chaos and conversation, I just feel…complete.

Rory's friends—*our* friends—head home, and Riley, Rory, and I get ready for Christmas Eve service. I've never gone, personally; growing up, my parents didn't go and thus neither did I, and then when I was on my own with Trace, we spent Christmas Eve with his friends. But apparently, for Rory and Riley, it's a tradition they've kept since Riley was a baby. Rory grew up going to Christmas Eve church with his mom, up until her death, and it was a tradition he himself has kept ever since as a means of remembering her.

We dress up fancy, Rory in a suit and tie, me in my best evening gown, a black number that's flattering but not exactly sexy. I help Riley find a suitable dress and tights, and do her hair in a fancy braid like mine.

The service is packed, and we have to park almost half a mile away. The sidewalk has been cleared, and most of the houses on the street as we pass by are strung with lights and festooned with wreaths, and trees glimmer and twinkle in the windows. It's cold, with a few small hard flakes of snow swirling in the air, not quite falling. Riley is between us, her mittened hands in ours.

We find a section of a booth near the back and sit together; I recognize coworkers from the school and their families, students with their families.

It's a candlelight service, and we sing "Silent Night" while holding small white candles with paper rings to catch the wax drips. The sanctuary is lit with the soft warm glow of the candles, and we all sing, and I'm holding Riley's hand and Rory is on the other side of her, his hand resting on the small of my back.

I have a family of my own.

It's enough to send tears of pure overwhelmed joy down my cheeks.

This is it: this is the future I saw, as a young woman. It's not with the person I'd thought it would be with—it's better.

The service ends and we tromp back to our truck. As I'm helping Riley up and into her booster, she looks at me. "Emma? Why were you crying? Are you sad?"

I kiss her cheek, nuzzle her. "No, honey. The exact opposite. I was so happy to be in that moment with you and your dad that it made me cry. You guys, you and your daddy, you make my life so complete. You make me so happy." I tap her nose. "And it's all thanks to you. Because you came into my room, that day, and befriended me. So really, I have you to thank. So…thank you, Riley Kerr."

She wraps her arms around me and squeezes tight. "It's because we're kindred spirits." She loosens her grip a little, and smirks at me. "Wanna know a secret?"

I nod. "Tell me."

"I knew Daddy would fall in love with you," she whispers.

I grin at her. "You did, huh?"

She nods. "Uh-huh. He was lonely. And so was I. So I thought if I was your friend, maybe you and him would be friends and if you and him were friends, maybe he'd fall in love with you, and then he'd be happy. And then we could be a family."

The visits from Mindy faded as abruptly as they'd begun—once she realized Rory was off the market and Riley wasn't going to suddenly and immediately develop feelings for her, she vanished. Riley wasn't surprised—a little hurt, and it prompted Rory to bring her to see a child counselor once a month. Rory was pissed about it, but once we settled into a groove as a family unit, he let it go.

We drive home in the snowy silence. The house is lit only by the tree. Rory carries a sleepy Riley inside, but instead of putting her to bed, he helps her off with her coat and we sit together on the couch, watching the snow fall, thick and heavy, coating everything with a fresh blanket of white.

He holds her on his lap, cradling her in one arm, and his other is around me. "My girls."

I stroke his beard. "Merry Christmas, Rory."

"Best Christmas of my life." He leans over, and I turn my head to meet him for a kiss, over the sleeping Riley. "Merry Christmas, Em."

"Best Christmas ever, indeed," I whisper. "But only the first of many."

"First of many," he echoes. "I'm excited for each and every one."

"Me too."

Epilogue

Christmas Eve, One Year Later

"YOU ALMOST READY, EM?" RORY CALLS.

"Almost! One sec!" I give the elastic band one last twist and snap it into place around the end of my braid, which drapes over my shoulder and down my chest.

Makeup? On point—some contouring, fierce red lips, some shading on my eyes. Strappy black three-inch heels paired with the real showstopper: a white lacy cocktail dress. It's tight, hugging my hips and thighs, and the hem falls a couple inches above my knee, with a halter neck leaving my back and arms bare, and a plunging neckline. It, along with the holly berry-red faux fur cape stole, were gifts from Rory, meant for me to wear specifically tonight.

Rory is going to have trouble in the pants region all evening, I think. Sorry, not sorry.

I grab my clutch and leave the bedroom. Rory is waiting by the front door, dressed in a tuxedo, with a thick, tan wool overcoat. His hair is somewhat tamed, pulled back into a low manbun—I've refused to let him cut it, because I just love him wild and kind of shaggy. His beard is neatly trimmed and groomed, and if I was close enough to kiss him, it'd smell like pine.

He watches me emerge, and his eyes go wide. "Holy shit, Em." He swallows hard. "You look...incredible."

"You picked the dress." I do a little spin.

"I won't be able to take my eyes off you," he murmurs.

I close the distance between us, rest my hands on his chest and bury my nose in his beard—pine. "That *is* the point, after all."

He just growls. "We'd better go, or we won't make it to our date."

"That would be a tragedy. You've been planning this date for weeks." His plans involve Riley spending the evening with Rebecca and Rob and their four-month-old baby boy, Rad. He won't say anything else, just *trust me—go with it.*

He laughs. "That was supposed to be a secret."

I just pat his chest. "You kept the details secret, but I know you've been planning something. I just don't know what."

"Good," he mutters. "Worked my tail off to make this a surprise."

He helps me put on my coat, a heavy black floor-length overcoat that will keep me warm despite my ridiculously small dress.

We head out to his truck—he finally upgraded earlier in the year, so it's a new F-250 with all the bells and whistles; the owner of the shop retired and sold the business to Rory. It meant a few months of insane hours, but it's more successful than ever. He still works on the engines part-time because he loves it, but now he can also run the fishing charters he's been dreaming of since leaving Maine, which is the other part of his business: Westport Marine Repair and Fishing Charters.

He holds my door open for me, hands me up. As I sit down and tuck the coat away from the door, I let it fall open, and decide to give Rory a little peek at my own surprise.

"Rory."

He's about to close the door, and pauses. "Yeah, babe."

I turn toward him to sit sideways on the seat, and part my thighs. "Merry Christmas."

I'm not wearing a single stitch under this dress, except the bra, which is a sheer lace number meant more as something for him to have fun taking off of me than anything else. The neckline is so plunging I'm wearing double-sided tape to make sure there's no wardrobe malfunction during dinner, or whatever he has planned for this date.

I can't believe I'm wearing this outfit—it's sexier and more revealing than anything I've ever worn, but I feel incredible in it, and his reaction is exactly what I was hoping it would be.

His eyes bug out. "Emma, good lord, woman." He leans into me, and his hands skate over my knees. "You're gonna kill me. I won't survive the night, knowing you're bare under that sexy fuckin' dress."

"Something to look forward to?"

He runs his hands up my thighs. "How am I supposed to walk away, now?" He bends over, kisses my thigh. "I might…" Another kiss, higher. "I might need just…a little…taste."

I lean backward and let him part my thighs, let him push the dress a little higher up. "Dessert before dinner?"

"Mmm," he murmurs, kissing his way to my core. "Exactly."

I cradle his head in my hands as he buries his face against my sex, wasting no time finding me with his tongue. "Did you think I would stop you?"

"Mmm-mmm."

"Damn right. Oh god, Rory. Yeah, just like that."

"Mmmm."

I'm so sensitive, so eager, so responsive to his every touch that it's seconds before I'm writhing against his mouth, coming apart in a series of rippling waves of climax.

He pulls away, once I'm finished and gasping, wiping at his mouth.

I pull him to me for a kiss. "Mmm. Now your beard smells like pine trees…and me."

He groans as I kiss the living daylights out of him.

"Em, Em…stop, stop," he says, pulling away with a laugh. "We have to go. Any other day, I'd say screw it, but to-night? I have plans that I'm not skipping out on." He kisses me again, and then backs away as if I'm a barrel full of explosives and he's a spark. "Later—I promise you, later, I'll let you tie me up with my own tie and do whatever you want with me for as long as you want. But right now, we *have* to get going."

I catch his hand. "Wait, hold on one second." I give him a devilish grin, grip his tie and pull him to me by it. "Is that a promise? You'll let me tie you up with *this*—" I tug on his tie "—and have my wicked way with you?"

He pinches my chin, kissing me while pinning my wrists together with the other to keep me from ripping his suit off right here, right now. "Yes, Emma, that's a promise," he laughs. "You horny little wildcat."

"Damn right," I say. "Fine. I'll let you off with a warn-ing, mister."

He turns me right way on the seat and buckles me.

Unexpectedly, we drive over an hour west, into the coun-tryside. Suburban sprawl gives way to spaced-out houses on several acre lots, which slowly give way to stretches of forest interspersed with open fields blanketed with snow.

I don't ask where we're going. I'm with my man, and we have Christmas carols playing softly on the radio, and he's holding my hand, and I'm still tingly from his ear-lier affections.

I'm just content to be in this moment.

We pull off the highway and onto a local two-lane road, which winds across the countryside, further away from everything. Here, the snow is thick, and deep. Huge pines line the road, and the fading late afternoon light is a wash of silver and gray on the fresh snow.

Once more, he turns off the road and onto an even smaller unplowed track through the forest. I am starting to wonder, now, though. He's in a tuxedo and dress shoes, and I'm in a holiday cocktail dress and a three-inch heel. Not exactly the right gear for traipsing through the forests of rural Connecticut.

Finally, the tunnel through the trees gives way to a clearing, and I gasp audibly. It's an adorable little log cabin by itself in the acre clearing. It's got big picture windows on either side of the door, and a deep front porch. It's strung with white lights, which glow off the snow and illuminates the clearing. The snow has been cleared around the porch, with salt down to melt it, revealing stone pavers. Smoke trickles from the river stone chimney.

It's something from a Thomas Kincaid painting.

"Oh my gosh, Rory. It's so beautiful."

He grins at me. "You like it?"

"I love it." I give him something between a happy smile and puzzled grin. "But…why are we here?"

He just winks at me. "You'll see."

He shuts off the motor, exits, and rounds the hood to open my door for me. Hands me down, buttons my coat against the cold, even though it's barely ten feet from the truck to the porch.

He takes my hand and we head up onto the porch. Above, the stars are infinite, shining and twinkling in the crystal clear December night sky. Through the window, I can see a portion of the fireplace, lit with a roaring fire, a live-edge floating mantle above it draped with lights and garland and holly, three stockings hanging from reindeer hooks.

Instead of opening the door and going in, he stops and faces me. Holds both of my hands, just stares down at me.

"Rory?" I ask. "Do you want to go in?"

He shakes his head. "Not just yet." A long pause. "Emma, the last year with you has been a study in happiness. You've made my life better in every conceivable way. You never cease to surprise me, and amaze me. You're always up for an adventure, no questions asked. You're the smartest woman I know, the most beautiful woman I know…" He inclines his face to mine, drops his voice to a murmur, "and the horniest, lucky for me."

I suddenly have a feeling what's about to happen, and I feel my throat swelling up with that hot lump of emotion—the lump is a hard hot knot of YES, waiting for him to ask.

"I wondered, before I met you, if I'd ever be happy again. Come to find out, not only could I be happy again, but I'd come to understand that I'd never really truly known what *real* happiness is. Not until you." He reaches a hand into his coat pocket and drops to his knee. Holds up a ring box, opens it—within, a round diamond glitters in a crust of smaller diamonds. "Emma Cole, will you marry me?"

I nod, blink tears. "Yes," I whisper. Try again, louder. "*Yes*." I laugh, then, crying and sniffling. "A hundred, thousand, million times, yes."

He stands up, slides the ring onto my finger; once it's on, I leap at him. He catches me, holds me against him and twirls me as he kisses me until I'm gasping, breathless, and so hot with need for him that I could lie down in the snow and take him here beneath the stars.

He sets me down. "I have one more surprise. It's through that door." He pauses. "This is the part I'm less sure about. I just…I hope it's what you want."

I can't fathom a surprise that I *wouldn't* want. "Okay?"

He opens the door, standing in it so I can't see in, yet. "You can say no."

"Rory, what's…I don't understand."

He inhales deep, holds it. Lets it out slowly. "Em, you said yes. A year ago, you told me you'd say yes even then. That I wouldn't have to wonder at your answer."

"I remember." I search his face, desperate now to know what's on the other side of him.

He takes both of my hands. "So now, I'm asking if you'll say yes…" He backs into the cabin, pulling me behind him. "To marrying me."

I already said yes, is on my lips—but the words die as I take in the scene.

Instead of a living room set, the interior of the cabin is set up like a chapel. A white archway is set up in front of the fireplace, woven with red and white roses along with garland and holly. Arranged in a single section, three antique church pews. On those pews, is…everyone. Rob and Rebecca, Charlie and Amy, Zeke and Allie. Riley is with Rob and Rebecca, but she's dancing in her pew, antsy and excited and too wound up to sit still. Also in attendance is my family: Mom and Will, holding hands, Eddy and Lacey and their twins, Dad—and yes, Margie; Nicky is there, too, between Dad and Uncle Will.

Say yes…to marrying me.

Right now, he means.

On Christmas Eve.

I take in everyone, the archway, Riley…and then Rory. Waiting, clearly on pins and needles.

I blink hard, shake my head with a laugh. "Rory, you're crazy." I yank him to me by the tie and kiss him. "Yes, Rory, of course. You did just say how I'm always up for an adventure, didn't you?"

He sighs in relief. "I was so scared it was a mistake. But it just…seemed right. A surprise wedding."

I laugh again. "You brought my whole family in?"

"The hunting trip I went on with the guys?" He'd taken a weekend away, a few weeks ago, ostensibly to go hunting with the boys. "We did go hunting…in Colorado, with your dad, Uncle Will, Eddy, and Nicky. To set this up."

It wasn't the first time they'd met, though, thankfully—Mom and Dad did end up divorcing over the summer, and oddly, after that, things improved between us all. The three of us spent a week in Boulder with my family, and Mom and Will came out to visit us over Thanksgiving.

I lean up and whisper in his ear. "If I'd known I was marrying you tonight, I probably would have worn panties. I thought this was just a fancy Christmas Eve date."

He growls a laugh. "Quite a surprise," he mutters. "No one but you and me will know."

I kiss him. "I'm truly and genuinely shocked, though. So surprised."

He touches my cheek; I feel everyone watching, but for the moment, I don't care. "Happy, though? You don't feel pressured into it?"

"No, not pressured. And yes, so happy. I want to marry you. I honestly was sort of expecting a proposal over the summer."

He grins. "I know. I could tell. I hated to let you down, but I was hoping this would make up for it. I just...the thought of getting engaged and then having to wait to plan a wedding? I want to be your husband. Right now, tonight."

"It's perfect." I frown. "What about the reception?"

He grins. "There's a barn out back, decked out for a party, catering and all. Warm, bright, airy, and there's not one but *two* Christmas trees. And everyone brought presents to exchange."

I laugh. "That's why you had me wrap yours early."

"Yup."

"You really did think of everything." I look around. "Except...who's officiating?"

He turns to face the room, tucks me under his arm. "That's another surprise."

Nicky stands up—my favorite cousin, tall, broad-shouldered, his beard long enough to braid with a decorative iron band binding the bottom, his hair shaved on the sides and in a ponytail on top. He's a wild child, my cousin, a little reckless, a little crazy, but he's got a kind heart.

"I'm an official licensed minister, cuz." He winks at me. "From a real in-person college, too, not just some online gimmick."

I can't help a laugh. "Nicky Cole—*you're* officiating my wedding?"

"Sure am, Emmy. I've practiced, too. This'll be my fifth wedding. I wanted to make sure I was good at it before I did yours."

There's a flurry of greetings, then, with hugs and congratulations all around.

Riley finds me last of all, wrapping her arms around my middle and gazing up at me. "I know you're not married *yet*, but...hi, Mom."

I sniffle back tears. "Hi, sweet girl."

She reaches up and dabs underneath my eye with a Kleenex. "No crying. You'll smudge your makeup."

I grin, laughing through tears, and tap her on the nose. "I'm wearing waterproof mascara."

"Oh."

I hug her tight.

From somewhere, a single cello plays "Silent Night."

"That's our cue, Em," Rory says.

As the song plays from the speaker in the corner, Rory and I take our places under the archway.

I wonder how he knew this would be the perfect wedding for me.

He knows I've already had the four-month engagement and the church wedding and the big reception—but how could he know that with him, this is exactly what I want? I didn't even know, until now. I wouldn't want it any other way.

Nicky's speech is short and simple. "I may be a wedding minister, but that don't make me a preacher," he says. "We're here because our girl Emma found the love of her life. And somehow, I don't think I'm the only one not surprised that she'd have a surprise wedding. I didn't even know that was a thing, and I admit I thought Rory was bug-shit crazy." He winces. "Sorry, probably shouldn't curse, huh?" A laugh. "But he knew his woman, and here we are." He looks at me. "You inspire me, cousin. I hope, someday, I'll find love like I see you and Rory have. But for now, let's get you two married, so you can start in on your happily ever after." He lets out a breath. "Okay, here we go." He looks to Rory. "Do you, Rory Emerson Kerr, take this truly amazing woman, my favorite cousin, Emma, to be your wife, for always and forever, through all things?"

Rory's eyes blur with tears. "I do."

"Knew it." Nicky winks at me. "And what about you, Emma Rose Cole? Do you take this man, Rory, this big, bearded, grease-knuckled fisherman to be your husband,

The world of *Wounded:*
Wounded
Captured

The world of *Stripped:*
Stripped
Trashed

The world of *Alpha:*
Alpha
Beta
Omega
Harris: Alpha One Security Book 1
Thresh: Alpha One Security Book 2
Duke Alpha One Security Book 3
Puck: Alpha One Security Book 4
Lear: Alpha One Security Book 5
Anselm: Alpha One Security Book 6

The Houri Legends:
Jack and Djinn
Djinn and Tonic

The Madame X Series:
Madame X
Exposed
Exiled

The Black Room
(With Jade London):
Door One

Door Two

Door Three

Door Four

Door Five

Door Six

Door Seven

Door Eight

The One Series
The Long Way Home

Where the Heart Is

There's No Place Like Home

Badd Brothers:
Badd Motherf*cker

Badd Ass

Badd to the Bone

Good Girl Gone Badd

Badd Luck

Badd Mojo

Big Badd Wolf

Badd Boy

Badd Kitty

Badd Business

Badd Medicine

Badd Daddy

Dad Bod Contracting:
Hammered
Drilled
Nailed
Screwed

Fifty States of Love:
Pregnant in Pennsylvania
Cowboy in Colorado
Married in Michigan

Goode Girls
For a Goode Time Call…
Not So Goode
Goode to Be Bad
A Real Good Time
Goode Vibrations

Billionaire Baby Club
Lizzie Goes Brains Over Braun
Autumn Rolls a Seven
Laurel's Bright Idea

Standalone titles:
Yours
The Cabin
The Parent Trap
Wish upon a Star

Non-Fiction titles:
You Can Do It
You Can Do It: Strength
You Can Do It: Fasting

Jack Wilder Titles:
The Missionary

JJ Wilder Titles:
Ark

To be informed of new releases, special offers, and other Jasinda news, sign up for Jasinda's email newsletter.